D1535095

Other books by Anne Britting Oleson

The Book of the Mandolin Player
Dovecote

Tapiser

Tapiser

Anne Britting Oleson

Bink Books
Bedazzled Ink Publishing Company • Fairfield, California

978-1-945805-94-3 paperback

Cover Design
by

Bink Books
a division of
Bedazzled Ink Publishing, LLC
Fairfield, California
http://www.bedazzledink.com

For Honora Lynch Carey, my grandmother, who published stories under the name Honor Bright, and for whom I wrote my very first book.

*Also, for Becky and John:
thanks always for letting me sit in the corner and write,
and for not poking the bear too much.*

Prelude

THE FIRST TIME she came across him in the garden, he dropped his charcoal quickly and hid the block behind his back, his green eyes guarded.

She curtseyed low. She had not laid eyes on him in so long. Since they had removed to the Marches ahead of his train, to prepare the house for his arrival.

"Mistress," he said after a moment.

She remained bowed.

"Rise," he ordered abruptly. His voice cracked. "I hate this."

She did not know what he should hate: the changing of his voice, or the awkwardness between them who had formerly been playmates. She straightened slowly.

His face was as flushed as bright as his hair, high tide in his cheeks. She felt her own skin warm. Her eyes fell on the block he'd attempted to hide.

"What do you draw?" she asked, hoping to divert attention.

"'Tis nothing," he mumbled. After a moment he held it out to her.

The study was recognizable as the flowered bank to his left; it was more than passable, though in some places the perspective seemed a little skewed. He must have seen some of her reaction in her face, for he snatched the drawing back.

"I shall never be as good as you are in all my days," he said in a low voice, then laughed, a small self-deprecating sound.

They had drawn together as children in the nursery. She remembered a time when, frustrated, he had torn her picture and had thrown the scraps to the ground.

"No, Your Highness, not so," she said quickly. "You are much improved over the last years. You will surpass me yet."

He lifted his face and smiled then, the crooked grin she remembered from those too-long-ago days. "You too are much improved, Mistress Beatrice. Never would you have been so politic."

The memory of the punishment for her temper at the tearing of her drawing lay between them.

"Will you sit?" he asked, moving aside on the bench. "Tutor me so I might become the artist I'd like to be."

He was laughing at his own wordplay. But she shook her head; she would not be drawn. They had been childhood nursery mates, but that had been long ago. "I would not presume, Your Highness."

His smile became a smirk. "I could command it."

In that moment, to her, he became king. He could command it of her, and she, as subject, would have no choice to obey. She looked at him through lowered lashes: the sun playing on his red-gold hair, picking out the gold threads in the sleeves of his doublet. He wore a crown, even when he did not.

She was abashed, and saddened.

She was saved from having to reply, if saved it was, by the sharp call of her guardian

"Where are you, Beatrice?"

"Here, Madame," she answered quickly.

In a moment she was upon them, holding out an imperious hand, her rings winking in the afternoon sun.

"Beatrice, I have been searching for you everywhere." She stopped at the sight of them, slipped into a graceful curtsey, and only rose again stiffly when he waved an impatient hand. Her sharp eyes flickered between the two, a suspicion Beatrice did not recognize then, but one which made her cheeks warm yet again. "You are wanted in the solar." Her tone was impatient; her tone was always impatient.

"I have delayed her, Madame," he said. "Do not chastise her."

A nod, a narrowing of the eyes. "By your leave," she said at last, her jaw tightening, "we will withdraw."

Beatrice sucked in a quick breath and curtseyed again, awaiting dismissal. Once away, her guardian held herself sternly, striding across the grass, and Beatrice had to hurry her steps to keep up. After one stray glance back, she cast her eyes downward.

His bright hair, his crooked grin. Though she knew she should not let it, she felt her heart quicken to see that he watched them even as they retreated to the door.

"I HAVE BEEN told," the wizened old man said, his black eyes darting to her face, her hands, to the other girls who were pretending not to listen. Master Arnaud: Madame had spoken his name courteously, but with a touch of disdain which was not lost on him. Master Arnaud: his words were heavily accented, a sound more guttural than French, yet not quite German. Flemish? She had to listen closely as he spoke. "I have been told that you have an eye for color."

She couldn't not imagine her patroness speaking of her with any such kindness, but she dared not look for affirmation. "My guardian is too kind," she demurred.

"Sit with me," he said, indicating one of the embroidered stools beneath the window. He swept aside the folds of his black coat, velvet, but slightly shabby at the elbows, she noticed critically. His words were a peremptory as any she'd heard that afternoon, though she sensed he was not of the same class as her guardian, and far below that—they were all far below that—of the companion of her babyhood. She

looked now to her guardian, who nodded once, her eyes hooded. Beatrice sat and folded her hands in her lap, waiting, curious, nervous.

He took a seat beside her, his black eyes never leaving her face. She schooled herself to remain impassive. After a moment he nodded.

"You keep your own counsel," he said. "That is good."

Now she saw that he held in his hand an embroidery hoop, and when he laid it flat on his lap, she saw that it was hers. A woodland scene in miniature: she had been attempting, with the stitches—and with marginal success—to represent the shades of green easing one into another, the way the light played upon the leaves.

"This is your work," he said, not looking at it, but rather, still at her.

"It is, Master," she said.

He ran a finger over the tiny stitches. She had been quite pleased with the work, despite pride being a sin; she had liked how the embroidery had come to fruition beneath her fingers. Now, under her newly-uncertain eye, she saw every unevenness, every awkwardness.

"You have how many years?" he asked.

"Fifteen, come midsummer."

He nodded, and there was a long pause as he dropped his probing gaze to the hoop. "You have much to learn, mistress," he said at last.

She hung her head. She knew that. Her guardian said as much frequently.

He touched her hand, a single tap from a single finger. She might have imagined it, had it not been as imperative as the rest of his manner.

"Your good lady wishes that I should teach you."

She lifted her eyes quickly, afraid that she had misheard. Master Arnaud was staring into her face again, and this time, the skin around his dark eyes was wrinkled, and his thin lips quirked slightly.

Part One
Tapiser

1

"YOUR GRANDMOTHER," ELAINE tacked on at the end of the conversation, almost as though unwilling to say the words, "would like to see you. Sunday afternoon. At four."

Over the phone, my mother's voice was thick with exhaustion and impatience. I closed my eyes. This was not an unusual occurrence.

"At the Willows. She says you haven't been in to see her since you've been back."

I'd been back nine days. Nine days of sorting out the new job at the library, of signing the lease on the efficiency apartment, hooking up electricity and internet. Nine days of becoming progressively smaller.

"I haven't had a chance yet," I said.

The sharp intake of breath, the sound I'd grown used to, having heard it since my childhood. The sound that usually preceded an angry outburst enumerating my faults.

"Mom," I said, cutting her off before she could wind up. "I've just got back to town. I've just found a place to live, and a new job—"

"Part-time," she scoffed. It was easy for her to change the direction for her anger and disappointment; I had so many faults, after all. Lately, it was leaving Rob—well, technically, he'd left me—and quitting my job at the university, and then returning home. *With your tail between your legs,* she had, predictably, said when I'd first told her. *Why couldn't you have stayed there and fought it out?*

"It's fine, Mom," I said wearily. "I'll go over on Sunday afternoon. At four."

THE PART-TIME job was enough for me at that point, though the head librarian at the community college, Madeline, had been insistent that it would become full-time once the end of August rolled around. Mostly I wanted to sit on the second-hand futon in my one-room apartment over my landlord's garage and think—or not think—about how I had failed, so suddenly, so thoroughly, in my life plan. I had had the tall, dark, and handsome husband (of whom my mother had actually approved), the house in Wilmington, a position at the law library. And then suddenly I had none of that, once Rob had decided he'd wanted something else. *Someone* else.

Why I had thought I could come home again, I couldn't begin to say. That I could come crying to my mother, perhaps? But that was wishful thinking, because I'd never been able to come crying to Elaine without a frown and a dismissal from her.

As for my grandmother, my mother's mother—that was far more complicated. I had seen her rarely when I was a child. Eleanor had owned a townhouse not far from our own home, though she was infrequently there; her work took her to New York, to Paris, to any number of exotic places I could only imagine. Her periods of residence at the house seemed random and sporadic. Only recently diagnosed congestive heart failure—she was nearly ninety, after all—had slowed her down. She had decided that the Willows was an appropriate retirement village for her: close to family, but not *too* close. When she had first taken up residence there, I had tried to imagine her in a crowded common room, playing bridge with some elderly partners with walkers and colostomy bags and fitful memories—but the image simply did not compute.

With a sigh, I reached again for my phone and entered *Eleanor—Willows* on Sunday's date in the calendar app.

2

"CAN YOU HELP me?"

I looked up from the cart of books I'd been organizing by call number, shoving the hair back from my face. The voice was deep, unfamiliar, and I had to keep looking upward, the speaker was so tall. He glanced uncomfortably to the bank of computers behind him and back again, running a hand through his blonde hair.

"What seems to be the trouble?"

He looked sheepish, the lines around his eyes emphasized by his frown. "I'm trying to upload a document to my online dossier, and I keep getting a failure notice."

I followed him to the computer. Squinting, I leaned forward over the work station for a closer look. "Have a seat," I suggested, feeling him looming over me, "and show me what you've tried."

He slipped into the chair, called up the dossier, and clicked through to an empty page. "It's my updated CV. I've taken down the old one—haven't had much luck with that version—and now I can't get the new one to upload."

"Show me."

I watched him click the button on the bottom of the page, and then call up his file again.

"That's your problem. Don't ask me why it doesn't work this way, but it doesn't. You need to go to the 'insert' drop-down and work from there." I pointed to a spot on the screen. "Once you've chosen the file and uploaded it, you won't be able to see it until you get out of edit mode." I stepped back to watch him move the cursor, then click, and click again.

"How do I get out of edit mode?" he asked, looking up at me. His eyes, I saw, were a brilliant sapphire blue, to go with the blonde hair.

"Click save."

Then his CV was on the screen before us. *Carwyn N. Grey.*

"Success!" he crowed. He smiled up at me. "Finally. Now I can finish up all these applications."

It might have been a dismissal, which was fine. I still had the cart of books to re-shelve before it was time to clock out and go home to the empty apartment. I smiled in return and headed back to the desk. Still, I couldn't resist a look back over my shoulder: I had the niggling sense that there was something familiar about him.

HE REAPPEARED AT the circulation desk just as I returned with the now-empty cart.

"Hi," he said. The sheepish look was back.

"Another problem?" I glanced back at the clock. It was four minutes to four.

He saw my look, and grinned. "No, not that. Or I should say—no, thanks to your help." He shifted his backpack up onto his shoulder. "I've got the applications out, and now all that's left is the waiting. So—I was just wondering—since you're off in a few minutes—whether you'd let me buy you a cup of coffee. To say thank you."

To cover my own discomposure—I wasn't comfortable with the idea of a date, even a coffee date, yet—I laughed. "I'm a librarian. It's what I do."

He tipped his head to the side. "Oh, come on. A cup of coffee. Over in the student union. Perfectly safe." His tone was teasing. Inviting. Despite myself, I kind of enjoyed his interest.

"I'll get my coat," I said.

ACROSS THE COMMON, after a soggy wet April, spring was finally making itself felt. Though the grass was still patchy with brown, the daffodils along the border had flowered out, yellow trumpets announcing their presence singly, and in pairs, and in a few spots, in battalions. The birds, which I had not noticed before in this awkward season, were riotous this afternoon. I lifted my face to the sun, shoved my hands down into my pockets.

"I'm Carwyn," he said.

"I know," I replied. "I helped you upload your resume less than an hour ago."

He laughed. It was a pleasant sound.

"Emily," I said. I pulled a hand from a pocket and held it out. Carwyn shook it as formally as one could without breaking stride. "Emily Hill."

The union was surprisingly quiet for this time of the afternoon; usually it was noisy with students finishing up the day's classes and straggling in for respite. I avoided it for just that reason. At the coffee shop, I ordered a vanilla latté, no sweetener, and Carwyn took his coffee black. We settled at a table near the window overlooking the pond. He dropped his pack into an empty chair and shrugged out of his denim jacket.

"Take your coat off and stay awhile," he invited, sliding into the chair opposite mine. I glanced up sharply—Eleanor had always said that, though she had always been the one on the fly.

I demurred. Now we were here, I was back to debating the wisdom of this idea. I thought of my apartment, the lumpy futon, the comforter draped over the end: in a matter of minutes, I could be home, huddled, safe. Carwyn Grey was a good-looking man—older, perhaps, than the majority of students I'd been dealing with in the library. Perhaps closer to my age, middle thirties. And pleasant. Yet my husband—my ex-husband—was a good-looking man, and pleasant. I took a sip of the too-hot latté and immediately regretted that, too.

"I don't bite," he protested against my unspoken hesitancy.

"You knew what time I got off work." The realization had come to me suddenly. I slid a sideways glance at him. "How did you know that?"

He looked out the window toward the pond, his face reflected in the glass. Did he always look so abashed? When he turned back to me, he wasn't smiling, but the skin around his eyes crinkled. "State secret," he said.

I should get up and walk out, I told myself. Part of me was that nonplussed. And possibly unnerved. The other part of me couldn't quite bring myself to do it. I drank my latté, slowly, debating, looking out at the late afternoon and the slanting sunlight.

He tapped the side of my cup, careful not to touch my hand. "Okay. I admit it. You probably haven't noticed, but I've been in the library an awful lot lately, working on that dossier, and those applications. I just finished my degree, and I need to be gainfully employed."

"Your degree here?"

He paused, then cleared his throat. "Well, no. At the university. But this library is closer to home. I've been spending a lot of time here."

"Spending a lot of time noticing when I get off work."

He had the grace to flush. "Well, you interest me."

There was not a lot to say to that, and I'd long ago got out of the habit of bantering in this way with men. I wasn't sure any longer how to play the game, what the rules were. They might have changed since the last time I was single, all of eleven years ago. I returned to studying the spring muddiness of the pond outside the window, lifted the cooling latté to my lips.

"You probably didn't even need my help uploading that CV," I said after a while.

"I probably didn't."

He was watching me. I could see his reflection in the glass. I drank some more of the coffee. Suddenly it was nearly gone—I tipped the cup back, and then it was. The cardboard made a peculiar click when I set it on the table between us.

"Would it make you feel better to know how long I had to work up my courage to ask you for that help?"

I couldn't tell whether or not he was laughing at me.

"It makes me uncomfortable," I said at last. I picked up my purse. "This whole conversation is making me uncomfortable, actually." I felt prickly and anxious as I got to my feet, and slightly ashamed, too, though I could not have explained that if I'd tried. "But thanks for the coffee."

Carwyn, too, stood. "Thank you for coming out with me. Can I walk you to your car?"

I shook my head. "No, that's all right. I'm fine. Thank you again." And I hurried off before he could protest.

3

SUNDAY AFTERNOON. I'D neatened my one room and bath, done my laundry, finished my shopping and put all the groceries away, so there was no excuse not to make my way to the Willows to visit my grandmother. Doing my duty, I supposed. Though why she was so adamant about seeing me (at least according to my mother), I wasn't sure. Eleanor's affection for me, distant at best when I was a child—she had seemed more interested in the boy who did her yard work, actually—had become even more strained when I had married Rob. *He's all wrong for you,* she'd declared, *all wrong.* But that had been eleven years ago. Perhaps she wanted to gloat over my divorce? Perhaps she wanted to welcome me back into the fold, now I'd rid myself of my matrimonial encumbrance.

The assisted-living facility was across town, beyond the sprawl the university had become. The Willows also sprawled: a central two-story brick pseudo-plantation house, looking somewhat out of place in this whitewashed New England town, surrounded by a series of low-slung duplexes and triplexes for the more independent of the retirees. My grandmother, I'd learned from my mother, had chosen to live in the main building, her lack of husband and congestive heart failure causing her to think a proximity to help, if necessary, to be a wise move. I parked the car in one of the spots signed for visitors and made my way through the wide front door.

"Mrs. Ludlow?" The front desk might have been that of an exclusive hotel, and looking at the receptionist, in her dark suit, made me feel frightfully underdressed in my jeans. She gestured down a long corridor to the left. "Suite 14. At the end of this corridor, take a right through the conservatory. It will be at the end of the south hall." She smiled professionally. Behind her was an AED station.

I followed her directions, and after one wrong turn beyond the conservatory, found the door to suite 14. I knocked a bit nervously.

"Come!"

Immediately I was thrust backward twenty-five years into my childhood: the peremptory tone was unforgettable. Not unkind—my grandmother had never been unkind. However, there had always been an unmistakable air of formality to her voice and carriage. Perhaps it had been all those years as a dancer. I had never had the courage to ask. I also had never disobeyed an order from that voice.

"Good," she said, looking up as she crossed from the tiny kitchenette to the chairs facing one another across a polished coffee table. "I'm so glad you've come at last, Emily."

I stopped, uncertain. Did I kiss her?

She was carrying a tray laden with a silver tea service. I rushed to relieve her of it, and set it on the low table.

"You're expecting me?"

"Elaine told me she'd spoken to you and delivered my invitation. So yes, I was expecting you."

Invitation. I had not experienced it as an *invitation*.

The certainty. It jarred—how well she knew me. Or at least, that I would fulfill her expectations. There was no question on her part.

Remember Rob, I thought. And then thought better of it.

Eleanor poured for both of us, adding milk, but quirking her eyebrows in surprise when I stayed her hand at the sugar. "You've changed," she observed dryly. "More bitter?"

"Probably." I blew across the lip of the cup she handed me. "Divorces will do that to a person."

My grandmother clicked her tongue. "I can imagine." She refrained from saying *I told you so*; that kind of thing was simply not done. It was enough that she had warned against marrying Rob all that time ago. She had been correct, that he was not, ultimately, the man for me—there was, to her way of thinking, no reason to belabor the point, as time had proven her right.

"I'm sorry," she said after a moment. Surprisingly, but gracefully. "I shouldn't be flippant. It's too soon, isn't it?"

I was not used to apologies from Eleanor, any more than from Elaine. We didn't, in this family as a general rule, apologize. One quick jab, and then out. I took a deep breath and let my eyes rove around the room, over the pieces Eleanor had chosen to keep, furniture familiar from visits to her townhouse when she had been in residence. The drop-front desk, the dining room chairs—though the table seemed smaller. Even the service from which we drank our tea was a memory from my childhood. I took a sip from my cup, my eye falling on the bit of the ornate bed frame visible through the slightly open bedroom door. I wondered whether the carved wooden chest was still holding pride of place on the bedside table.

"Tell me about it, if you wish," Eleanor suggested, her green eyes warmer than I remembered. "If you feel up to it. If it helps." She turned her cup gently on her saucer. "I have no advice. Only commiseration."

It might have been the first time my grandmother had invited a heart-to-heart. So I suddenly found myself telling her, about Rob and Michelle and the law library, and how, suddenly, at thirty-two years old, I had no idea what I wanted anymore.

She nodded. "So you came home."

"To regroup." How do you tell someone like Eleanor—Nora Ludlow to the people in the know in her field—that you suddenly came to realize that, without your husband, your acceptance among friends of long standing was totally superficial? "To find out who I really am."

My grandmother took a final sip from her tea cup and set it aside. As she leaned back in her chair and folded her hands in her lap, the light gleamed on the coronet of braids wound around her head, and her narrow face took on an almost regal cast.

"Oh, no, Emily," she said firmly. "You are, to put it plainly, the queen of your own destiny. It only remains for you to realize that destiny."

Her words, which should have been reassuring, instead sent a chill through me.

4

"YOU'VE BEEN TO see Eleanor," Elaine said over the phone. It was not a question.

"I have," I replied cautiously.

The telephone call, at eight, was early for me. I used to go to the fitness center at the university before work when I'd lived in Wilmington, but that habit, like so many which I'd thought important, had been discarded by the wayside. Instead, I'd fallen into a pattern of walking around the neighborhood, sometimes as far as the river, after dinner. In place of dinner, some days. I used to like to cook, too, but now there was no one to cook for.

There was a pause. My mother would be getting ready to go into the law office at nine; I could imagine her choosing her earrings, tucking her silk scarf into the neckline of her conservative blue suit, brushing back her red-gold hair, so like mine, but trimmed severely short.

"What did you talk about?"

I did not, at first, want to admit that I'd poured out my innermost soul to Eleanor; it had been so unlike me, and would probably just make Elaine resentful that I had not told her the things I'd told her mother. Even that thought made me feel guilty, though.

"Me," I said finally. "Rob. Michelle. Divorce."

The monumental sigh was a blast in my ear. "You should have fought for him, Emily."

That's what I got; that's what I expected. "Two against one, Mom. I would have lost anyway." I glanced at the clock. This had to be a new record for phone calls spiraling into the void. "Listen, I'm getting ready for work. Maybe I could come over tonight and we could talk. Have a pizza or something."

I could feel her drawing back.

"Not tonight," she said quickly. "Soon. I'm busy tonight."

Elaine had always been busy.

"About your grandmother, though," she said.

"What about her?" I couldn't help the peevishness in my tone. At least Eleanor had time for me.

"Just be careful."

5

BE CAREFUL.

I was still pondering my mother's cryptic warning when I got into the library just at ten to find Carwyn at the computers. I paused in the double doorway, surprised that he had not sensed my appearance—he seemed attuned to my comings and goings, a thought which did not make me entirely comfortable. Right now he was leaning forward, frowning at the monitor before him, clicking between a website and a document. Every so often he would frown, bite his lower lip, and tap rapidly at the keyboard.

I watched him curiously. There *was* something familiar about him: I couldn't shake the idea. The way he moved? The way he smiled? He wasn't smiling now, as he worked. I wondered if it was still the online dossier giving him trouble. I could see the curving of his jaw from this angle, the blonde hair curling slightly into the back of his neck, the width of his shoulders. As I stood there, he leaned back and stretched his arms over his head, fingers splayed. He must have felt my eyes on him, for he half-turned, hands still aloft, and grinned.

"Caught me," he said.

"Good morning," I answered. Madeline passed, nodding, glancing pointedly from me to the clock. I hurried to the office behind the circulation desk to shed my coat and purse.

I HAD BARELY time to hang up my things on the hook before Madeline called back to me. I stuck my head out.

"This man says you've been helping him?" she said, sounding a bit miffed. "I offered to answer his question, but he seems to think you're familiar with his work." Her lipsticked mouth thinned into a line.

Carwyn smiled angelically. "Hello, Miss Hill."

I felt my cheeks grow warm. "I can take it from here," I said, tossing a rueful smile in my boss's direction. "What is it that you need, Mr. Grey?"

He led the way to the computer where he'd been wrestling with his work. His résumé was open again.

What do you need?" I asked again. I thought he'd told me his applications were all finished.

Carwyn rested his hand on the back of the desk chair. "Well, nothing here, actually."

"You lied again." I rolled my eyes. "And now Madeline is pissed off at me."

He winked. "I didn't actually *lie*. I do need to ask you something, and I didn't really want to ask your Madeline."

"What is it, then?" Still in work mode, I stepped closer to the screen, frowning. *Carwyn N. Grey.* The résumé looked the same as it had the last time.

"Would you consider going out to dinner with me?"

The question threw me into momentary panic, which gave way almost immediately to embarrassment. A date. A man was asking me out on a date. How long since that had happened? Since Rob, of course, since before we'd married, which was odd in and of itself. I wasn't married anymore, so I was allowed to respond to the overtures of a handsome man. At the same time, I still cowered before the ugliness—at least in my estimation—of the divorce; I backed away quickly from those overtures.

"Just a date," Carwyn urged, as though reading my thoughts. "Dinner. A movie. Not a big deal."

"I don't know." There were quite a few things I didn't know; how to respond to the offer was one of them.

Carwyn held up both hands and took a step back. "No worries. Maybe some other time."

He seemed genuinely disappointed, and suddenly I did, too. I choked back my misgivings and spoke before I could change my mind.

"No," I blurted. "Let's do it. Friday night?"

An enormous grin broke out over his face. He held out a hand, and I shook it. Then he raised his eyebrows, pointed randomly to the computer screen, and gave me a thumbs up. When I was about to speak, he muttered, "Your boss is giving us the evil eye. I hope she can't read lips." Then more loudly, "Thank you, Miss Hill. I think that'll work."

A COUPLE OF nights later, at the condo, Elaine slid her spare key across the breakfast bar to me. Almost reluctantly, I thought. But maybe I was just being too sensitive.

"You could have," she said, not for the first time, "stayed with me, you know."

Mixed signals. Passively, aggressively, expressing disappointment at my not doing the thing she had never suggested I should do. While delivering the key to her house as soon as I'd settled into my new place.

"I mean"—and she actually sniffed, brushing back her hair—"an efficiency?"

"It's all I need," I told her. Again. And it was. Coming from the big house in Wilmington, with all those rooms Rob and I had planned to fill eventually (the *eventually* never arriving), compacting in upon myself was almost welcome. I hadn't taken anything from the house; I'd let him sell what he didn't want—which was most of it—and we split the difference.

Elaine peered at me closely. "This probably isn't healthy. Have you seen someone? This sounds like depression to me."

"It's not, Mom," I said wearily.

But she continued on, roughshod. "You had everything: a handsome husband, a good job, a nice house. And you gave it all up. Really, that's not healthy."

"I didn't give up the marriage," I protested. Angrily. I couldn't make her listen. "I've told you. It was Rob's decision to get done."

As for me, I had thought it just a rough patch, albeit longer than any we'd had previously. Until the evening Rob had come home, his usually warm brown gaze shifting to the side, and said we needed to talk.

"I liked him," my mother said peevishly. "I thought he was a good man. Good for you."

Like I needed—what? Someone who would be good *for* me, not necessarily *to* me. Like I was somehow unbalanced.

But I took the key to the condo and jimmied it onto my keychain, all the while wondering why I'd thought coming back here would be a good idea. I fished my own spare key from my pocket and clanked it across to Elaine.

"It didn't work," I said shortly. "Rob wanted a divorce, so I let him have one, and then I needed to get away from a life where I didn't fit anymore." I sighed, throwing the keychain into my bag with more force than absolutely necessary. "Frankly, I was hoping for a bit more sympathy from you."

It was a good thing I was over the initial crying stage. Elaine would have been decidedly no help there at all.

"Especially since you, too, have lost your husband," I pressed.

"It's not the same," she shot back. "I was young. I had a child."

"And he died," I added.

"Yes," Elaine said, turning her face away as she always did, as though my bringing up my father's death had wounded her again. "He did. And I don't want to talk about this."

Always her response.

I should have known.

When I left—I had to be at work at the library early the next morning—the phone was ringing. My mother waved me out before answering, and as I made my way down the carefully-swept walk, I heard her say two things: "she's just leaving" and "not well."

I pretended it didn't bother me all the way to the car.

7

THE ONLY TIME it was possible for me to get to the Willows that week was on Thursday evening, because I'd volunteered to work end-of-academic-year inventory over the weekend, and because of the date on Friday night. If not then, I wouldn't be able to get back to see my grandmother in more than a week, and a niggling anxiety told me that was too long.

On this particular evening, the front desk was occupied by a dark-skinned man with close-cropped hair, rather than the officious woman I'd grown used to from the weekends; he made a bit more of an attempt at friendly conversation that the woman usually did. Trying to hide my impatience, I signed in on the visitor's log and set off, striding purposefully along the corridor and to the conservatory.

Eleanor's door, as was usual, was propped open, and a slight breeze moved into the corridor, carrying voices in conversation. I checked my wristwatch doubtfully, but it was well past time for the health care supervisor's visit. Uncertain, I paused just outside the door, listening.

"—pleasant," my grandmother was saying. "You know I always enjoyed finding out what you were up to when I returned home from a staging."

"Listening to your stories was what made me want to travel."

A man's voice—definitely not the health care supervisor's. Familiar.

"I'm glad you were finally able to. And I'm always glad when you come to tell me about your adventures, as I'm no longer able to be an adventurer myself."

There was a clink of tea things, a sound I recognized easily from the last several Sunday afternoons shared with my grandmother. *A cuppa:* I could hear the old woman's ironic words in my head, could see the curious way her lips twisted. I stood frozen, listening, feeling guilty for listening. Something in me felt strangely betrayed, though I could not for the life of me tell why. It was a familiar feeling, and unwelcome. That Eleanor would be having an evening tea party with someone, someone who wasn't *me*—and yet that didn't even make sense. In all the time I was growing up, my grandmother was frequently traveling, and when not, had frequent visitors. Even having taken up residence in this assisted living facility surely had not changed the fact that the old woman knew many people, and would have visitors other than me. Yet how soon I had adopted an unwarranted sense of my own importance in her life.

More clinking, a cup against a saucer. "Earl Grey," said the male voice appreciatively. "Thank you. I've had Earl Grey since those days in your parlor, but it's never been quite the same. I guess you and the tea will forever be connected in my mind."

My grandmother laughed. "Oh, you were always such a dramatic child."

I felt the dawning knowledge deep down, but still refused, for a moment, to recognize the voice. Someone my grandmother had known as a child. Someone my grandmother had had in her parlor. *Someone.*

"But I was able to be, with you," the man said. "And I have always been grateful for that freedom."

Then I knew.

THE SCENE AS I remembered, playing out in several minor variations:

I had stopped in at the townhouse one afternoon after school, when my mother had a partners' meeting and wouldn't know. Elaine had a just-in-case-key, which I had purloined from the kitchen just that morning, and now I let myself in through the side door. I heard the talking from the front room—Eleanor called it *the parlor*—and something made me think to muffle my footsteps as best I could on the hall rug. He was always there, it seemed, the boy who mowed her lawn, who clipped her hedges, and who came in for tea afterward. He was there now.

"Oh, yes," Eleanor was saying, "he was a very hard task master. He demanded perfection. Always."

"Like you?"

He was Nick, then: the boy from down the road, the youngest of a big family . . . or perhaps there was a younger one? A sister? At some point my grandmother had hired him, and then he'd become a fixture. In the way of self-righteous awkward put-upon children, I'd resented that.

Eleanor had laughed at whatever comparison Nick was suggesting. "I learned from the best," she told him. "I was indeed very very lucky." And yet, when I thought about it, there was an odd note in her voice which belied her words—as though she believed it was not luck but her just deserts which had delivered her into the hands of the very hard task master, which had enabled her to learn from the very best.

"Will you dance for me now?" Nick asked.

Surprised by his forwardness, I crept closer to the parlor door.

"One of his?" my grandmother asked, amused. "Or one of mine?"

"Yours."

And then, shockingly, I heard it: the whisper of her footsteps as she danced. I moved closer to the door and peered around the corner. In the stage formed by the bow window at the front of the room, Eleanor stood with her arms upraised, fingers curled gently, eyes closed; then she moved, her upper body suggesting a narrow tree in the wind. There was something commanding, regal, in the way she was both herself and something other than herself. I was barely aware of Nick on the Queen Anne sofa, his expression rapt.

My gasp shattered the moment.

"Emily," my grandmother said, opening her eyes. "What a surprise. Join us."

"No. Thank you. I just—" I stumbled awkwardly over the words, tangled by my grandmother's dancing, by Nick her audience, by feeling that I was not supposed to be there. "I'm sorry—you're busy—" And I fled.

Thinking about that, I was ashamed of my own reaction, and at the same time, defensive. The dance had made me uncomfortable then, and the memory made me uncomfortable now.

CARWYN.

I felt the ground slip beneath me in the way it had in those early days of my husband's betrayal. *The things I knew, I didn't know at all.* Carwyn was in my grandmother's suite now, having tea. Carwyn, who had been Nick then, had known my grandmother as a child. He had never said anything. But then— had he even known that the old woman and I were related? I thought back to our discussion over coffee, over computer monitors: surely I had not mentioned my grandmother to him. But I wasn't sure. He had seemed familiar, but the new name had thrown me off; it was such an unusual name that I would have remembered anyone called that. *Carwyn N. Grey. N* for *Nick*, obviously.

No need to panic. No need to get wound up about anything, either. I forced myself to breathe slowly: how angry was I? I could feel my heartbeat, huge in my chest, a sure sign of the confusion and fury I'd been feeling off and on for the past several months. Over-thinking, something I'd done quite a bit since the night Rob and I *had to talk*. Right now, I simply had to see what Carwyn had to say for himself, before I decided upon my reaction. I took a deep breath, then stepped forward to knock on the door of the suite.

The conversation broke off abruptly.

"It's just me," I announced, stepping into the room, immediately recognizing the inanity of the words.

"So it is," Carwyn said, setting his cup and saucer on the coffee table and rising from his chair.

He did not look at all surprised to see me.

Neither did my grandmother. Eleanor looked up and smiled. "Emily. I didn't expect you until Sunday." She too set aside her teacup. "Join us. Let me get you a cup."

Carwyn waved the old woman back down as she began to rise from her chair. "No, let me." I watched as he moved without hesitation to the cupboard to the left of the sink, where he withdrew another cup and saucer. This he brought to Eleanor, who poured a dollop of milk into the cup and filled the rest with tea, just as I liked it. No sugar. Bitter.

I set my purse on the occasional table near the door and drew up the chair my grandmother indicated. Wordlessly I accepted my cup and saucer.

"You know Nick," Eleanor said.

My eyes shot to his face. Carwyn seemed unconcerned. If anything, a bit amused.

"I don't know him *as* Nick," I said slowly.

Eleanor dipped her head in acknowledgement, or perhaps apology. "No, no, my mistake. He goes by Carwyn now." She bestowed a smile upon him. "I can't quite get my old brain around that, of course." Back to me, as though participating in a game of conversational tennis. "He was Nick as a child."

As if that explained everything.

I took a sip of the tea. It was still hot, but not uncomfortably so; I wondered how long the pot had been sitting on the low table between the two. The silver gleamed, and I could see myself, distorted, in the pot. Probably she had Nick— Carwyn—over to polish the silver now she no longer had lawns for him to mow.

Boy, that was catty.

"I didn't expect you, my dear. Not that you're not welcome—I'm always glad to see you." My grandmother's words and smile were warm, but there was a question. "But you're such a creature of habit—"

I shrugged noncommittally. "I'll be working all weekend. I won't be able to be in on Sunday."

"And we have a date tomorrow night, Emily and I," Carwyn added. His eyes crinkled at the corners, as though daring me to deny it.

"We *might* have a date tomorrow night," I shot back. "I mean—I made a date with a guy named Carwyn, but I'm not sure who the hell you are."

At this he laughed outright. "*Touché.*" He held out a hand. "Allow me to introduce myself. Carwyn Grey. Carwyn Niclas Grey."

"Formerly Nick?" I shook his hand, albeit suspiciously, looking down at it as though it might hold a snake or a knife.

"Until my father died." His smile shadowed a bit. "Then there was no confusion. He was the first and the best Carwyn."

After a pause, Eleanor lifted the teapot again. "Top you off?" She poured and set the pot aside, then turned back to us and smiled almost proudly. "And so you have a date tomorrow evening. Isn't that just lovely? Where are you going, do you know yet? Have you decided?"

Again I shrugged, feeling more than a bit embarrassed. More than embarrassed: in need of escape. Eleanor might not have thought Rob was a good choice for me, but she certainly seemed pleased that I'd agreed to a date with Carwyn. Nick. Her favorite.

"Dinner," Carwyn was saying; he seemed unaware of my reaction. "A film, perhaps. What would you suggest for a restaurant?"

But Eleanor only held out her fine-boned hands, helplessly, palms up. "Oh, heavens, I don't know. I very rarely went out when I lived here before. I saved all those adventures for traveling."

"Better restaurants where you were going?" His tone was light, teasing.

"Foolish young man," Eleanor admonished. "When you're traveling, all the restaurants are better. You know that. Adventure tastes good."

He saluted the rightness of the judgment by lifting the teacup to her before taking a drink.

I found myself glancing from one to the other, envious of the ease of their teasing. It was, I realized jealously, the ease of long familiarity. A long familiarity I did not have with either of them, and the jealousy made me edgy. Angry.

I was surprised at how naturally the anger came.

"I'LL WALK YOU out to your car," he said, once the tea things were washed and put away.

"You don't need to." My jaw felt stiff, from trying not to grind my teeth.

The mood had changed. I had changed it and couldn't change it back, even had I wanted to. The anger was old, and all the more dangerous because of its smoldering.

"Emily," my grandmother interjected impatiently. "Don't be a stick."

So at Eleanor's urging, I allowed Carwyn to play the gentleman. The night was cool, it being a damp spring; we bid the man at the front desk a good evening and let ourselves out into the parking lot. For a long moment I stood next to my car, key in hand, and looked back toward the front door. Somewhere far below University Hill, a siren wailed before trailing off in the distance.

"So I didn't tell you everything," Carwyn said at last, shuffling his feet in the dirt on the pavement.

I refused to look at him.

"No, *Nick*, you didn't."

"In my defense, I thought you'd recognize me."

I laughed shortly, a bitter sound. "I haven't seen you in twenty-odd years. You've changed a bit—and I don't just mean your name."

"You haven't changed much at all."

I didn't know why this should make the heat rush into my face.

"So," I managed after a moment, "you knew all along who I was in the library."

His silence was admission enough.

Anger wouldn't let me think of another thing to say—or rather, it got in the way of organizing my furious thoughts into any coherent words. He had set me up. I couldn't help but think that. And yet—why on earth would he do such a thing? We hadn't laid eyes on one another in more than twenty years, and even then the only point of congruence had been my grandmother, a woman who, at that time, had been far more interested in Carwyn—Nick—than she had been in me, her own grandchild.

"She didn't like me better," he said now, and his apparent ability to read my mind just added to my anger. I snorted.

"Emily," he said, and his voice hardened. "When I was a kid, she helped me. More than I could ever tell you. She understood things about me that my parents didn't, or wouldn't, or couldn't. I was grateful that she let me do yard work for her, that she let me keep an eye on the house when she was in Europe."

"She paid more attention to you than to me."

"Have you ever asked her about that?"

"No," I shot back, defensively, as though he had probed a sore spot. Which he had.

He put out a hand, and I stepped away, not wanting him to touch me, not wanting him to release me from the anger that had taken hold, and not really knowing why I should hang onto it, either.

"You know she's had a less than comfortable relationship with your mother for years."

"Let's not bring my mother into it."

But he had, and now there was another thing I couldn't ignore, working its way up through the sludge of memory. My mother's voice on the phone, impatient, as though delivering a message grudgingly: *your grandmother wants to see you.* As though shunting off a responsibility, but not happy about doing so.

"And she's always thought you've avoided her, perhaps because of that."

"Stop." I pressed the button on the key fob to unlock the car, then jerked the door open, a clear dismissal. "You don't know about me. You don't know about my mother. You don't know any of us—you're not family." I slipped into the driver's seat and slammed the door, but not quickly enough to shut out his last words.

"I know Eleanor," he said.

8

"YOU HAVE TO at least let me explain," he said the next afternoon, holding out the single daffodil.

I stared at it, my hands resolutely by my sides. The yellow trumpet blared from the spray of white petals edged with the tiniest band of red. I knew exactly which bed on campus he had picked it from. Just another sign, I decided, tugging the edges of my anger around me, of his nature: stealing flowers from a community college flowerbed.

"I don't have to let you do anything," I said firmly. I shoved my hair back behind my ears and bent back to the book cart.

"Emily," he said. That was all.

"And I don't know why you think I'd still be interested in going out this evening with you. I really don't." My voice was rising, and I caught myself, stopped the torrent of words that burbled in my throat. *No need to make a scene in the library.* A glance around told me no one seemed to have noticed. Yet.

"Because you're curious."

His mouth quirked in that way I'd first found interesting. Attractive. I looked away again quickly.

And he was reading me correctly, damn it. That made me even angrier, though the feeling now had a rusty quality to it, as though it was past-dated. From last night, of course. But anger was the only thing I had left on my side—I had learned this since the divorce—the only thing that kept me moving, one foot in front of the other. I had to hold it close.

"Aren't you curious to know why I was there last night?"

"No." It was a lie, and he knew it. I pulled a book from the pile on the desk, scanned it with the hand-held, and found its place on the cart, where I shoved it in, perhaps a bit more roughly than it deserved.

"Last night—the night you just happened to be going to visit, even though everyone knows you usually visit on Sundays?"

"Everyone *does not* know that." Another book scanned and slammed. I turned my back on him.

Carwyn seemed to have all day. He appeared intent upon waiting me out. For the first time ever, I wished for Madeline's hovering, disapproving presence. But then, what would I say to her? *Madeline, Carwyn's being mean to me.* Yeah, that would work.

There were no more books on the desk, so I unlocked the wheels of the cart, kicked at them bad-temperedly, and pushed the load of books out into the stacks. Not a lot this afternoon, but then, hardly anyone signed out books anymore; I had to pass by the banks of computers where students squinted at the screens instead.

He was following me, daffodil in hand.

Halfway along the first row, I stopped to pluck a book from the cart for re-shelving. Then I whirled on him, volume in hand like a weapon.

"Don't you have somewhere you have to be?" I hissed.

He only shrugged. "Not yet." He held up his hands. "No job offers yet."

"I hope you applied for positions far, far away."

Rather than annoy him, my responses seemed to delight him. He laughed. "Everywhere, actually. But I'm here now, and you're almost off work, and I brought you this flower, and you know you really just want to come out with me and have me explain all of this." He held out the daffodil again, and when I did not take it, set it lightly on the book I still held in both hands. "Because you're curious, Emily. You've always been curious."

"Not about you."

"Fair enough," he replied. "But you want to know how it transpired that you and I are standing here in the stacks of the community college library, arguing about something that doesn't really matter."

His eyes were sky blue. And steady. His gaze this afternoon was unabashed. Teasing, even, now that he no longer was pretending to be someone else, a stranger. I bit my lip, looking down at the poor illicit daffodil, sacrificed as a peace offering I was refusing to accept.

"Over something that's *never* really mattered," he added.

Again I half-turned, dumping the daffodil on the cart before slipping the book into its place on the shelf among the rest of its fellows. I wanted to remain angry, but suddenly I was exhausted: the effort was just too much. There was a weariness between my shoulder blades that weighed me down.

"Let me help you with these," he said quietly. "And then we can get out of here."

"I DIDN'T DRESS for it," I said, climbing out of the passenger seat of his Celica at the curb.

"Because you weren't going to come out," Carwyn said. He flicked the lock on his key fob, then pocketed the keys. "It's all right. This isn't an overly dressy establishment. Just good for dinner and a drink is all."

"And an explanation," I reminded him darkly. "You're doing all the talking, and there had better be a lot of it."

I followed him around the corner of the building to the heavy front door. He held it for me. Inside, a waiter at the bar acknowledged us with a lift of the chin, then grabbed a couple of menus.

"Carwyn," the waiter said.

"Were you able to save me the rear booth?"

"Come on back."

It was a relatively small place, with an ornate bar to the right, some hightops down the center, and booths along the left-hand wall next to the windows. At the front, a tiny raised stage held a rather placid string band. Friday evening, early, but still noisy, no doubt from the end-of-the-week beer crowd; I could see why the rear booth would be the one of choice for any kind of conversation. I slid across the seat and ordered a Smithwick's from the menu printed above the bar.

Carwyn nodded approvingly. "I like a girl who doesn't drink yellow beer."

"It's my grain serving for the day. And it matches my mood." I opened the menu on the table before me and studied it pointedly.

After the waiter returned with our pint glasses and took our orders, I folded my hands on the scarred wood and cleared my throat. "The floor, Carwyn—*Nick*—is all yours."

He took a long sip from his Guinness, then set the glass down in the dead center of the coaster. "I knew your grandmother when you and I were kids," he said slowly.

"Better than I did."

He held up a hand. "We'll get to that." He was staring down into the stout as though the answers to all the questions in the universe could be found in its black depths. Suddenly he laughed, a sound nearly drowned out by a wave of noise from the bar. There was a soccer game on the television overhead, but European, I noted, so *football*. "It's suddenly so complicated, now that I'm trying to explain. So many layers."

"Start by telling me: you two kept in touch? All these years?"

"You were the one who went away, not me." Carwyn shrugged. "Sorry. That came out wrong. But you have to understand that Eleanor was the one who encouraged me to go to the university once I got out of high school. No one else did. She's the one who sparked my interest in the world, sending me all those postcards when she was off on her productions."

I sank back against the hard wood of the booth. "I didn't know she sent you postcards, too." The postcards had been a mixed bag for me: she was thinking about me, she was far away. I was ambivalent about them, but they were mine. This just seemed like another betrayal.

He nodded. "They were a kind of life-line when I was a teenager. Someone out there cared that I did well. Someone out there was encouraging me." He tipped his head, smiling gently, but his eyes were focused on a memory, not on me.

The idea gave me pause. That Carwyn had lived the sort of life where encouragement was in such short supply that he looked forward to each postcard from a woman in a faraway place, cheering him on. I hadn't really needed that encouragement, had I? My mother, thought distant and mostly angry, had always had expectations, and I had known what they were. College, a decent job, marriage, children. At least, I thought bitterly, I had fulfilled *some* of those.

"And then Eleanor was back, and this time for good." Saying those words seemed to pain him, as though he were looking at a bleak future, one in which the source of his courage was no longer there. He coughed, took another sip from his pint of Guinness. "I helped her sort out her house. There wasn't much, really—she had been down-sizing for years, and knew exactly what she wanted to keep, what she wanted to give away." His lips twisted for a moment, and with a shock, I realized it was an expression of disgust. "She offered most of it to your mother."

"Who probably turned it all down flat," I rejoined.

"Yes. Elaine didn't want it. She already had enough in her own house." Carwyn shook his head. "Your mother—"

"I know. The most unsentimental person I've ever known. She's not into things with history." I sighed, turning my glass around on its coaster. "I rather wish she'd saved some things out for me—my apartment's rather bare—but I guess none of us knew"—and I looked away quickly, toward the band on the tiny stage—"that I'd need anything." Nobody had known I'd need anything, save that Rob might have had an inkling at some point.

Carwyn cleared his throat. "Yeah. I'm sorry about that, Emily."

"Another thing Eleanor told you about?" The betrayals were coming thick and fast, and they tasted of bile in the back of my mouth. Even taking a drink of my beer did not allay the taste.

"She mentioned it," he said evenly. "When she mentioned you were coming back home from Wilmington." This time his smile was sympathetic, reassuring. "We didn't talk about it in depth, don't worry. Some things are best left alone." He held up his left hand, his ring finger bare. "My divorce, too. Except that Eleanor told me it was for the best."

"Eleanor was glad you divorced? She passed that judgment on you?" There was a bit of satisfaction to be had from that, anyway.

"Made me furious, let me tell you. I stayed away from her for a long time, I was so angry." He sighed ruefully. "She said Melanie was all wrong for me."

"Wow." Just like my grandmother's judgment about Rob. *All wrong.*

"Well, she was right, I suppose. It's been four years. It's just that in the midst of the break-up, that might not be exactly what you want to hear from the one person you thought always had your back. If you know what I mean."

The waiter reappeared suddenly, carrying plates. He set the burger and sweet potato fries down in front of Carwyn, the chicken pesto wrap in front of me.

"I think another Guinness, Justin. Another Smithwick's for you?" Carwyn indicated my suddenly nearly-empty glass, and I nodded. "Thanks, Justin."

The waiter moved off again into the rising din of the swelling Friday night crowd.

"Good thing we got here when we did," I observed, plucking the toothpick from my wrap and setting it aside. I could no longer hear the music from the front.

Carwyn glanced back over his shoulder. "True. Though I wasn't sure we would get here to begin with." He winked. "It was a toss-up between this, you turning me down flat, or you punching me in the face."

"I've never punched anyone in the face."

"There's always a first time."

I lifted the wrap gingerly and took a bite. Chicken, pesto, bacon, lettuce. A combination I'd consider punching anyone in the face for. Nice, but messy. I wiped my mouth with the napkin. "Keep talking," I said, uncertain as to whether I wanted to know anything else, but—I had to admit it—Carwyn had been right, and I was curious. "You knew I was coming back from Wilmington. Eleanor told you."

"Yes."

"She told you I'd be working at the library."

He made a face, dipping a sweet potato fry into his pool of catsup. "Not at first. I saw you working there, and thought I recognized you. So I asked Eleanor, and she said yes, that I was right, and that it was you."

"So you *were* stalking me."

Carwyn ate the fry, followed it with a bite of his burger and the final drink from his pint. "Kind of sounds like it when you put it that way, doesn't it?" He looked vaguely uncomfortable. "To be fair, I have been legitimately working on my applications. The internet's better than it is in my apartment."

"Maybe you should get better internet."

He laughed. "Beggars, as they say, can't be choosers. I've been stealing internet from the Dunkin' Donuts downstairs for the past couple of years. Don't tell."

"Thief."

"Better believe it."

Justin returned, deposited their new pints, and whisked the empty glasses away with him.

"I was working up my courage to talk to you."

"Horse hockey."

"It's true."

I didn't believe him. I took another bite of the sandwich, got pesto on my face, and wiped up quickly with the napkin before anyone noticed.

"Eleanor said she thought we should become reacquainted. That we had so much in common."

Suddenly the anger was back, flooding up the back of my throat. I felt my temperature rise. "Great. So now she's playing matchmaker between me and her favorite."

"Stop it," he flashed, his anger rising to greet mine. "You've really got to get over this put-upon idea that you're some sort of runner-up in your grandmother's affections. You're not. If you only knew how much she wished you two were closer when you were a kid—"

"You talked about me. Not just lately. Back then."

"That's not the way it was."

"Bullshit. That *is* the way it was. That's the way it is. And I've heard enough."

I threw my napkin on the table, grabbed my purse, and hurled myself out of the booth.

"Emily—"

But I was out of the restaurant and into the street. I never looked back.

IT WAS ONLY about a mile and a half back to the campus lot and the car, and I was used to walking. I kept my keys between my fingers as a weapon and strode purposefully, but the streets heading up the hill away from the river were well-lit. Still, I was grateful when I noticed the police car cruising along in my periphery. It went up a few blocks, then turned and came back.

"Are you all right, ma'am?"

The cruiser had slowed, the officer rolling down the window.

Did I not look all right?

I paused, nodding. "My car's up here at the community college. Just walked out on a bad date."

The officer scanned the street. "Do you need a lift?"

I shook my head. "Thanks. I'm all right. It's just up here."

There was a squawk from the police radio. The officer looked down at his computer, then back up. "You have a phone?" When I pulled it from my pocket, he smiled. "Good, then. Call if you need us. I'll be around the neighborhood."

Still, by the time I reached the lot beside the library, I was sniffling and battling tears. I dragged a sleeve across my face as I slammed a thumb into the "unlock" button. Overhead a light buzzed and flickered, and I realized that my head was pounding. The drink, the anger.

When I got home, I poured myself a shot of whiskey, a double, and downed it. After a moment, I felt it coming back up. I barely made it to the bathroom in time.

9

THE STRIDENT RING of the phone cut through my confused and ugly dreams, and I knocked the cell onto the floor as I groped for the light on the table at the end of the futon.

"It took you long enough," Elaine said.

I fought through headachy grogginess to consciousness. "Mom. What is it?"

"Your grandmother. She's at the hospital. She complained of chest pain and shortness of breath, and they decided to transport."

There might have been the slightest trace of panic in my mother's voice, a note that was tamped down firmly.

"Are you there?"

"I'm on my way. I'm in the car. They just called from the Willows."

"Okay. Let me get some clothes on. I'll meet you there."

I stumbled out of bed. I was still fully clothed, but my shirt felt clammy, and smelled of sweat. I stripped it off, threw it aside, and grabbed another tee-shirt on the way to the bathroom. There I splashed water on my face and dragged my fingers through my tangled hair. My mouth tasted foul, my tongue thick and furry. I uncapped the mouthwash and took a gulp straight from the neck of the bottle, swished and spat. My purse and keys were on the counter; I shoved my feet into flip flops and was out the door.

MY MOTHER WAS perched on the edge of a salmon-pink plastic chair, her long fingers snapping and unsnapping the clasp on her bag. She looked up as the doors slid open for me. Her lips were pursed tightly.

"Don't say it." I held up a hand. "I got here as fast as I could."

"You look like it," Elaine said.

"Of course I do. It's the middle of the night, for crying out loud." I took the mint green chair next to her. "Where is she? How is she?"

Elaine only shook her head. "I don't know. They're running tests of some sort. I haven't seen her." She sniffed, and I glanced at her. But she looked away, her short hair swinging forward to hide her face.

A television hummed on the far wall. A woman and a man, seated behind a desk, seemed to be arguing. My eyes felt hot and gritty when I rubbed them. Not for the first time, I regretted the whisky. My stomach was roiling.

"Was it a heart attack? What happened?"

"I don't know. I don't *know.*"

Elaine's voice was shaking. She lifted her head, and I noted the heavy lines to the sides of her eyes, between her brows. Without makeup, my mother suddenly looked her age, and I felt an unexpected twinge of sympathy. I reached out impulsively for her hand; but Elaine quickly opened the purse and withdrew a tissue, which she used to dab her eyes.

Nice dodge, I thought bitterly. I shoved my hands into my jacket pockets.

"Mrs. Ludlow?" A man in blue scrubs approached. A stethoscope hung about his neck; an ID swung from the hem of his shirt. His eyes were red-rimmed beneath the tumble of his dark hair.

Elaine stood. She tucked the tissue back into her purse. "Harris. Eleanor Ludlow is my mother."

I stood silently, hovering behind her shoulder.

"It's not a heart attack," the doctor said.

"What, then?"

"Atrial fibrillation." He brushed his hair off his forehead. "In short, an irregular heartbeat." He held up his hands. "*Not* immediately life-threatening."

The mask of impatience I knew so well now slipped down to cover my mother's relieve. "I sense a 'but' coming," she said.

The doctor looked at Elaine appraisingly. "If untreated, a-fib can lead to damage that can result in a heart attack, or, more likely, a stroke. Your mother did absolutely the right thing in calling for help from the people at the residence."

"So what's the plan now?"

"Well, we've regulated her heartbeat with electrical impulse, but in many patients, that only holds for maybe eighteen hours. So I'd like to admit her and keep her for observation."

Elaine nodded, but I could still feel the tension emanating from my mother. "And if that doesn't hold?" I asked.

The doctor, for the first time, let his eyes flicker to me. "And you are?"

"Eleanor is my grandmother," I said. "I'm Emily Hill."

Now the doctor glanced quickly around the waiting room, his eyes roving over the late-night sparseness. "Are there any more of you? Mrs. Ludlow's husband, maybe?"

Elaine's mouth tightened. Her eyes flickered at me for the briefest moments—I nearly missed the look—before returning to the doctor. "My father is dead. We are the only family. But—the treatment?"

Her brusque manner seemed to annoy the doctor. His tired eyes narrowed. "We might need to consider some drug therapies. The biggest concern is making sure that the upper chambers of Mrs. Ludlow's heart empty as much blood as possible. If it pools there, there's the danger of clotting and stroke."

"Can we see her?" I asked. My voice was barely above a whisper.

Eleanor might die. My grandmother might die.

SHE LOOKED AMAZINGLY small in the midst of the clicking and beeping and whirring machinery. Her eyes were closed, an oxygen tube snaking into her nose, and her hair was a disordered white cloud which she no doubt would hate, had she been aware of it. Her left hand was clenched, at her side, into a fist. Beside the bed, a nurse checked first one monitor, then another; then, with a faint smile, she slipped out of the darkened room.

Elaine gasped one time, and then her jaw returned to its former hardness. My instinct, once again, was to reach for her arm, but, as if sensing this, Elaine moved quickly away, to stand by the bedside, her hands clutching the rail.

"I'm not dead yet, Elaine," Eleanor rasped.

I remained just inside the door, in shadow. I kept my eyes on my grandmother, feeling the unreality of the situation. I could not remember—not recently, not from childhood—a time when I had seen this woman so still. Even in the dim light, her fine papery skin seemed brittle and grey, parchment grown old. Only the fist gave a hint of the woman I was used to. I felt a panic, and looked around desperately for some reassurance.

"You're not dancing," Elaine retorted, a bit more sharply than was warranted with a nearly ninety-year-old hospitalized woman. Now I felt awkward, in the presence of the fraught relationship between these two.

"It's been a long time, Lady of Shalott, since I danced in the middle of the night."

"Don't call me that."

A silence fell between them, uneasy on my mother's part, exhausted on my grandmother's, and filled only with the clicking of the monitors. A sudden beeping surprised them, and the nurse appeared, adjusting, pushing buttons, gliding away again.

"If all you want to do is argue, Elaine," Eleanor said slowly, "then go home. I'm tired." She blinked once, twice, and then closed her eyes again. "Come back in the morning."

"Mother—"

"And send me Emily," Eleanor added. "I want to see her."

Sucking in a harsh breath, Elaine turned away. At the door she hissed, "You're up, then," and yanked the handle. The door swung shut behind her.

Gingerly I moved to the bedside. Like my mother, I found myself gripping the rail for support.

"Why do you two do that to each other?" I whispered at last.

"For the same reason you two do that to each other." Eleanor's eyes flickered open briefly. There might have been the ghost of a wry twist to her lips, but in the dim light it was hard to tell. She sighed. "Sit, Emily. Sit and stay with me until I fall asleep, will you?"

"Yes." I dragged a chair forward and sank into it, now leaning my head against the top rail. I reached for Eleanor's hand, still fisted; at the touch, my grandmother loosened her grip on whatever compelled her, and twined her bony fingers with mine.

AT SOME POINT toward morning, I woke to find my grandmother's eyes upon me; our fingers were still entwined.

"I'm sorry that you ever thought I didn't love you." Eleanor smiled weakly, and there was something in it that made me uneasy. "I've just been worried. About your future. Your destiny."

I blinked groggily. The headache remained, scraps of black gossamer at the periphery of my thoughts. My tongue still felt thick. "I don't understand."

She didn't answer.

Confused, I leaned back in the chair and fell into an uncomfortable sleep.

10

THE VIBRATING OF my phone in my pocket woke me to muted sunlight falling through the heavy curtains at the window. My back and my neck were killing me. Eleanor was eating breakfast daintily from a tray.

"I've saved you some toast," she said, when she noticed my waking. "And marmalade." She indicated the tray with a hand, and caught up the oxygen tube and frowned. "I wish they'd take this ridiculous thing out. It's in my way."

I fumbled for the cell phone, but I'd missed the call by the time I was able to focus on the screen. *Damn.* Madeline. My boss. I looked at the time: 8:44.

"I was supposed to work this morning," I said, pressing the key to return the call. "I'm already late." While I waited for Madeline to pick up, I reached for the triangle of toast.

"You can go to work," Eleanor said. "I'm fine here. They'll send me back to the Willows soon enough. That handsome young resident told me so. While you were sleeping." Her eyes traveled to the door, as though the handsome young resident would appear there at her will; her expression was curious, thoughtful. "He seems to think sometime later this afternoon—he wants to keep the heart monitor on until then, and make a decision about *drug therapy*, as he calls it."

The phone clicked at the other end. I quickly explained the situation, holding out the toast for my grandmother to spoon a dollop of marmalade onto it. "I'll need a quick shower," I told Madeline, "and a change of clothes. Can you give me an hour?"

When I rang off, I wolfed down the toast. Eleanor buttered and marmaladed the second triangle and handed it to me wordlessly.

"Thank you for staying with me, dear," she said as I gathered up my purse and jacket.

I pulled up short. "What time this afternoon?"

"I'm sorry?"

"What time is that handsome resident going to spring you? You'll need a ride back to the Willows, won't you?" I wondered whether Elaine would come, to take her mother home, and decided not to think about that scenario.

But Eleanor shook her head. "Carwyn can come for me. Call him for me, won't you? Tell him what's happened."

I felt my spine stiffen, and was swamped by a sudden rush of empathy for my mother. *Carwyn. Damn his eyes.* Always Carwyn. I sucked in a breath and nodded. Eleanor could give with one hand and take with the other, and enjoy every moment of it.

"And tell him not to worry. You know what he's like."

I wished I didn't.

It wasn't until I was pulling out of the hospital parking garage that I realized that Eleanor had a perfectly good telephone on the bedside table in the hospital room.

"EMILY," HE SAID. "Thank God. When you walked out last night—"

I brushed past his relief. "Eleanor told me to call you."

He actually laughed. "That woman. Always organizing things."

"She's at University Hospital, and she wants you to give her a ride back to the Willows this afternoon."

"The hospital?" His tone shifted immediately to concern. "What's happened? What's the matter?"

"She also said to tell you not to worry—she thought you'd react this way."

"*Tell me what happened.*"

"A-fib, the doctor said. They kept her overnight for observation."

"What does that even mean?"

I sighed impatiently. "It means she wants you to go to University Hospital and pick her up this afternoon and bring her back to the Willows. I'm sure she'll tell you everything you want to know then. She just ordered me to relay the message to you."

"Emily—"

"Listen. She wants you, not me. She told me to go to work. So I'm going to work. And I've got to go now." I jabbed the red icon on the screen, cutting him and any other noise he chose to make off, then tossed the phone over into the passenger seat.

11

"IT SEEMS," ELEANOR said, crossing to the sofa and lowering herself stiffly, leaning heavily on the onyx cane—a new addition, "that I have angered everyone: you, your mother, Carwyn."

Settled, she held up the cane and glared at it as though at her worst enemy; and perhaps, for a woman who had spent her professional life as a dancer and choreographer, it truly was. She set it aside and crossed her ankles delicately. The feeling that had surprised me upon seeing her in the hospital bed now returned. When had Eleanor become so small? She seemed to have diminished, and being released from the hospital had not mitigated that shrinkage. At least, however, she was fully dressed, her hair carefully wound in her accustomed coronet.

"I'm nearly ninety, you know," she said, raising her elegantly shaped eyebrows. She might have been reading my mind. "This aging business is not unexpected. However, it is still annoying." She sighed. "And I fear it will only get worse."

I brought out the tea tray and set it on the table before my grandmother. Then I slid into the chair on the other side.

"Play mother, Emily, will you, please?" she requested. "Milk for me. And one sugar."

I leaned forward, poured the milk into the teacup first, as I knew Eleanor preferred, and dropped in one lump of sugar with the silver tongs before filling the cup with steaming tea. I handed the cup across, then poured my own. Today I wanted it black. *Black as my heart. And just as bitter.*

"I've angered everyone," Eleanor repeated. She smiled, not looking in the least repentant. "But I'm an old woman. A very old woman. And the rest of you are just going to have to humor me."

I wasn't going to ask. I wasn't. And I did. "How have you angered Carwyn?"

The look my grandmother cast me was reminiscent of Carwyn: *you're curious.* Her lips quirked slightly.

"He's angry that he wasn't informed straight away when I was transported. He's angry that I only wished him to give me a ride home. *You only think of me as a cabbie,* he said, or something to that effect. *Not a person with feelings.*" Eleanor's tone was a sharp imitation of Carwyn. She sighed again, sipping at her tea. "I'm sure he'll come around. It's just so tiresome that he's that sensitive about everything." Again she sipped from her cup, looking archly at me over the rim. "It's tiresome that you're so sensitive about everything as well." She laughed mirthlessly. "You two are so much alike. It's as though you were made for each other."

I set my own cup in its saucer with a decided click. Ready to protest.

"I'm an old woman, Emily," Eleanor reminded me.

"One who knows how to push my buttons," I countered.

"Drink your tea."

Quite frankly, I had never felt less like drinking tea. I set the cup and saucer carefully on the low table. What I wanted, really wanted, was to throw both pieces across the room, smash them to smithereens.

"And when you're done," Eleanor said slowly, as though coming to a very great decision, "I need to show you something. Something very important. I shouldn't have left it this long, but I had to be certain." She drained her own cup, then, surprisingly, turned it over on the saucer. She lifted it, and the tea leaves made a pattern against the glaze. She stared down at them, her lips twisted slightly. Studying the arrangement, she frowned, then set both cup and saucer aside on the tray. "It's time."

"What do you mean, it's time?" Despite myself, I leaned forward to look at my grandmother's saucer, but could not see anything but the damp mush of tea leaves. They meant nothing to me, told me no secrets. "Time for what?"

Eleanor took up her napkin and wiped her fingers carefully, delicately. The frown still wrinkled the papery skin between her pale brows. "I need you to go to the bedroom and bring the small wooden chest from my bedside table. You know the one." She looked up, and her green eyes blazed as brilliantly as emeralds in her sudden excitement. "It's time," she repeated, more to herself than to me.

Puzzled, I did as I was told. The bedroom, when I let myself into it, was dark, the curtains pulled against the daylight, and it smelled of rosewater. As my eyes adjusted, I made out the table, the lamp, and then the dark squat box. The one I remembered from childhood.

"Get the key, too, Emily," her grandmother called. "In the case in the top drawer of the table? It has a ribbon on it."

I flicked on the lamp and opened the drawer. Inside was a pad of paper, a collection of pens, a small coin purse. I twisted the clasp of the purse and found the key, a wisp of worn red velvet tied to it. The chest, when I picked it up, was heavier than I expected, and rough beneath my hands, carved all over its sides and domed lid. I cradled it against my chest and pulled the door closed behind me.

"Are we finished with the tea things?" my grandmother asked, though she clearly was. She held her hands out for the box. It was an order, and I delivered the chest, then removed the tray to the kitchen counter. Once the table was clear, she set the little casket in the center, but kept both wrinkled hands on it, as though afraid it might escape. Or as though it were her child, the one she dearly loved. "Sit down, dear," she commanded when I returned, but she did not look up.

I slid back into my accustomed chair, my own hands crossed in my lap, the key on its ribbon cradled within them. After a moment Eleanor pushed the wooden casket toward me and withdrew her hands, wordlessly. A surrender.

The box was small, perhaps fourteen inches long and half as wide; it stood perhaps eight inches high at the highest part of its curved lid. The wood was darkened to a soft patina by age, the carvings rubbed in places so as to be nearly indistinguishable. There might have been animals: a dragon, some kind of giant fish, a serpent. An enormous bird with its wings spread wide. For a long moment I did not dare touch it. I squeezed the key, feeling its metallic bite in the skin of my palms.

"Open it," Eleanor said. Her voice was low, almost reverent with a barely-controlled excitement.

I didn't know why, but my hands were suddenly shaking so much that I dropped the key to the oriental carpet. Awkwardly I leaned forward to grasp it by the ribbon, then held one hand with the other in an attempt to steady myself enough to slot the key into the wrought-iron lock at the front of the casket. It turned easily.

"Open it," Eleanor whispered again.

Something in the light of the room seemed to have shifted. It seemed darker, the afternoon more ominous. Portentous. The sound of my own breathing was loud in my ears, overlaid with the ticking of the clock on the bookcase. I licked my dry lips, and, my hands still shaking, I lifted the rounded lid and looked inside.

Pictures. There were many, and they were old. Most of them seemed to be of the same person. I reached inside and pinched a small black and white print on a heavy card between my fingers. In it, a sailor in a white jumpsuit leaned against a wall, his arms crossed over his chest. He was squinting into the sun, a crooked grin playing about his mouth, a cap over his blonde hair. He looked somehow vaguely familiar, and yet I was certain I had never seen him before. I turned the card over, but there was nothing written there save the date: 1956.

"Who is this?" I asked.

Instead of answering right away, my grandmother held out a hand. I placed the photo gingerly into her palm, and she wrapped her fingers around it as though cradling an egg—something that would break if handled too roughly. Her expression softened into a fine blend of happiness and sadness.

"It's your grandfather," she said at last. She caressed the card with a finger, tracing the face in the photograph, the crooked smile. "The only man I've ever loved." Her own lips curled gently, but she handed the picture back suddenly, as though she could no longer bear to look.

Grandfather. He had died young, I knew, long before I myself had been born— like my own father. Growing up, I had wondered about him frequently, but had never quite dared to ask, knowing what happened when I asked Elaine about my father. Later, I had wondered why there were no pictures of him anywhere, not on the wall in my grandmother's townhouse, nor atop her piano. Now I found myself staring more intently at the black and white print, at the face, at the smile.

Maybe they just weren't happy together, my mother had said shortly, the only time I had asked her. *I really don't remember.* And then, *I don't want to talk about it.* That was Elaine's standard response to all of my most important questions.

Yet the look on Eleanor's face, as she had gazed down at the man in the picture—there was love there, I thought with a shock. But then I quickly backtracked: who was I, after all, to know what love looked like? I had thought I was in love with Rob, and he with me; how little I had truly known about that. Still, the look that had flitted across my grandmother's face, the half-happy, half-sad expression: wasn't that love? *Wasn't it?*

"I don't even know his name," I said. I bit my lip, looking down at my grandfather, my mother's father.

"Nolan," Eleanor supplied.

"Nolan Ludlow." I tried the name out in my mouth, listened to the sound.

"No," Eleanor said. "Nolan Harris."

It took a moment to register what my grandmother was saying.

"But—your name isn't Harris. Though my mother's last name is."

Eleanor didn't even blink. Her gaze remained steady and intent. "She has her father's name. I thought it would be best on her birth certificate."

The 1950s. I tried to imagine what it would have been like then, the conservatism, the Eisenhower stiffness. I shook my head.

"You kept your own name?" I knew my grandmother had been somewhat of a Bohemian, a world-traveler, a dancer and then a choreographer when she no longer danced. Something of a radical, in the days of Mamie Eisenhower. "When you married?"

Was that amusement flashing across Eleanor's wrinkled face?

"Oh, but I never married Nolan," she corrected.

I felt my jaw drop.

"Come, now, Emily," my grandmother said impatiently. "Surely you realize that marriage is not necessary—and sometimes not even feasible—for pregnancy and childbirth."

The light in the room was still odd, as though muted as for the coming of a thunderstorm. Every sound magnified. But there was no thunder. There was no slash of rain. Only the steady tick of the clock, and the rush of blood through my own ears. *Time,* I thought illogically. *It's all about time.* But I had no idea what I meant. I glanced up from the photograph of my grandfather, my mother's father, my grandmother's lover but not her husband, and felt the world go all strange.

"Does my mother know?" I realized how stupid that question was as soon as it was out of my mouth. I wished I hadn't packed the tea things off to the kitchen; I wished I had something normal in my hand, a teacup—something that would ground me in the familiar world. Instead, this photograph: *my grandfather.*

"Does Elaine know what? That her father and I never married? Of course she does. She never mentioned that to you?"

Suddenly my mother shifted into focus, like a set of pictures clicking into place in a Viewfinder. Elaine and Eleanor—I could not remember a time when my mother and grandmother had gotten along, had had the smooth kind of mother-daughter relationship I saw in the parents and grandparents of my school friends. It was all flint against flint, with resulting spark and frequently fire.

"She's angry—angry that she's illegitimate," I said. A realization.

Eleanor clicked her tongue impatiently. "Such a judgmental word, 'illegitimate.' There was nothing illegitimate about Nolan and me: we loved, we had a child. We loved the child." She sighed. "But you're right, even though you really haven't thought this out fully. Your mother would use that word, because your mother would make that judgment. In fact, your mother *did* make that judgment. And I fear she has never forgiven me for it."

My father is dead, Elaine had told the doctor at University Hospital. In light of this revelation, a painful choice of words. A self-protective choice of words. She could simply have said *my mother has no husband,* but had chosen not to.

"I'm feeling a little floored myself," I said weakly. My words seemed foreign, not quite my own.

"Well, as they say," my grandmother said, her voice still ripe with impatience, and imperative, "get over yourself. This isn't about you. Or, rather, this part isn't about you."

I still held the photo, still gazed down at this, my first introduction to my grandfather. *Nolan Harris.* A sailor. On his white sleeve, some stripes; I knew nothing about rank and insignia, so could not tell what that meant. He was handsome, though. Dashingly so. Debonair. Blonde, light eyes that, seen in the black and white photo, were obviously a brilliant blue.

"My mother said he had died," I whispered.

"Yes." Eleanor tipped her head back and looked away, the only clue that she might be close to crying. "Yes, Nolan is dead. We had kept in touch, of course."

Of course. "What does that even mean?"

The look my grandmother now cast on me was pitying. "He asked me to marry him. Several times. Before Elaine's birth, and after. For many years."

It seemed the perfect romantic solution, as far as I could see. "But you didn't. Why not? Why didn't you? If you loved him? If he loved you?"

Eleanor shook her head. "You're so like your mother in this, and I hope you get over it. I didn't marry Nolan because I didn't need to marry Nolan. I didn't even want to marry Nolan—or anyone else, for that matter. I didn't need to be married. I only needed to have a child."

The force of the words, and the meaning behind them, took my breath away. I could only stare at my grandmother.

"In any case, after I refused him that one last time, he married someone else. An Englishwoman. He lived, ironically, outside of Ludlow, until his death." Eleanor sighed yet again. "I kept in touch, but of course it wasn't the same. And I'm sure Viviane made him a good wife, and made him happy. I couldn't ever make him happy, because I wanted too much."

"From him?"

"From the world." Eleanor made a strange gesture, holding out her hands as though grasping the world within them. Again, the stern, regal look.

"And my mother? Elaine?" I took a long deep breath, feeling a pang of sympathy for Elaine where I was certain none had ever been. "Did she keep in touch with him?"

Eleanor shrugged. "That was information she has never shared with me. I rather imagine she was as angry with him as with me, but she has always refused to listen to my story." She pursed her lips. "She hasn't a sympathetic imagination, your mother. I don't know how she managed to escape that particular curse"—another quirk of the lips—"but I suppose her lack of imagination carries its own kind of curse."

For a long moment we fell silent, but it was an uneasy silence. I felt cold, colder than I had since the evening Rob had sprung his news on me, that he wished to divide everything we owned and sail off into an unencumbered future with Michelle. The world was a confusing place, I found myself thinking. I was unmoored and uncomfortable.

My hands still shaking, I slipped the photograph of my grandfather back into the wooden chest and moved to close the lid.

"Not yet," Eleanor said, raising a commanding hand.

I couldn't help it: I jerked away from her as though she were delivering a blow. "What else?" I demanded, a little wildly. "What else?"

"A latch," Eleanor said. "Under the lid. Run your fingers under the lid."

I darted a look to my grandmother's face and then down again, and I did as I was told. At first I felt nothing—but then the skin on my finger caught on the tiniest metal protrusion.

"You've found it." It was not a question. "Good. Press it sideways."

The catch dug into my finger. I felt more than heard the miniscule click. Eleanor leaned forward and pulled the lid toward her, opening it to its fullest extent. A panel, hidden until this moment, fell open.

"What is it?" My voice sounded like a croak in my own ears.

A bundle wrapped in yellowed cloth lay in the cavity.

"Go on," my grandmother said, her eyes blazing again with that excitement. "Take it out. Gently, though."

The cloth was ancient, soft, worn: muslin? I lay the small packet on the table before me and unwrapped it. A rolled scrap of what at first looked like embroidery lay inside, the colored threads faded to various extents, tangled in ways that seemed to have no order.

"Unroll it," Eleanor said. "That's the reverse. You need to look at the front."

"What is it?"

This time Eleanor did not answer, but waited, her hands, twisted together in her lap, the only clue to her internal agitation.

I spread the muslin over the table top and unrolled the embroidery slowly, carefully. I had no idea how old the piece was, but it was obvious that the hands that had created it were long since dead and gone. It was also obvious that the piece had been kept, lovingly, perhaps secretly, for much of its existence. The front, when I finally saw it, was also slightly discolored from age, but not appreciably faded. And the small scene depicted made me gasp aloud at its life, its energy.

"This—this embroidery—" I managed. My mouth might have been filled with marbles.

"Not embroidery," my grandmother corrected. "Tapestry. Woven on a hand loom."

It was no more than a foot square. The foreground featured a cherub, wings unfurled, but shaded ever so finely to suggest the motion of flight. A halo crowned its head, unnecessary with the blaze of reddish-gold hair. Surrounding the figure were tiny roses of red, of pink, of white, among finely-figured and veined leaves.

"What *is* this?" I gasped. "Where did it come from? How do you have it?" I knew nothing of tapestry, or of weaving in general, but I knew the piece of work I was looking at was invaluable.

"It was given to me by my mother before she died," Eleanor said slowly. "And when I die, it will go to you."

"Me? Why not my mother? She's next in line."

Eleanor's jaw hardened, her eyes narrowing. For a moment I thought I saw fury there, and disappointment. "Your mother has made it plain that she wants nothing to do with this." Then the expression disappeared, much as though a blind had dropped. She forced a smile, which didn't quite reach her eyes.. "That means it goes to you at my death. But now—*look* at it, Emily. *Look at the cherub.*"

I lowered my gaze again, leaned closer, my hands pressed together between my knees. The tiny angel, I realized as I studied the fine work, did not have the doughy baby features so common in Renaissance paintings I had seen with similar figures: the lips were full and generous, curving in a smile that could only be described as sweet. The nose was finely chiseled, distinctive, and the eyes a brilliant blazing green. It was not a generic face, but must have been easily recognizable to anyone who had ever beheld it in life. A portrait. And capping that clear high forehead, the crown of red-gold curls.

The weaver, it was plain, had modeled the cherub on someone he had known. Someone, I thought—and then quickly dismissed that as a trick of romantic fancy—whom he had perhaps loved. Again I leaned over the piece, scanning the brow, the chin, but time and time again, feeling my eyes drawn to the flaming hair, woven, as the wings, with shades such as to give the appearance of motion.

"Where did she get it? Your mother? She didn't weave this?"

"No," Eleanor said, with a shake of her head. "Oh, no, my dear. Look at it. It's much older than that. *Much* older."

I couldn't take my eyes off it, and the more I stared, the less able I felt to breathe. This is what *breathtaking* really meant. I put a hand to my chest, where I could feel my heart pounding against my ribcage.

"My mother inherited this from her mother, who had it from my grandmother, and so all the way back to the woman who wove it. The woman who was the tapiser."

I looked up to find my grandmother's gaze leveled on me. A brilliant green gaze, the green of emeralds in firelight. The color of my own eyes. The color of the eyes of the cherub in this bit of tapestry.

"Who was she?"

The moment should have been punctuated by a roll of thunder, a flash of lightning. Instead, there was the stillness, which stretched and grew, elastic and fertile.

"She's lost," Eleanor said slowly. "I don't know much about her, and I don't think my mother or grandmother did, either. They passed on what they knew, only a few things, which I'll tell you in good time."

"But it was a *she*. It was a *woman*."

"Yes," my grandmother said. "That's the most unusual thing about it—if you look to the history, Renaissance tapisers were, by and large, men."

"But how do you know? How can you be sure?"

Now Eleanor leaned forward stiffly, and pointed with a lacquered nail to the lower edge of the small tapestry, where a tiny black line—a line I had first thought to be veining in the leaves—formed itself, as I peered closer, into three words finely stitched across the green. I squinted, trying to make them out.

"Here." From the drawer in the coffee table, my grandmother produced a small magnifying glass. With its aid, the three words sprang out.

Creavit ex Beatrice.

A signature. My Latin was rusty, but the meaning was clear. *Made by Beatrice.*

"Beatrice."

"Your grandmother, however many generations removed."

I stared at the little cherub, the blue eyes, the gold hair. Slowly, barely thinking, I reached back to pull the elastic from my own hair, which tumbled down around my shoulders, wild, unruly. The same color.

12

I LAY IN bed for a long time, comforter pulled up around my chin, trying to make a nest for myself; every time I rolled over, the futon squeaked. I couldn't sleep. When I opened my eyes to stare at the ceiling, I could imagine the tiny tapestry floating in the darkness.

Creavit ex Beatrice.

Passed down from mother to daughter. From Beatrice? To her child, her grandchild, her great-grandchild, all the way through the years to Eleanor, her daughter Elaine, her granddaughter Emily: me. In the darkness I traced the bridge of my own nose, narrow and straight. Patrician, Rob had once called it, in the days when he still thought about me. The same nose that had, apparently, graced the face of someone Beatrice had loved enough to want to memorialize in the cherub of the tapestry. Her child? A daughter, always passed down to a daughter.

"But—my mother?" I'd asked again.

"She knows I have it. She doesn't want it."

"I don't understand."

"Your mother understands her own motivations, and that has to be enough for all of us." Eleanor looked away, her jaw hard in judgment. "The tapestry is yours at my death."

Regardless of what Elaine wanted, I knew one thing of myself: I *did* want that tapestry. I wanted to touch it again, to examine it at length, in the way I had been unable to do that afternoon. At the unexpected knock at the door—two sharp raps, followed by a lighter, single one—my grandmother had leaned forward and gently, swiftly, rolled the tiny tapestry in its muslin cover and replaced the entire packet in the hidden compartment of the wooden casket. She'd shut the lid, turned the key, and indicated that I should return both to the bedroom, all before clearing her throat and calling for this new guest to enter.

Carwyn. Of course. I had felt his eyes on the back of my neck as I slipped into the bedroom, clutching the little carved chest in my arms protectively. I did not know what he had noticed, but I did know this: my grandmother had not wished Carwyn to see the chest, nor its contents. Something in that gave me a surprising satisfaction. The casket and the tapestry were secrets my grandmother had shared with me—and not with Carwyn. Apparently that was one thing I got, that he didn't.

13

IT WAS THURSDAY, not Sunday, when I pulled the car into the lot at the Willows, slotting it in between a red Ford Explorer and a white plumber's van. It was also early afternoon, which was why I was at a loss. When I'd returned from lunch, Madeline had called me into the office, her face strained.

"I've got to cut back your hours," she said without preamble. She held a pen in her hand, and did not seem to notice that she was clicking it over and over nervously. "It's the budget. There are overruns, and apparently library services are where the administration is taking up the slack." She clicked the pen a few more times, then held it up to look at it as though it were some sort of foreign body she'd never seen before. She set it aside abruptly on the desk.

Maybe in September, she'd said. Now I sat in the parking lot at the Willows, having no idea what to do with myself—unemployed. Unmarried. Unable to figure out which end was up. I'd thought to go talk it out with Eleanor—Elaine, even had she not been at the office, would not have been a sympathetic ear—but now I didn't know why I'd believed that to be a good idea. Leaning my head against the steering wheel, I reached over to rifle through the mail I'd picked up at the post office box. A flyer, an ad for classes—oh, the irony—at the community college, the electric bill, and a heavy envelope from Rob's lawyer, for which I'd had to sign at the counter. Inside, a reckoning of the final division of our mutual property, and a check. A very large check.

I folded it up carefully and put it inside my wallet, inside my purse. At least I was saved for the time being. I wouldn't starve, nor be living in a box on the side of the road.

Just something else to talk to Eleanor about.

EXCEPT THAT SHE was on the way out.

"I'm sorry, my dear," she said. "I've got an appointment with the eye doctor."

"Do you need a lift?"

She raised a hand and dismissed the offer with a wave of her fingers. "Carwyn's taking me."

Of course.

"Just close the door behind you, will you, dear?" she said, kissing my cheek on the way out, leaving behind the smell of powder and rosewater. "And come back soon. We have much to discuss, you and I."

With that I was left alone in the front room, with not even the ghost of the old woman's crafty smile. I lowered myself onto the sofa, trying not to look at the bedroom door, but failing, as I knew I would. The bedroom door behind which the chest and its contents lay. I realized that I was playing with the clasp of my purse, and clenched my hands in my lap. There was no one here, I reasoned, and Eleanor had told me the tapestry would be mine eventually. Looking at it wouldn't hurt. Just looking at it one more time.

Abruptly I stood to cross the room, where I pushed open the door. The carved casket was right there, on the bedside table, where I'd replaced it at Carwyn's entrance the other day. I sat on the bed and lifted the chest onto my lap; the box, though small, was heavy in my hands, and warm, like a live thing. The key was in the drawer, tucked into the change purse, and I drew it out by the faded ribbon. I slotted the key into the lock and lifted the cover. This time I ignored the photographs—my grandfather's face stared up at me reproachfully—and slid my finger along the underside of the lid until I found the catch. I pressed it; the panel released.

The box and the contents are yours.

Really. There was nothing wrong with taking another look. Then I would put it back. Just one look. That was all.

Then the rolled muslin was in my hand. I felt a shock run through me, holding it, as though it were electric. I drew in a sharp breath, shutting my eyes, willing my hands to stop shaking.

The box and the contents were mine.

Again I took a deep breath.

The knock on the outer door startled me. Awash in guilt, I shoved the cloth into my purse and dropped the lid of the box back into place.

"Mrs. Ludlow?" It was the dark-skinned man from the front desk. I recognized his voice. The woman had been at that post when I'd come in, and I was momentarily confused. Quickly I swept the key back into the coin purse and shut it in the drawer. Then I went to the bedroom door.

"She's not—" I stumbled, started again. "My grandmother's not here. She's gone to the eye doctor."

The man's eyes roved up to my face, which felt suddenly hot.

"Of course," he said noncommittally.

"I'm just leaving," I said.

14

I MADE IT back to my apartment, though I couldn't remember how. I know I drove too fast. Once in the driveway, I waited in the car with the doors locked, watching the street, until I was certain there was no one around. At the door at the top of the stairs, I twisted the key hurriedly in the Yale lock, whimpering in frustration as it stuck like always. Inside, I threw the bolts and hooked the chain, then stood with my back against the door, trying to catch my breath.

I had never stolen anything before.

I was shaking, and I clutched my handbag to my chest, trying to control my reactions. I had never stolen anything before, and this was not just *anything*. It was invaluable. And it belonged to my grandmother. I closed my eyes tightly. The blood was still pounding in my ears. No one knew, I tried to tell myself. There was no way anyone could tell just by looking at me that I was a thief. Slowly I forced myself to cross the living room to the futon. I sank down onto it and set the purse on the end table gingerly, as though it contained a bomb.

A bombshell, I thought, and let out a hysterical giggle that turned into a sob.

I HAVE NO idea how long I sat staring at my handbag, unable to touch it. Unable to open the clasp, to withdraw the rolled cloth. The afternoon drew into evening, and the light from the windows next to the door moved across the floor and up the wall. I had the sense of something huge, something far larger than myself, and at the same time I had no idea what that meant. Something I had thought I had the courage to consider, back when I held my grandmother's wooden casket on my lap, but which I knew felt was more frightening than I had first imagined.

Who am I? I wondered, and at the same time mocked myself for the hysterical question that was. *What am I?*

I could just take it back. I could sneak the roll into the box when my grandmother was out of the suite for another one of her many and various appointments. Or I could admit to the old woman that I had stolen her secret. Something in me shied away from that, however: how disappointed Eleanor would be with me—and suddenly that mattered. After all these years of pretending to myself that my grandmother's approval was not important to me, I found myself wondering what could have possessed me, to make me risk throwing our tenuous relationship away. Yes, that mattered, so much.

15

I DIDN'T GO back to the Willows the next day. Nor the next.

Saturday afternoon, I was coming out of the supermarket into the first truly warm day of the season, which made me feel no better about myself at all, when I thought to turn on my phone and check for messages. There were four missed calls from Carwyn, all time-stamped within the past hour. Standing with the car door open, I trashed them, one after another, without checking to see whether he'd left voice mail. I couldn't handle him right then. I shoved my sunglasses onto my nose; I had a splitting headache, one which had followed me now for two days. Slinging the two bags into the passenger seat, I slammed the door and buckled up.

The phone vibrated in my hand.

Not Carwyn this time. My mother.

"Mom—"

"It's your grandmother again," Elaine said without preamble. "This time they think it's a stroke. University Hospital."

"Give me ten minutes."

I ACTUALLY MADE it more quickly than that—every streetlight between the grocery store lot and the hospital seemed to turn green just as I approached. I flicked the key fob and locked the door on my groceries as I sprinted toward the double doors of the emergency entrance.

"They gave her aspirin therapy before the ambulance came," Carwyn was saying to my mother as I skidded to a stop in the waiting room. "But her eyes— she was talking to me, and she seemed really agitated, and then she just . . . stopped, and her mouth was open, and her eyes seemed to roll sideways."

He clamped his mouth shut when he saw me.

"How is she?" I demanded. "Where is she?" *De ja vu.*

"The doctors are with her now," Elaine said. She lifted her chin. Her back was ramrod stiff, but she held herself as though it took a huge effort. She clutched her purse in both hands with a strangling grip. "They told us to wait here."

"Us?"

"Carwyn was already here."

"I followed the ambulance."

His voice, I realized, was shaking. I glanced at him sharply. He looked frightened.

When he reached a hand toward my arm, I sidestepped quickly, a gut reaction. Then I stopped, watching my own mother's nervously twisting hands, and knew where I'd got my own mannerisms, my own techniques for avoidance. It wasn't time for anger, I tried to convince myself, it wasn't the time. I put a hand on Carwyn's arm. His gaze flickered down, then back up to my face, surprised. His skin was shockingly cold.

"She was there, Emily," he said, bewildered. "And then suddenly she just—wasn't."

I found myself nodding. I bit my lip, then pressed his arm, not knowing what kind of reassurance to offer, or if to offer any at all.

Elaine, however, raked us both with a glance. "Well, aren't you two just adorable," she said acidly, and whirled to throw herself into one of the orange plastic chairs.

I squeezed my eyes closed for just a moment. "Mom—"

But Elaine pointedly picked up a magazine from the table beside her and flipped through the pages.

SHORTLY AFTER NINE, the doctor came for us.

"You'd probably better come," he said. "I'm afraid all we can do now is make her comfortable, and wait."

"Is she conscious?" Elaine asked. The ice had not left her voice.

"Will she—recognize us?" Carwyn asked.

The doctor shook his head. "I don't think so. But you never know."

He led the way along a confusion of corridors, through doors which swung closed behind them with a hush. Carwyn stayed close to me, perhaps hoping I'd provide a lifeline; his skin seemed to give off wave after wave of cold, as though his heart was having difficulty pumping enough blood to keep him warm.

The room was dim, only a single light on, the head of the bed left in shadows. Again I was struck by the smallness of my grandmother's body under the sheet, the frailness, as though she'd hurried the process of shrinking toward nothingness. It was a morbid thought, and my mind shied away from it. Monitors beeped and clicked, and my eyes traveled to the one registering the old woman's slowing heart rate.

Elaine pulled one of the chairs forward to the side of the bed and sat, her spine stiff and straight, her shoulders back.

"I'll find you another chair," a nurse murmured, and disappeared from the room.

"Can you hear me, Eleanor?" Carwyn asked. "We're here. Your daughter, your granddaughter." He coughed. "And me. Carwyn. Nick. Can you hear me?"

"Don't be a fool. You heard the doctor. She can't hear you." Elaine's face was drawn, angry, grief-stricken—and frightened, too, I thought. And something else. Remorse? Regret?

Which made sense. I probed my own fear as I might a toothache. I had not thought as much about my grandmother over the past several years as perhaps I ought to have; like my mother, I held on to my own kind of resentment. Until recently. Until the past couple of weeks. Now I looked back over the past I shared with Eleanor, sporadic and at times distant, and felt guilty. I had cheated myself. For years, and now there was no longer any time to make up for it.

And the last thing I had done was to steal from her.

I pushed that thought away.

"Nick."

It was little more than a breath, but in the near-silence, it was unmistakable. Carwyn stepped to the rail, leaning over the bed.

"I'm here," he said.

Her eyes remained closed, and her thin chest rose and fell under the sheet, her lungs laboring despite the oxygen tube snaking up her nose. Her fingers, though, scrabbled at the air, trying to find a grip on something. Life, maybe.

"Tell her," Eleanor whispered.

"Who? Tell who?"

"Mother?" Elaine interjected.

"Emily—"

"She's here." Carwyn edged back, and I drew closer to the dying woman, leaning forward, taking the veined and gnarled hand in mine. Eleanor's skin was colder than Carwyn's had been.

"It's me, Eleanor," I said, my voice uncomfortable and thick in my throat. "I'm right here. Tell me what you want."

The breaths were rasping, painful. Eleanor opened her mouth, but for a while no more words came. Just the breathing, the clicks and beeps.

"It's yours now," she gasped out at last. Her eyes fluttered, then the lashes settled again on her cheeks, strangely dark against her pallor.

I looked around frantically. *The tapestry?*

"What is? What's mine now, Eleanor?"

I thought Carwyn, behind her, had become still, stiff. At the other side of the hospital bed, my mother had drawn back slightly, her jaw hardening.

The last word was barely audible. I leaned closer, straining to hear.

"Responsibility."

I felt the single word as a punch to the gut.

"Yours."

Then it was all confusion, as the monitors went haywire, as nurses and the doctor crowded into the room. I thought I heard Elaine cry out *Mother*. The bony hand in mine went slack. Carwyn gripped my shoulders. I could only stare, straight ahead.

The responsibility is yours.

FOUR BLURRY DAYS.

After Eleanor's death, I stumbled back to my apartment and collapsed onto the futon, my head pounding and my vision misty. When I struggled from sleep in the early hours to use the bathroom, I found the headache pain had moved down behind my right eye, and my nose stuffed. I'd been breathing through my mouth, and my lips were dry and already cracking. A cold, I thought, and willed myself not to cry anymore, because that only filled my sinuses. I gulped down some Tylenol with a glass of water that did nothing to assuage my dry mouth, and fell back into bed.

I woke again later in the day to find the sheets tangled and sweaty. My head felt like a boulder, and my eyes were gummy. I was in the bathroom, splashing cold water on her face when my phone rang: twice, three times. Five, ten.

"What took you so long?" Elaine snapped.

"I'm sick, Mom."

"So are we all. I need your help planning this funeral."

"Really sick. I think it's a sinus infection."

"Make an appointment, get some antibiotics, and come over. I need your help." Though Elaine sounded as impatient as always, there was a new quality to her voice, a vulnerability, that she seemed to be working hard to suppress.

"Call Carwyn. I'll give you his number."

My mother sucked in a sharp breath. "I don't want to do that. He's not family. He doesn't need to be part of this." Her words echoed my feelings since the evening I'd first come across Carwyn at the Willows; but somehow, now, most of my resentment had drained away. There were other things to think about.

"Eleanor would want him."

"Eleanor, in case you've forgotten, is *dead*. My *mother* is dead."

With that, the phone line went silent in my ear.

Sighing, I poked through my contacts for the number of the campus health center, and gave them a call.

I WAS ABLE to get an early appointment, and made a stop at the pharmacy on the way to my mother's condo. There was a strange car in the second spot before the door, and I had to drive around to the overflow lot beyond the last building in the complex and walk back. As I approached along the sidewalk, the blue Impala pulled away. Of course. I felt an incredible urge to flip off the silver-haired man at the wheel, but instead was wracked with a sudden cough, and decided, clutching my sides, that it was not worth the effort.

Elaine was waiting, holding the door open. She peered into my face critically. "God, you are sick, aren't you? You look terrible."

"Who was that, Mom?" I was still gazing along the street after the Impala.

"Come inside," my mother urged. She led the way down the hallway toward the kitchen at the back. "Just a friend," she tossed over her shoulder. "Stopped by to see if he could help."

He's not family, I almost shot back, but thought better of it. Whoever it was, he'd gone, after all. He wasn't sticking around to help with the planning.

"I want it small," Elaine was saying. She moved the tea kettle to the burner on the stainless steel stove unit and turned on the heat under it. "The service. In St. Michael's. Closed casket, then cremation, and burial in Holy Cross."

"St. Michael's?" I felt shaky and feverish and wondered whether I'd heard correctly. I slid onto a stool at the marble-topped counter and drew the prescription from my jacket pocket. "Holy Cross?" I was confused, too. "The Catholic cemetery?" I had never once heard my grandmother talk about religion, or God, unless it was to take the name in vain. I had never once heard Eleanor speak about attending church, St. Michael's or any other. I myself had no memory of church as a child, not even for Christmas or Easter.

"She was baptized a Catholic," my mother said. "And those are the instructions in her will."

I frowned. My grandmother had been baptized in the Catholic church, had borne a child out of wedlock, and now had left a request to be buried with a Mass, in the Catholic cemetery. It wasn't as though Eleanor had behaved throughout her life as a particularly devout person; it wasn't as though, as she lay dying, she had requested the last rites to be administered. None of it made sense, no matter how I turned the information over and over in my mind, examining it from every possible angle.

"Can she do that?" I asked. "Can we do that?"

"I've had the funeral director call the Diocese. They've said yes." The kettle on the burner whistled, and Elaine moved to pour hot water over the tea bags in the cups on the sideboard. She brought a dark blue mug over to me at the counter. "Drink this. You look like you need it. Like you need the entire pot."

"Sinus infection. I told you." I attempted to draw the steam up into my nose, but was too stuffed up. I held up the white bag holding the prescription. "The health center prescribed this. Three days of mondo killer antibiotics." I tore open the packet and drew forth the orange bottle, peering at the directions. "One by mouth for three days. Take all prescribed medicine." I popped the safety top and shook one out into my palm. I blew on my tea, then took a careful sip before tossing the enormous pill into the back of my mouth. It went down hard. I took another sip of tea, but not so carefully this time, and burned my tongue.

"Just don't give it to me," Elaine said darkly. "Whatever it is."

"It's a sinus infection, not a cold," I retorted. Having learned my lesson, I blew on my tea again before taking another drink from the mug. "What about the newspapers?"

"Taken care of. Through the funeral home."

"Which newspapers?" Eleanor had lived here in town, but had spent much of adult life traveling, working in Europe. Paris, Rome, places which, to me, remained unexplored. Then I frowned. "You wrote it?"

"Eleanor wrote her own. She had it with her will. In which, by the way, she leaves you everything."

I waved that off. "I don't need anything." I held out a hand expectantly. "The obit?"

Tightening her lips, Elaine slid a legal-sized manila folder across the countertop, then turned her attention to her own tea. Hesitantly, I opened to the first sheet of paper.

Nora Ludlow died Sunday, May 7, at University Hospital, surrounded by those she loved. She was born Eleanor Cynthia Wood in New York City, August 7, 1927, the only daughter of Cordelia Wood and Cecil Furness. A dancer, she studied at the American School of Ballet, later finding work with Balanchine in his theater productions, before becoming a member of the Corps de Ballet at the Ballet Society and later at the New York City Ballet. It was at this time that she adopted her professional name, Nora Ludlow.

With the birth of her daughter, she turned from dance to choreography, creating pieces for the Ballet Russes, Sadler's Wells Ballet, and many other companies of international renown. Her work enabled her to befriend and support artists from all over the world, something for which she was ever grateful. In her later years, she retired to Connecticut, where she was able to spend time with her family. Nora leaves behind her daughter, Elaine Harris, her granddaughter, Emily Hill, and a special family friend, Carwyn (Nick) Grey. She was predeceased by her parents, and, in 1982, by Nolan Harris, Elaine's father.

I looked up from the paper in my hand. "That's all?"

My mother shrugged. "That's all she wanted to say, apparently." She lifted her teacup, then set it down again without drinking. Her eyes darkened. "At least she had the grace to mention my father. Nolan." She spoke the name as though rolling marbles around in her mouth, awkwardly, experimentally.

"The only man she ever loved." I spoke the words aloud, but heard them in my grandmother's voice. I stared into my tea.

"Don't kid yourself," Elaine said viciously. "Your grandmother didn't love him. Nor me, nor you, nor even that Nick, either now or when he was a kid. Your grandmother didn't know how to love anyone."

I reared back, surprised and horrified by the bitterness of the words. "That's pretty harsh, isn't it?" I asked when at last I could find my voice.

My mother looked up, her face still hard, and she seemed aged by the anger. Still, the look in her eyes was pity. "Your grandmother has always had one leading passion. One. She lived her entire life in the service of that passion. She did her best to inflict it upon me. And God help you, Emily—if she tried to ensnare you with it as well."

"What do you mean?" I felt suddenly cold, despite the fever; I looked down at my arms, I had goosebumps. "Do you mean her dancing? What? She's dead, Mom." I swallowed. "I don't know what you mean."

Abruptly Elaine pushed away from the counter and crossed to dump her nearly untouched tea down the drain.

"Then you're lucky, Emily," she said with her back to me. "You're very, very lucky."

My mother's head was bowed, her hands gripping the edge of the countertop. And then, shockingly, her shoulders were shaking. Elaine was crying.

WE ORDERED PIZZA, and I fell asleep on the couch.

Late in the night I awoke to find myself beneath a downy coverlet, but sweating with fever. *Tylenol*, I thought, and, as my eyes adjusted to the dimness of my mother's living room, I swung my legs down and tried out the steadiness of my feet when I stood. I wasn't wearing a watch, and my phone was in my purse in the kitchen, so I had no idea of the time. Navigating by touch, I slipped along the hall to the half-bath at the foot of the stairs. The pills were in the cabinet over the sink, and, cupping my hand beneath the faucet to catch enough water to chase them, I gulped them down. The effort made my face hurt, and made me dizzy. I had to lean against the doorframe for a moment to get myself back on an even keel.

From the bedroom overhead, I heard my mother's voice.

"—No, I didn't. I was going to, and then—I just don't know. It was too much. Too damned much."

There was a long pause.

"I know she's old enough. Of course she is."

Me? I thought groggily. *I'm thirty-two. Of course I'm old enough.*

"I just need more time," Elaine was saying. "I've got to get through this first." Another pause.

"I'm sorry. I know. I just needed to talk to you." My mother coughed, and her voice softened. "I just needed to hear your voice."

The softness, and the implied intimacy, made me uncomfortable. I fled back down the hallway to the living room and the couch, where I burrowed under the comforter and squeezed my eyes shut.

In the morning, I awoke and could not be sure what had been real, and what had been a dream.

18

THE FUNERAL HOME'S limousine slid up to the curb before St. Michael's, and to my surprise, there were far more people there than I had expected. The director held the door open and handed out my mother first; I clutched my purse with one hand, took the man's arm, and allowed him to help me to the sidewalk. The air seemed sharp, though the sun shone brightly overhead. People pressed toward us. Strangers. Someone had a camera.

"I wanted this to be small," Elaine hissed.

"I'm sorry," the funeral director said, his voice solemn as he leaned forward solicitously. "The obituary was picked up by the wire." He gestured to his dark-suited colleagues, then held out an arm to guide them toward the steps. "Ms. Ludlow was well-known in certain circles."

Then we were inside, led down the aisle to the front pew. The casket, gleaming and speckled with prisms from the stained glass windows, rested before the altar, closed. I breathed a sigh of relief. Elaine had said the casket would be closed, but somehow, I couldn't bring myself to trust my mother in her anger. The pew was hard against my back. Not for the first time, despite that anger, I wanted to reach for my mother's hand; but I knew just how unwelcome the gesture would be. If I could just hold something—someone—the curved arm at the end of the pew wasn't it, not the hymnals stacked next to it. Someone warm. Alive. Human.

Still I stared at the spatter of colored light falling across the casket: reds, blues, greens. The colors moved. Undulated. The organist played somberly in the background, and it grated. I was grinding my teeth; I tried in vain to relax my jaw. I turned away from the casket, looking over my shoulder instead. Two rows back, across the aisle, Carwyn sat at the end of the pew, nearly unrecognizable in his dark blue suit and tie. His chin slightly raised, he stared toward the great rose window above the altar, but, feeling my eyes upon him, he turned his head to meet my gaze.

I bit my lower lip. My feelings toward Carwyn were muddled; but right now, every emotion was dulled, far away. With an unsteady hand, I indicated the space in the pew beside me. His glance flicked to Elaine, her unblinking eyes, her adamantine jaw, and back.

Please, I mouthed.

Slowly he stood and crossed the aisle. I inched aside. He sat.

Elaine glared and turned away.

I SLEPT THE clock around. The sinus infection had exhausted me, despite the antibiotics, and the funeral hadn't helped. When I woke, though, the following afternoon, my head was lighter, and I could breathe. My eyes no longer felt as though they were bulging from my head. I showered, dressed in a sweatshirt and shorts—the last of my clean clothes—changed the sheets on the futon, and opened the windows to let the apartment air out. The thin curtains fluttered in the breeze. Somewhere along the cul-de-sac below a bird sang, and another answered. The air smelled of lilacs when I headed out to the laundromat.

I'd returned, washed all the dirty dishes, and was turning the last of the glassware upside down on the sideboard to air dry when the doorbell rang. A glance at the clock—just after two, but I hadn't been expecting anyone. "Who is it?" I called, wiping my wet hands down my shorts.

"Me. Carwyn."

"Hold on." I drew back the deadbolt and opened the door.

He was back to normal: Oxford shirt, jeans. The dark suit and tie of the funeral were gone, and somehow that relieved me. He jerked a thumb over his shoulder to a red pick-up truck against the curb below. "I've got your grandmother's desk. From the Willows. The rest is in storage, but Eleanor said you were to have this. And a carved chest from the bedroom, but I couldn't find that."

For a moment I could only blink. *It will be yours at my death.* But Eleanor had not mentioned the desk to me—only the chest from the bedside table. And that had disappeared? I glanced at my purse on the counter, where the roll of tapestry still reposed, because I could not think of any safer place for it, and irrationally had wanted it to stay close to me anyway. The chest was gone. Had the tapestry remained in its hiding place, it too would have disappeared.

"It was just there," I said stupidly. "I saw it. Last week."

Carwyn held up his hands. "It wasn't when I emptied the room. I looked especially, because Eleanor had told me—before she died—and I never thought—there would be so little time . . ." He looked away. "I guess you need to check with the Willows to see if anyone knows anything. Was it valuable?"

I shrugged. "I don't know. It was old. She'd had it forever." I had no idea whether it was the original hiding place for the tapestry, or had become that later. "It was full of pictures of my grandfather."

"I'm sorry. I'll go look again if you want."

I shook my head. "Let's not worry about it now." Standing at the door, I was beginning to feel a little light-headed. I put a hand to the frame and looked down to the road at the pick-up. "That's not your car." I didn't even know why that suddenly mattered to me. Or if it did. My ears were ringing.

"Borrowed it," he said. "To bring the desk."

"Ah." I attempted to gather my wits. "Do you need a hand?"

Carwyn glanced down at my bare feet before turning away. "Get some shoes on if you're coming out here. You've been sick."

"You sound like my mother," I complained.

He threw an ironic glance over his shoulder. "No, I don't."

The desk, from Eleanor's front room, was wrapped and padded in a quilt. Carwyn didn't need my help carrying it, so I was reduced to holding the door for him. He deposited it in the middle of the floor, unknotted the thin ropes, and pulled the material aside.

"Where do you want it?"

I looked around helplessly at the efficiency apartment, seeing it as from a distance. Despite the lack of furnishings, there really was not that much room. "I don't know. I mean—I didn't realize either—that Eleanor—" And I caught my breath, pressing a hand to my lips. "I'm sorry."

But Carwyn shook his head. "Don't be. I know what you mean."

The tears had started, however. The tears that had not come before, because I had been beyond tired, because my sinuses had ached and my throat had been dry and my heart had been sore. I put my other hand on the fine-grained cherry of the desk and felt the warm tracks along my cheeks, tasted the saltiness in the corners of my mouth.

Carwyn stepped forward, rested his hand gently on mine.

20

THAT WAS HOW it started.

In the fading evening light, I lay on the futon, hand to my lips, which did not feel like mine.

What are you doing? Carwyn had asked. *Emily?*

But I had leaned into him, tracing his lower lip with my tongue.

I hadn't thought about Rob, hadn't thought about anything but Carwyn, and then simply—hadn't thought. He had stepped back, his blue eyes gone dark and probing.

What do you want from me, Emily?

In one motion I had pulled the sweatshirt over my head, then dropped the shorts to the floor. Naked, I had stepped to him, run my hands into his hair, and then pulled his mouth to mine. After that, we hadn't spoken.

Now I could hear the water running in the shower. I had felt him climb from the futon, but had not opened my eyes. I listened, remembering his hands on my skin, winding through my tangled hair. I stretched beneath the sheet, then slowly got to my feet to pad to the bathroom door. It creaked gently when I pushed it open. The tiny room was steamy, the mirror over the sink filmed over.

"Emily." Carwyn's voice was strange, as though he'd forgotten how to speak.

I didn't answer. Instead, I slipped the shower curtain aide to join him in the stall. The hot water ran over my shoulders and breasts. I tipped my head back and let it soak my hair.

"Jesus, Emily," he breathed. Then his mouth was at my throat, his tongue trailing along my collarbone. "I don't know what the hell is going on, but I don't care." His hands slid down the length of my back, I moaned, and he repeated, "I don't care."

WE MADE LOVE in the shower, then toweled each other off before moving to the futon once again. The room was growing dark; night drew on. We slept, woke, made love again. Somewhere, after midnight when we came wildly together, I felt it.

A tiny ping, like a bell ringing in the far distance.

Interlude

"NO," MASTER ARNAUD protested in exasperation. "No, Beatrice. No, a thousand times." With his cracked and yellow nail, he picked at the weft. "This is not the way."

She dropped her hands into her lap and lowered her head. "Then I don't know the way, Master." She felt the hot tears behind her lids and willed them—unsuccessfully—not to fall. From the other end of the solar, where the ladies were gathered about her guardian, she could feel that woman's eyes upon her, and she turned her face away.

There was a long moment's pause. Then the wooden bench creaked as Master Arnaud lowered himself to sit beside her. Wordlessly unraveled her weaving of the morning, weaving which did not meet with his approval. It was rough work, she realized, the work of an untutored child.

"I'm sorry," she whispered, hands still clasped in her lap.

"Ah." He continued to pick at the faulty threads. "It pains me, young one," he said, his voice softening and full of sorrow. "Pain."

"I know."

"No, Beatrice," he said again. "You do not know. You cannot. And you will not until you feel the fire of this passion." He rewound the bobbins in his gnarled hands.

She lifted her chin and stared at his wizened face beneath his black cap.

"Is this your passion?" she asked, aware of her own impertinence, but at this point, beyond caring. "The weaving of tapestries?"

The old man wound the brilliant colors around more bobbins before pausing to answer, the rainbows vibrant in his palms. He held them up for her to see. "The colors are my passion. The colors of the world. The shades of people and the truths they tell. The colors of the lies they repeat to get themselves through their lives."

Beatrice slumped again. "I do not know what you mean, Master."

He faced her with kind, but sad eyes. "The colors are a river," he said slowly. "They flow forward through time. You and I will never see where they end, if they end at all. You and I are only channels through which they pass."

"You talk in riddles," she protested.

He lifted her hands and set the bobbins in her palms. "I am an old man. You are young. You must discover your passion, and you must protect it against all who would take it from you and destroy it. Remember that, young one. Find your passion and protect it with your life."

Part Two
Ludlow Women

21

THE MORNING WAS clear, and as the plane followed a path, for its approach to Heathrow, along the Thames, I pressed my hand to the window and looked down on familiar landmarks. The sun was already high, and the airplane trailed its own shadow. I loved this approach, loved it especially when the air was clear; it was somehow like coming home. I wondered whether my grandmother had loved it this same way; whether she had loved flying into Charles du Gaulle or Leonardo da Vinci or Pulkovo. Not for the first time in the past several days, I swallowed back my bitterness at not paying more attention to Eleanor when I'd had the chance. Now, all that was left was guessing.

So much to think about, and so much I could not allow myself to think about. When the plane taxied to a halt at the terminal, I retrieved my backpack from the overhead bin and waited for the aisle to clear. There was no hurry; there was nowhere I needed to be urgently. Except Ludlow, but the town had not gone anywhere since Eleanor had chosen to name herself after it, and would still be there whenever I reached it. There was no rush. Not yet.

My suitcase, small and electric blue, circled around the baggage carousel, and I grabbed it before turning to UK Border. Non-EU, nothing to declare: the green exit. The line snaked back and forth between the velvet ropes, and I followed a balding man in a tan jacket without thinking. Two steps forward. Two more. Two more. When at last I was directed to a kiosk, my passport and Customs card were sweaty in my palm. I hoped the woman in the booth didn't mind.

"Reason for your visit?"

"Pleasure," I lied. I tried to look happy.

"How long will you be in the country?"

"Two weeks," I said.

I had no idea, when I had pressed the purchase button on the website, why I had chosen that particular length of time. No conscious reason. No plan. However, the money had been in the bank—or would be soon—and Madeline had made clear that there would be no need for me until mid-August, if at all. There wasn't a reason, but I didn't need a reason. I simply needed to be away, where no one knew me, where no one would ask questions.

"Visiting friends?"

"Exploring historical sites," I corrected. Did I even know anyone in the UK? I didn't think so. Except—*Viviane*.

ON THE TRAIN from Reading to Newport Gwent, I connected my iPad to the wifi and began searching for Viviane. *Ironically, outside of Ludlow*, Eleanor had said in passing. Perhaps my grandfather's wife still lived there; but then, she'd be how old? If she was around the same age as Nolan and Eleanor, she'd be closing on ninety as well. She might long ago have packed it up to live in a care home, as Eleanor had done; she might long ago have died. She might have remarried, have an entirely different name. It might have helped to have Viviane Harris's maiden name, but though I wracked my brain, I could not remember my grandmother mentioning it. The task of finding her seemed daunting. Yet also immeasurably important. I tucked my ticket under the corner of the iPad so I wouldn't be distracted when the conductor appeared, and opened Google.

I was still searching at Newport Gwent, where I had to change trains for Ludlow. Impatiently I scanned the overhead notice board—I'd arrived at platform 2 and needed to go up to the overhead walkway and cross to platform 4. Shrugging my backpack further up onto my shoulder and jamming the handle back down into the blue suitcase, I moved to the stairs. Hurrying—I wasn't sure how much time I had to get to the far platform, and, now that I was here, I couldn't bear the thought of waiting for a later train.

"Ludlow?" I asked the closest guard as I bumped down to platform 4.

"This one, love," he said cheerily, pointing to the train idling to his right. "Just made it, then."

I climbed on, found a seat at a banquette—complete with USB connectivity for the low battery—and resumed the search for my grandfather's wife. *Somewhere outside Ludlow. Ironically.*

And somewhere outside Ludlow, after downing a particularly unpleasant cup of tea from the trolley, after massaging my temples and pressing my eyes closed against the glowing of the screen, I found Viviane Harris.

22

MY ROOM AT the ancient half-timbered hotel had a fireplace and a four-poster bed. The window overlooked the main street and another age-old inn. I deposited my backpack on the chaise at the foot of the bed, stepped past the table and armchairs into the window recess, and looked down. It was late in the afternoon; traffic, both auto and foot, was brisk in the street. Everyone seemed to have a purpose. I leaned my forehead against the cool glass and felt the exhaustion of travel wash over me: from embarkation on the plane the previous evening, to landing and customs and the bus, then trains, I had been awake for more hours than I could count. Somewhere out there was the woman my grandfather had married after the mother of his child had rejected his proposals, but with my stomach growling uncomfortably, it was obvious that I could make no advances this evening. Even if I could figure out how to make those advances.

Hello, I'm Emily.

Hello, I'm your step-daughter's daughter.

Hello, I don't even know what the hell I'm doing here.

I felt like crying. But I wouldn't, because crying got me into trouble. It was only the tiredness and the hunger, I consoled myself. And probably hormones—but I wouldn't think about that.

The obvious choice was a quick wash, a change of clothes, and a search for food. However, the whirlpool bath was enticing—what on earth was it doing in this inn?—and I allowed myself to be enticed. It was late when I made my way to the terrace for bangers and mash, and a sad gaze at the pulls from the Ludlow Brewing Company.

23

I WENT FIRST to the castle.

I wasn't really sure why. I wasn't sure, come to think of it, why I was even here, except that there was a nagging feeling, somewhere in the back of my mind, that I was missing some vital piece of information, about Eleanor, maybe about Elaine, possibly even about myself. And that there was no other place to start the search. Eleanor, back when she was barely in her twenties, had chosen to mark her life path by changing her name to Ludlow. Something here prompted that. Something that had, eventually, sent Nolan Harris to the town and ultimately into the arms of the wife who was not Eleanor. It was a mystery—it was a *hole* in the way that I understood the world, and now, more than ever, I needed to fill that hole. I needed it desperately.

It was something to focus on.

I wandered along the High Street, both excited by the prospect of the castle walls ahead, and reluctant to reach them. What if I got there and found—what? My grandmother's secret, whatever that might be, emblazoned at the top of that round tower? Around me, the market crowds washed back and forth, and I paused momentarily to examine a rack of Indian cotton tunics more to slow my steps than out of any real interest.

"What color, love?" the vendor asked, a man in a tweed waistcoat, smiling broadly. "That purple now—that'd go a treat with that Pre-Raphaelite hair of yours."

I felt my face go hot. "Just browsing, thanks," I said quickly, and moved away from the racks, past the next stall, and the next. The smell of old books, a mustiness I usually loved, assailed my nostrils, and for a moment I felt queasy.

Not now, I whispered to myself, and wondered what I meant.

I walked on, looking up again toward the castle at the curve of the street. What if I got there and found *nothing?* The gray stone walls, surrounded by the greens of the grass, of the various trees, kept their own counsel, and gave away nothing. But what were they supposed to reveal to me? I felt a sudden anxiety, along with the queasiness. Still, perhaps I would stumble upon some insight once I'd made it through the gate. *If in fact this was my grandmother's Ludlow.* I wiped the back of my hand across my suddenly sweaty brow.

There was a café just inside the castle entrance. Relieved, I slipped in and bought a bottle of water and a fruit scone, then found a seat on the terrace. Just nerves, I told myself, feeling prickly over my entire body, as though every hair were standing at attention. I could see nothing, as I gazed around the outer bailey, that would have unsettled me so. But there was a sense of expectation I couldn't explain to myself. *What is it, Eleanor?* I asked in my head. *What am I supposed to see?* Something told me I was on the right track. *What am I supposed to know?* The grass in the bailey smelled of a fresh clipping and glowed in the morning sunlight; the air was warm, but the smallest of breezes caressed my still-warm cheek, for which I was grateful. I drank deeply from the bottle, broke off a piece of the scone as though sharing communion.

Eleanor had been born and baptized a Catholic.

Eleanor had been buried a Catholic.

Why was I suddenly thinking about that? What had it to do with anything? But now the niggling thought had pushed its way to the fore, so I turned it over in my mind. Not for the first time. Suddenly, though, I wondered why I had not thought to ask whether my mother had been baptized in the Catholic Church. Unless they didn't do that in the fifties, when Elaine was born, with illegitimate children? Surely, though, that would have been the next logical question—but when my mother had dropped the bombshell about Eleanor's funeral preferences, I had been too shocked, or too much *in* shock, to think of it. For half a moment I considered calling my mother and asking, but then I realized that it was not quite six in the morning in Connecticut, and Elaine would hardly be appreciative of a call at that hour, waking her up to ask if she were officially Catholic.

Am I?

I set the scone down on the paper plate and found myself looking around at the other tables, where only a few people sat: a couple leaning close, a woman with a small child at the table and another in a push chair. Another small earthquake in my thoughts; my mouth had dropped open, and I must look slightly demented. Well, I felt, suddenly, slightly demented.

A question I had not even thought of. *Ever* thought of.

I went over it again. I had not grown up in any particular church, but had not considered that odd. I had never felt especially religious, and Elaine certainly never discussed religion, any denomination, nor the Bible except as literature. Easter and Christmas had not been marked with attendance at any service, so there was nothing at all to hang a sort of belief on. That Eleanor had felt so strongly about being buried from the church indicated at least a strong possibility that she had had Elaine baptized there, if it would have been allowed. Would it? However, that Eleanor and Elaine had had such a fraught relationship might have led Elaine to discard the idea of any such baptism for her own child. Still, one could never really tell what drove someone to do, or not to do, any particular thing. The only real way to find out, I knew, was to ask Elaine outright, but my own relationship with my mother was so uncomfortable that I shied away from such intimate questions.

I looked down at the scone. In my agitation I had crumbled it to tiny bits on the paper plate. I wasn't even hungry now. Tucking the water bottle into the front pocket of my purse, I stood to throw the trash away.

24

AT THE TOP of the steps, the rooftops opened up before me, and out behind the outer bailey, the town spread out in hues of grey stone and red brick and green trees, the market stalls pointing the way back up the High Street toward what I knew were the half-timbered walls of my hotel. The square tower of St. Laurence's Church, with its four spires, rose among the buildings crowding up to its walls. A single cloud scudded across the impossible blue of the sky to the north; the wind up here was more brisk, whipping my hair around my face no matter how often I shoved it behind my ears. Fighting vertigo, I clutched at the stone wall with both hands. Everything below was so small, a doll's village. If I squinted against the sun, I could almost imagine myself a sentry, keeping guard some five hundred years in the past. Almost. I shivered, hunching my shoulders inside my jacket.

At some point Eleanor must have stood up here and looked down upon the town from which she had drawn her name. At some point, Eleanor must have come here, searching for something. What could that have been? Would I recognize it when I came upon it? I circled the platform slowly, scanning the ground below, scanning the horizon. To the west, the River Teme wandered out of those Welsh hills and into Shropshire, though I could not really see it from this vantage. I looked down into the inner bailey, at the round chapel, and beyond that—I consulted the brochure I had picked up at the entrance—the block of buildings formerly housing the solar, the great hall, and the Tudor lodgings. I drew on vague memories of what I had learned at some point, of Ludlow being the seat of the Council of the Marches, and of poor Arthur Tudor honeymooning at the castle until he died, not long after his wedding. I leaned against the parapet, studying the end of the block of buildings: thick walls, no roof, windows long since gone. He had lived in those blocks with the teenaged Katharine of Aragon, had entertained and perhaps governed from that great hall in the center, while his young wife had kept company with her ladies in the solar at the far end. Sad, that all the plans so carefully laid by Henry VII had come to naught with the death of the Prince of Wales—until his younger brother Henry had been shuffled quickly into his place, to take his castles, his responsibilities, and his wife.

I sighed, and once again fought back the surprise of tears. What was going on with me? I was not a crier, and this was getting ridiculous. Still, I knew all about carefully laid long-term plans, those laid and then smashed to pieces by the cruel hand of fate. At least in my case it wasn't death, unless you counted the death of love. At least in my case it had just been divorce, something Arthur's younger brother and the wife they shared knew all about.

The sound of laughter drifted up the stairs behind me, a shout, and then another shout in answer. Quickly I scrubbed at my eyes with the back of my hand, hoping the wind would account for the flushing I felt in my cheeks, then wondering why anyone would care. When the family—mother, father, three kids—erupted from the stairwell, I nodded quickly and dodged back down, leaving the platform to them.

BEATRICE.

I caught my breath, standing near the well at the side of the inner bailey. Above me the stonework towered, but I suddenly couldn't look upward for long without feeling dizzy, a reverse sort of vertigo. I wished I'd eaten that scone instead of tearing it to bits and throwing it away; food might have steadied me. The walls were swirling above me, and I closed my eyes momentarily, but that only made it worse. I opened my eyes. I took a step toward a flight of stone steps leading upward into the great hall, then another step, and then found myself half-staggering, half-falling to an awkward seat on the worn tread. Gasping for air, I dropped my head to my knees and prayed I wouldn't be sick. The birds in the trees outside the curtain wall seemed suddenly shrill and piercing, the sun jabbing sharpened knives into my eyes.

Beatrice, I thought again. Unless that wasn't my own voice I was hearing.

Creavit ex Beatrice.

I clutched my purse, still containing the bit of tapestry, convulsively to my side.

"Miss?"

At first, clenching my fists against my ears to deaden the clamor of the birds, I did not register the voice. Then came the hesitant touch on my shoulder.

"Miss? Are you all right, miss?"

"Beatrice," I whispered. My lips felt numb.

"Your name is Beatrice? Do you need me to call someone, Beatrice? Are you here with friends? Do you need medical attention?"

The voice was a woman's, calm, businesslike. The touch on my shoulder became firmer.

I gulped. *I didn't think it would be like this,* I thought nonsensically, *at least not this early, not this soon.* I took a deep rasping breath. Another.

I lifted my head and saw that my would-be rescuer wore the uniform I had seen on the ticket-sellers at the entrance. She wore a name tag, too: *Katti.* Her hair was dark, but silvering along her temples, and she had laughter wrinkles around her eyes. She looked reassuring: eminently capable and good-natured.

"Thank you," I mumbled, wiping a hand across my brow and finding it sweaty again. "I'm okay now. Just vertigo."

"Would some water help, do you think? Something to drink?"

I fumbled with the catch of my purse's front pocket, and drew out the bottle I'd purchased in the café. I managed a half-smile, then realized that the woman was waiting, watching me expectantly. Measuringly, as though I might regress and pass out, sprawling on the grass at her feet. I uncapped the bottle and lifted it to my lips. The water was warm now, but I felt the need to reassure the woman by drinking it down. I immediately felt the need for more. But I also felt better. Calmer.

Katti was smiling encouragingly.

"Beatrice—"

I shook my head. "Actually, I'm Emily."

If the initial expression that flashed over Katti's face was one of puzzlement, it was quickly replaced by one of professional kindness. "Sorry. My mistake." Katti looked at her watch, then tapped the radio strapped to her belt. "Perhaps I should just call for someone to check you over," she suggested. "In case it's heatstroke."

Again I shook my head. "No, no, that's not necessary. It was just momentary. I made the mistake of staring up at the towers and just got a little dizzy."

"Maybe you'd like to come sit in the office for a bit until you feel better?"

It was obvious that this woman, kind as she was, would hold on like a terrier unless I took direct action. I recapped the bottle, then got to my feet, holding myself steady by sheer force of will. "Thank you. Really. Thank you." Smiling with what I hoped did not quite resemble rictus, I tucked the empty bottle back into my purse. "But I'm fine. I'll just—try to find my friends." I waved a vague hand toward the interior of the great hall. "They're around here somewhere."

Katti did not look entirely convinced—I'd always been a bad liar—but had no choice then but to let me go. Still smiling stiffly, I raised a hand in farewell and concentrated on steadying my walk as I climbed the rest of the stairs. I felt the woman's eyes on my back until I reached the inside and ducked behind the wall.

IN THE TUDOR apartments—so identified in the brochure—I found a seat on a stone bench in an arched window embrasure and leaned against the cold wall, my exhausted gaze on the round chapel just across the grass. I no longer felt dizzy, but I felt drained, as though enervated. I closed my eyes, leaning my head back, feeling the coolness through my hair.

This time there were no words. No sound, either, though confusingly, I was sure there should have been. What there was—was sadness. Huge, overwhelming sadness. It washed over me from all directions, heavy, crushing. I crossed my arms over my stomach as though for protection, but the sadness was inside me, part of me, part of my history, of the whole world.

A single sound which might have been a whimper escaped from my mouth, and I fled from the apartments, fled from the castle, not stopping for breath until I was in the street.

25

I HAD A sleepless night.

After breakfast the next morning—a full English, to avoid the queasiness of the previous day—I ordered a taxi for ten. Seven miles, I had discovered in my research, give or take a bit. When the cab arrived, I slumped into the front seat and repeated the address I'd committed to memory. I had no idea how long I would be on this errand—perhaps it would be a fool's errand, and I would wind up with the door slammed in my face—nor how I'd get back to the hotel, but at least those were puzzles that were easily solved, unlike all the puzzles I'd been left with since Eleanor's death.

"Friends out there?" the driver asked, dropping his sunglasses onto his nose and pulling away from the curb. This morning, like the previous morning, was brilliantly sunny.

"Relatives," I answered. "Of my grandfather."

"Expecting you?"

"No."

"Surprise, like?"

I nodded. I hoped it wouldn't be too much of a surprise. I had decided not to call ahead, though part of me was uncomfortable about the incredible rudeness of that. But, I kept telling myself, I simply wanted to see this woman. Viviane Harris. To lay eyes on her. If Viviane chose to speak to me, that would be a bonus. However, if I opted to call and then have Viviane hang up the telephone on me, we'd never meet face-to-face.

"You look nervous," the cabby observed. He turned the wheel, took a left.

I glanced down at my hands, clenched together and wound within the strap of her purse. Taking a deep breath, I straightened out my fingers and examined my nails. "I am, rather. We've never met."

The driver's eyebrows climbed above the rims of his sunglasses. "Could be awkward, that."

"I hope not," I said.

HE LEFT ME off at the Baker's Arms on Green Lane, pointing further up the road between the hedgerows. "Follow this way until the road forks, and then bear left." Thanks to the beauty of Google Earth, I knew what the house looked like from the road, stalker that I was, and recognizing it would be no problem. As the taxi disappeared back down the road, I looked up at the front of the pub, still closed this early in the morning, and wished it otherwise. If ever anyone could have used a drink for false courage, I would be that one.

Just as well, I thought bitterly, and walked on.

The road was narrow, no more than a lane, the trees forming an arch overhead; the ground was speckled with prisms of sunlight that danced on ahead of me. The morning was warming, and I felt the sweat prickle on my skin, but I couldn't be sure whether it was from the heat or from nervousness. I strode on purposefully, still biting my lip out of nerves.

Then suddenly the house appeared on my right, a gateway through the shrubbery leading up to the front door. Further along the lane was a slight turn-in for a car, though it was empty now; more than likely there would be a more commonly used side door there. My steps faltered. I was here, now, finally, and I was unsure which door to approach; would it even matter, if there was no one home? The front door seemed too formal, the side door too familiar. As I pondered, the side door opened, and an elderly woman stepped out onto the porch.

"There you are," she called cheerfully. "I was wondering how long it would take you."

I stumbled on the dirt verge. "Hi," I said, my voice unnaturally high and loud. "I'm Emily."

"I know exactly who you are," the woman said. She gestured with a long-fingered hand. "Your hair gave you away. Come in and have a cup of tea with me."

26

"MY HAIR?"

Viviane smiled. She had brought the tea tray to the table in the sunny end of the open-plan room, and now sat with her legs tucked up beneath her on the deep sofa. *Don't mind my informality,* she had said, laughing. *My house, my age.* Despite her protestations, she did not look to be quite the age Eleanor had been; she might have been in her seventies.

Now she sipped her tea. "Of course. Pre-Raphaelite hair, Nolan used to call it. Your grandmother had it, too." She ran her hand up into her own short silvery hair. "Your mother, too, perhaps?" She raised her eyebrows. "I've never met Elaine."

"My mother has always kept her hair really short," I said. The conversation— the morning—was going far too quickly for me. Whirling. Difficult to follow. "But yes. It's the same color."

"Ah." There was a wealth of understanding in her tone. She seemed sad, but only for a moment. Viviane appeared to be a woman with a wealth of good nature. Irrepressible. The smile broke forth again. "That's a shame. It's glorious. You Ludlow women are so lucky. My own daughter ended up with my dark hair."

Ludlow women. I set down my teacup. *My own daughter.*

"That's how I've always thought of the girls: the Ludlow branch of Nolan's family tree, and the Harris branch. Though I know your mother was given the name Harris."

"She still keeps it," I said. "I think it means something to her, but I'm not sure what."

Viviane leaned forward and poured a bit more tea into her cup, then held the pot aloft toward me, and I declined. "Nolan always worried that Elaine was so angry." She sighed. "It's rather sad to go through life in such a fury, don't you think? So little time, wasted on an anger that gets you nowhere."

I gave Viviane a curious look. Younger than Eleanor, yes, but somehow lighter, as though she carried far fewer worries. My grandfather's second love.

"You have a daughter," I said slowly, trying to retrace our conversational steps.

"Your mother's half-sister." Viviane nodded, her dark eyes on my face. "So you have an aunt."

The idea slid me toward the damned tears that seemed never to be far away these days. "An aunt," I murmured, looking over Viviane's shoulder at the trees outside the tall windows. "I never knew." *So little time, wasted.* "Does my mother know? Have they ever met?"

Again, the fleeting sadness. "I assume she knows, though they have never met. No, Katharine is much younger than Elaine, by ten or fifteen years, I think, so that makes her ten or fifteen years older than you." She spread her hands out. "We've never had terribly much money, and working for the Trustees as she does, Katharine has never had much time, either, and so she has never gone to the States."

"And Elaine has never come here."

"No."

"Because she's always been that angry."

Vivian lifted her cup to her lips. She took a drink and gazed thoughtfully at me before speaking. "I think that's the reason." She sighed. Then she smiled. "But you're here now. Nolan's granddaughter. And so lovely. I'm so pleased you've finally discovered us and come."

Such an open-handed, open-hearted welcome: I had no idea what to make of it. I couldn't think I'd ever felt this kind of enthusiastic embrace, one that expressed pleasure at my presence without demanding anything in return. Even Eleanor, in the past months, seemed always to have an underlying agenda, something going on beneath the surface which was, even with her death, unclear. Perhaps even more so now.

The responsibility is yours.

"Thank you," was all I could manage.

"You are very welcome," Viviane replied. "And you are very welcome here." That smile again. "Nolan so would have loved you. And I hope that you'll stay at least until my daughter comes home from work this afternoon. You two really should meet properly."

"Properly?"

"Oh, yes." Did Viviane just wink? "You met her yesterday. At the castle. She told me all about it. As soon as she described your hair, I knew it had to be you. And I knew you'd be along eventually."

"HELLO, MUM," CAME the voice from inside the house.

"In the garden, Katti," Vivian called through the open double doors. It was late in the afternoon, and after a walk to the pub for lunch, and a bit of desultory gardening, we were relaxing out on what Viviane called her terrace.

Indeed, it was the kindly woman of the previous day. As she breezed through to the garden, she was peeling off her uniform jacket, then unpinning her name tag. She smiled when she saw me seated in the cane chair with her mother, a smile, when I thought about it, that mirrored Viviane's. Wide and welcoming.

"You made it," she said. She did not seem at all surprised.

I flushed.

Katti pulled another chair over to us and sank into it, blowing her dark hair away from her forehead.

"This is really weird for me," I said.

"She didn't know about you." Viviane's voice was rich with disapproval. "Nor, I gather, about me, until fairly recently."

Katti reached across to pluck some grapes from the bowl on the table between us. She popped one into her mouth. "That's absurd. Really absurd." She turned her brown eyes to me. "I probably shouldn't say that about the Ludlow women, but they surely have quite a bit to answer for."

"Katti," Vivian said reproachfully.

"No, Mum, it's true and you know it." Katti held up a square capable hand, a grape held between two fingers like a totally useless weapon. "We are family. And *someone's* anger and secrecy has kept us from knowing each other for years."

She was, of course, right. The confusion returned to the forefront of my thoughts. *Whose* anger? The net spread wide. I thought of my own anger, resentment at my mother's distance and disapproval, at Eleanor's preference for Carwyn when we were younger. Anger and confusion about the way I felt weirdly manipulated into this—relationship—with Carwyn. Guilt about what I had done to him. With him.

Katti was still looking at me with those frank eyes. "What's the matter? Did I upset you by saying those things?"

"Let the poor woman be, Katharine. She's had a surprising and possibly trying day."

Katti was immediately contrite. "My mother. She only calls me Katharine when she's angry with me." She leaned forward conspiratorially. "My dad wanted that name for me. I think Mum wanted me to be named Pansy or some such thing."

"Katharine!"

Katti winked. "See what I mean?" She ate some more grapes. "No, really, Emily. You don't look especially well this afternoon, and you surely didn't look well yesterday. I was quite concerned." In fact, she looked concerned now. "I saw you run out of the castle after we talked, as though the hounds of hell were on your heels."

Viviane drummed her fingers on the arms of her chair. "Fishing for information like that isn't very attractive, my dear. If you want to know something, ask straight out." She turned to me. "And if you feel it isn't any of her business, tell her so."

It occurred to me just then why my grandfather must have finally given up on Eleanor and turned to Viviane: her good-natured straightforwardness must have come like the proverbial breath of fresh air to him after the archness that defined my grandmother's branch of the family. It certainly was refreshing to me.

Katti, however, was sighing mightily. "All right, Mum. Emily, are you sick?"

I took a deep breath, considering. I could dump my sad life story on them here and now; but old habits were easier to fall back into. "Shocked. More than anything."

"Were you sick yesterday, when we first met?"

Beatrice. Creavit ex Beatrice. Out of habit I glanced around for my purse, but it was in the house. "Not sick. Not really. Shocked, like I said. The place—the castle—seemed weirdly familiar to me. If that makes any sense at all." I closed my eyes, imagining myself back there. It was not comfortable. "I've never been there. I'd never seen the place. Then I got there, and—it was as though I knew where I was. As though the castle was waiting for me." The words made little sense, but somehow were true.

"Like I was waiting for you today," Viviane suggested.

It really was comfortable here with these two women. I leaned back in the cane chair, looking up into the canopy of trees overhead, the way the leaves shifted and whispered in the afternoon sunlight. It was pleasant not to have to feel defensive, not to be dismissed out of hand. "No. That was different." I frowned. "*Your* waiting for me made sense after you explained about Katti. There was—there is—no explanation for the feeling at the castle. I was . . ." I flailed for the words, and they did not come easily. "There really isn't any other word for it. I was *spooked.*"

Katti's full mouth curved at the corners, though her gaze remained sympathetic. "So I guess what I saw was someone walking over your grave?"

"Good heavens, Katharine! What a thing to say," Viviane exclaimed.

Rolling my head against the back of my seat, I saw my mother's half-sister, so unlike my mother, watching me curiously. Yes, Katti seemed to understand far more than anyone else had yet. It was comforting, but unnerving.

27

ON THE DRIVE back to Ludlow after dinner, I asked the question which had been nagging at me all evening. "Have you always known about me?"

Katti slowed the car, flicked on the directional as we came to a corner. "Oh, yes. Dad made no secret of your mother, and neither did Mum. I gather Dad kept in touch with Eleanor."

"And your mother was okay with that?"

Katti laughed, and there was genuine merriment in the sound. And love. "I don't know if you noticed, but my mum is okay with everything." More laughter. "Accepting, I guess is the right word. I do believe that she is the wisest person I have ever met."

"My grandmother told me—when she finally told me about Nolan—that he was the only man she ever loved."

"He was immeasurably lovable, Dad. You would have liked him." Katti sighed. "I miss him, you know. Mum misses him, too. Dreadfully. And it's been more than thirty years since he died."

There was no expression of resentment in her words, or in her tone. I glanced over at her profile, lit in green by the dashboard lights.

"What?" Katti laughed, catching the look.

"I—don't know. It's just strange." I frowned. "That I said that about Eleanor, and you didn't even flinch."

Katti shrugged and turned right, leaning forward to check for traffic around the hedgerows, though the glow of headlights would probably have given it away anyway. "Dad had an incredible capacity for love, you know. He loved Eleanor, but he came to love my mother, too. He had room in his heart for all of us. And then, of course, they had me. I consider myself incredibly lucky in my parents."

The sudden ache in my chest made me lean back against the headrest with a sigh. "I envy you."

"Why? Tell me about your parents."

What was there to say? "My mother—your half-sister." I took a deep breath, and started again. "I'm sure she loves me. She's my mother; of course she loves me. But I don't think she likes me all that much. She disapproved of my career choice. She liked my ex-husband, and blames me for my divorce. I can't remember a time when she wasn't hypercritical." Perhaps, I thought after the words tumbled out, that it wasn't overly loyal to my mother to speak this way to someone I'd just met. But it didn't feel as though we'd just met. Somehow, it felt as though I had been born into the wrong branch of the family, and here, with Katti and Viviane, was where I really belonged.

I felt the slight but strong touch on my shoulder.

"That's a shame," Katti said quietly. Then, after a moment, "And your father?"

I sniffed. "I never knew him. He's dead."

"Oh, love," Katti breathed. "I'm sorry."

We drove on in silence for a while, then Katti reached out a hand to push the CD into the dashboard player. She adjusted the volume, and we were immediately surrounded by the sound of a muted trumpet.

"It was a long time ago," I said. But in a sad voice, because the warmth and love in Katti's tone, when she spoke of her parents, made it obvious what had been missing.

"You had Eleanor?"

"Not much. She and my mother didn't get along—I suspect now that it had something to do with your father, her father—Mom felt cheated. Deprived." I thought of my mother's last judgment on her mother, and winced. "She said, when my grandmother died, that Eleanor had never loved any of us, that she had one passion only, and the rest of us were just peripheral."

"The dancing?" Katti asked. Up ahead, Ludlow glowed on the horizon. "The choreography. She really was quite well-known. World-wide. In certain circles." She laughed, a small self-conscious sound. "I led such a boring life growing up. I used to look for articles about Eleanor, at the library. To live vicariously through her, I guess. My strange relationship to her was the secret I kept close when I was a snotty-nosed dissatisfied teenager."

"I can't imagine you were that," I said. "I thought my mother was talking about the dancing, when she passed that final judgment on Eleanor. But I'm starting to wonder."

A few more turns and we reached the front of the hotel, hulking over the street as it had for centuries.

"It's a mystery," Katti said. "And a tragic one."

"Yes."

Suddenly Katti leaned over and kissed me on the cheek. "But that's in the past. You and I—we've found each other, and we've got a lot to time to make up. So let's make it better, shall we?"

28

AT FOUR, I was waiting at the gate before the restaurant across from the castle.

"You could come to the gatehouse and meet me," Katti had suggested, but I had demurred and she had not pushed it.

Now my aunt—no, I couldn't really call Katti that—was crossing between the cars, one hand raised in greeting, the other clutching her purse strap across her plump form.

"Sorry I'm late," she said breathlessly when she reached the pavement.

"Don't worry," I replied. "It's not as though I'm on a strict schedule."

Katti put her arm through mine. "My car's along here at the car park. But before we go to the house, we're to have tea. Mum has giving me talking points."

"That sounds ominous."

Katti laughed and led the way down the pavement. Overhead, the sky was growing dark, threatening rain. "I've got a place in mind for cream tea. Have you ever had a cream tea? We could have just gone to the castle Tea House, but somehow I sense that isn't the best plan for you."

"No." As we reached the car, I glanced over the roof at Katti, the lifted eyebrows in that frank face indicating undisguised curiosity. Katti unlocked the doors and we climbed in.

"You never told me why you ran out of there the other day as though the Hound of Hergest was on your heels," Katti said as she turned the key in the ignition. Rain spattered on the windshield; we'd reached the car just in time. "You can give me the story over tea. I think it's probably important." She looked both ways and pulled out into the street, then took the right and followed the road around the castle walls. As we approached the river, I put out a quick hand.

"I need to go stand on that bridge," I said.

"All right." Katti drew the words out as though to request further explanation. When I didn't deliver, she shrugged and pointed across the river. "There's a bit of a place to park the car on the other side. Hold on." The rain was still spattering against the windshield, desultorily, unable to make up its mind. "You're going to get wet." Nevertheless, at the far end of the stone bridge, she pulled over and parked. We got out. Katti looked up once into the drizzly sky and pulled the hood of her jacket up over her tumbled dark hair. "Are you going to take a photo?"

I shook my head. I shoved my hands into my own jacket pockets and crossed the road, following the stone to the bridge parapet. Above us, against the roiling sky, the castle towered. Midway across, I placed my palms against the rough stone and stared down at the murky water, pocked with quickening raindrops. It did not seem deep, nor particularly fast-moving.

"Is this the original bridge?"

Beside me, Katti also looked down into the Teme. "No, this one was built in 1823—or at least that's what we tell people at the castle." She adopted a tour-guide voice. "On much earlier, possible Medieval bridge piers, however." She glanced up into my face. "Why?"

I wasn't sure why I had asked, or why it mattered. I was uncertain, now, why I was even standing on this bridge. I had felt compelled. I looked up again at the castle walls, thinking of the flood of sadness I had experienced there, leaning back against the stone, inside the window embrasure. There had been something, when I'd first seen the bridge over the Teme, that had called me to it. Now that something had faded—was gone save for the palest memory of it.

"I don't know," I whispered, my voice barely audible even to me over the hush of the river and the birds in the trees along the banks. I closed my eyes, trying to *feel* something. Somewhere there was a ghost of that sadness, but it was suddenly overlaid by anger, and determination, a familiar sense, which at first I could not place.

She doesn't love any of us. She only has one passion.

"Eleanor," I said, the word jerked from deep within. I turned confused eyes on Katti. "It feels like Eleanor here."

WE SHOOK OFF the rain and doffed our coats, finding a small table close to the screened fire.

"Tell me about the Hound of Hergest," I suggested after the waiter had taken our cream tea orders and sailed off.

Katti looked up, surprised. "Is this a diversionary tactic? We're here to talk about you, not about some blasted beast." She sighed mightily in feigned impatience. "Mum gave me—"

"Your mother gave you talking points. I know. I know all about it." I glanced out the window to the side, spattered and streaked with rain, at the drowned garden. "But it's not really a diversion. Not really. You brought it up, the other night, and again this afternoon. You said, and I quote, that I was fleeing the castle as if from the Hound of Hergest. I take it that's not a basset hound you're talking about."

The waiter reappeared with a trolley, from which he transferred a large teapot, cups and saucers, plates, and various other accoutrements. Then he delivered the *coup de resistance,* a multi-tiered cake stand, covered with pastries nestled in frilled wrappers. Mission accomplished, he trundled the trolley away again.

"Shall I be mother?" Katti asked. "How do you like your tea?"

"Black today, I think."

Katti grimaced. "Obviously not from this side of the pond." She poured me a cup, then fixed one for herself: cream, sugar. She set the pot aside and stirred her tea gently with her spoon. "All right, I'll humor you on this. The Hound of Hergest is a mythological black dog which is said to terrorize the hills, tearing out the jugulars of unsuspecting travelers caught on the holloways after dark."

"Oh. Like the Hound of the Baskervilles."

Katti nodded. "It's said that Conan Doyle did stay in this general area and might have picked up the myth—and then just transplanted the big black dog into Devon."

I sipped my tea. It was quite hot, but between it and the fire, I thought I might, at some point, feel warm and dry again. Outside, the rain splashed on.

"The good news," I said after a moment, choosing a scone from the cake stand, and reaching for the jam pot, "is that I really had no fear the other day of having my jugular torn out at the castle."

"We frown on that sort of entertainment," Katti said, nodding. "Would you care to tell me what had you running, then?"

"Is this part of Viviane's script?"

"No." Katti, too, selected a scone. "I'm going off on my own here. But—for some reason, I can't help but think it's important information." She split the scone, and slathered it with cream.

Again I turned to watch the rain, heavier now, stream down the glass. Outside, the garden had smeared into a late Monet painting, colors everywhere, shapes indistinct. "It was the sadness," I said slowly. Katti said nothing—appeared to be waiting. "Do you ever feel it? That a place has been imprinted with a feeling? Imbued? The stones in the Tudor wing—I was sitting in the window bench, and suddenly I just couldn't bear it."

"I know the place." Katti held the scone before her, but looked past it, as though having forgotten all about it. Her dark eyes were on my face. "I've sat there any number of times in the years I've been working at the castle. But I've never felt anything like that."

"You think it could happen, though, right?" I felt defensive and a bit desperate. "You think it *did* happen to me."

Katti nodded. "Oh, I don't discount those things. I'm just not one of the people fortunate enough to be sensitive to them." Her mouth quirked at the corner. "Dad always said I was far too practical for that sort of thing."

Another sip of tea. "I don't know if *fortunate* is quite the word I'd use," I said wryly. I sighed, set the tea cup aside again for the scone. I finished off the half in two bites, and used the cloth napkin to wipe the strawberry jam I knew was on my upper lip. Then I went for the second half. "You saw me running. Hell, when I felt that, I got out of there *fast*. I mean, I really couldn't bear it."

"The sadness?"

"The sadness. It soaked out of the stones and into me and I couldn't breathe." The memory forced me to set the scone on the plate and cover my face with my hands. "It was that thick, Katti. It was suffocating me. If I'd stayed there, it would have crushed me to death."

Katti spun the cake stand slowly, staring at the pastries, still without seeing them. "It's not *your* sadness."

"I don't see how it could be. I'd carry that with me, wouldn't I? If I tried to run away from it, it would keep up. If you know what I mean."

Katti's brow creased in thought. She stopped turning the cake stand, only to spin it in the other direction. "True. And you told me you felt Eleanor on the bridge, all angry and determined, so it's not her sadness in the castle. Whose could it be, do you suppose?"

A practical approach to something which had nothing to do with practicality. I wanted to leap across this table and hug this woman. How long had it been since someone had taken my concerns seriously, without dismissing them as fancy? And this particular concern—even I had difficulty accepting the validity of the feeling, though I knew what I knew; I knew what I had felt.

Which made me think of Carwyn. I bit my lip. He'd taken me seriously. But I forced the thought of him away resolutely. I had burned all bridges with Carwyn, tentative as they had been.

Katti was eyeing me with the openly curious gaze I was beginning to know so well. She said nothing, merely selected a tiny cake from the stand and set it on her plate.

"Does there have to be someone specific?" I asked at last. "Couldn't I have just felt some general sadness? I mean, it's a castle. A thousand years old. There have been a lot of people in that castle in all that time."

Katti poured more tea into her cup, then topped off mine as well without asking. She set the pot down and signaled to the waiter for more hot water. When he had flitted off on his errand, she lifted her hands, waving her thoughts into some sort of order. "But the sadness was *that* intense. Despair. Right? So intense you had to run from it. Concentrated. I don't know much about these things, but that indicates to me that it's the impression of a single person. Someone suffering an incredible grief."

It made sense. I cupped my chin in my hands and leaned my elbows on the table.

"Tell me about the bridge, though," Katti suggested. "Your grandmother on the bridge."

I frowned, trying to parse it out. "Not despair there. Not grief. More like a bit of sorrow, and then washed out by determination. If nothing else, determination spells Eleanor to me." I rubbed the furrows out of my brow with my fingers. "I felt her—I was sure I felt her—on the bridge. Not like she was there with us, not like a haunting. That wasn't it. But she had been there. At some point." I rubbed my eyes, which felt gritty. "Oh, I wish I could ask her these questions, now that I'm here, now that I've met you. She was here at one point—when she was young, maybe very young—and I think that time, when she was on the bridge, looking up at the castle, was when she decided to remake herself as Nora Ludlow. So she could remember that moment. When she *knew.*"

"But what did she know?"

"Therein lies the question."

29

"MUM," KATTI CALLED when we entered the house. Just as she had the previous evening, and just, I was certain, as she had every day before that.

"In the sitting room," Viviane called. "I have a fire going."

"Take your wet things off and go through. I'll take your bag upstairs." Katti paused on the first step. "It's the small bedroom. I hope you don't mind."

I looked at her in disbelief, and after a moment, Katti laughed and bounded up the staircase.

Viviane was seated in a wing chair before the wood burner, book in hand. She looked up and smiled as I entered. "So you came," she said easily. "I'm delighted."

I felt warmed by the welcome, and the fire. "Katti was very persuasive."

"Come. Sit. I pulled up another chair, as I was so hoping you would agree to our invitation. And here you are."

There were in fact three chairs grouped comfortably around the fire. I sank into the one across from Viviane. "You were quite confident." I wasn't exactly sure how to feel about that.

Viviane waved the judgment away. "Not even the slightest. But I'd hoped. You seemed to fit so well with us when you were here yesterday. And why should you spend all that money on lodging and food when we have a perfectly good room for you here?" She marked her spot in the book with a small card, and then set the volume aside on a pie-crust table. "Katti gave you tea, did she? But you might want something stronger now that you're home." She glanced toward the front window. "Such a miserable afternoon. Just bucketing down out there."

"I'll get it, Mum," Katti said, entering. She'd changed out of her work clothes, and now wore jeans and a soft blue pullover. She crossed to the drinks table in the corner. "What'll you have, Emily? Mum always has Scotch."

She seemed to take my silence as assent.

Katti handed drinks around, and then took the chair between us. She stretched her legs toward the fire and sighed. "There. This is nice. But we'll just have to find another chair once Helen gets back." She rolled her head against the high back of the chair, to look over at me. "Helen's in Zurich right now."

"Until Monday, isn't it?" Viviane asked. She reached out to pat her daughter's arm comfortingly. "She'll be back soon, love."

"I know." Katti put her own hand over her mother's and sighed again.

I buried my nose in the Scotch and breathed deeply; I hadn't heard that that would do any harm. I longed for a sip, just one, to let the fire slip down my throat into my stomach to warm me. "Who is Helen?" I asked.

Katti blushed, holding out her left hand. For the first time I noticed the ring: a small purple stone in a silver setting. "My fiancée. Helen is my fiancée."

Viviane laughed. "She keeps saying that like it's hard to believe."

I set my glass aside and caught Katti's hand in my own. "Let me look at that." In the warm light, the stone winked in its silver setting. "It's beautiful, Katti." I looked up into her proud face and swallowed back my sudden envy at the love there. I wanted that. I thought I had that. "She has good taste, this Helen. In jewels and in women. Have you a picture of her?" I looked up to the mantle over the wood burner, which was bare, other than a clock.

Katti leaped up and crossed the room to a breakfront. She collected one framed photo from the desk, then paused and picked up a second before returning to her chair. "This is Helen," she said, handing the oval frame to me. In the photograph, Katti and another woman looked up at the camera from below, holding hands, both smiling broadly at some wonderful joke. Where Katti was dark with wide apple cheeks, Helen was blonde, her hair swinging back from her uplifted chin in a pageboy cut, her green eyes wide and surprised.

"You look so happy," I whispered, because I couldn't trust my voice not to break. I stared down at the two smiling women in the picture, wondering what it would take to have someone look so happy to be in my company. I thought of Rob, thought of the wedding album I'd left behind at the house in Wilmington. I wished I could remember the photographs in it, but they were all a blur. Had I ever looked as happy as this in my now-ex-husband's company? Had he ever looked this happy in mine? Did he look this happy now, in Michelle's company?

I had to stop thinking like that, I told myself sternly. This wasn't about me.

But Viviane had noticed, with her sharp eyes. "What is it?" she asked gently.

"Katti and Helen," I said, still whispering. "They look so happy. So in love."

"We are in love. And we are happy." Katti took the photo from me, and replaced it with the second frame she had gathered from the breakfront.

I blinked rapidly. I would not cry, I told myself fiercely, I would not, not again. I would be happy for Katti. Slowly I took a deep breath and let it out again, before turning my attention to the second picture. This one was in a more old-fashioned, ornate frame, and the man and woman, dressed in wedding finery, were also holding hands. I looked into the dark eyes of the woman, then up at Viviane.

"You," I said.

"And Nolan." Viviane sipped delicately at her Scotch, the glass glittering in her hand. "On the day we were married."

Nolan Harris was taller than his wife, and stood with his free arm around her protectively. This was recognizably the same man from Eleanor's photographs, but now he had aged, with gray in his hair and a slight stoop to his shoulders. His smile was gentle. Hers was radiant. He appeared several years older than Viviane, which made perfect sense now that I thought about it: if Nolan and Eleanor were of an age, he would have been around ninety now, and Viviane could not be much more than seventy. I glanced between mother and daughter, calculating.

"I'm forty-seven," Katti said.

"And I'm seventy-two," Viviane added cheerfully. "You've figured it out." She held out a wrinkled but steady hand for the photograph, and then gazed down at her dead husband lovingly. "When I first met him—it was in a tearoom over in Bewdley—he was sad. Heartbroken, you might say. But he was kind, and handsome, and I decided then and there that he was the one I wanted. The only one I wanted."

"Heartbroken?"

Viviane cradled the frame in her hands, still smiling. "Oh, yes. I think he'd finally come to understand that your grandmother was adamant, and would not spend her life with him. He'd come here, to Ludlow, to come to some sort of grip with that reality. And here I was. It was the most fortunate day of my life, when I found him at the table next to mine."

"You made him forget?"

Viviane laughed, the sound of bright bells. "Oh, not right away—and never completely. He took a bit of convincing. After all, he'd spent all those years chasing the dream of your grandmother, and dreams are very difficult to give up on. But—"She laughed again. "I knew what I wanted, and I persisted. Because I am a very practical and determined woman."

The two women before me were so much alike: my grandfather's wife, my grandfather's child. *Practical and determined.* I supposed Eleanor was also practical and determined—I'd felt the determination on the bridge that very afternoon— but her passion, according to Elaine, had been singular and different, *not* a husband, *not* an especially close relationship with children or grandchildren.

Not children. Not grandchildren. *Child. Grandchild.*

The thought had been niggling, and now rose to the fore. Child. I was the only child of an only child of an only child. How far back did that go? I had no real knowledge of my grandmother's family—had my great-grandmother, too, been an only child? Her mother before her? So hurt and resentful had I been growing up, that I'd never thought to investigate my family tree. Looking at these new-found relatives, on the male side, I wondered what else I had been missing.

"I'm feeling a bit dozy, sitting in front of this wood fire," Viviane said suddenly. "I think a bit of a light supper might be a good idea at this point, and an early night."

"I'll get it, Mum. You sit." Katti stood, collecting the glasses. "You can help, Emily—you're going to need to figure out where we keep things in this house, since you'll be staying."

I got to my feet to follow, hoping they hadn't noticed my untouched drink, but Viviane stopped me before I followed Katti from the room. "I'm glad you're here, Emily. I'm glad you decided to accept our invitation. It just seemed so foolish to have you staying at a hotel when you could be with family."

Her smile was warm, and I returned it before heading to the kitchen.

30

"WHY WERE YOU in Bewdley that day?" Emily asked, handing the daisies she'd clipped to Viviane, who added them to the riotous bouquet she held in her gloved hands. "That day, when you met my grandfather?"

"Chance," Viviane answered. She nudged the flowers with a finger, rearranging them in her grip. "I was on a ramble with some friends from Astley Cross, and we walked into the village at about tea time and decided to have a cuppa before returning home." She smiled at the memory. "Four of us, all windblown and muddy, but the proprietress was a friend of one of the girls, so she didn't mind us. It was a blustery sort of afternoon, and we were the only customers aside from the one man who sat alone with the newspaper at the next table."

"And that was Nolan."

Viviane crossed to the cane chairs and settled herself into one. A pitcher stood on the low table, and she leaned forward to arrange the flowers in it. Then she sat back to look at her handiwork with a critical eye. "Some more of the purple, I think, Emily," she said, pointing to the border. "Cut the stems long, would you?"

I brought them to Viviane, who worked them into her arrangement carefully, eyeing each addition before inserting the next stem.

"I think that's good enough, my dear," she said at last. "Now come have a seat with me for a few minutes." She checked her watch. "Katti and Helen won't be along for another hour, at least."

I did as I was told. The rain of the past few days had finally ended, and the sun rode high and warm in the afternoon sky. I wiped a hand across my brow. "However did you manage to strike up a conversation with him? A spare guy by himself at another table, when I'm with my friends . . . even if I were alone, I don't think I'd have the courage to make the approach."

"Oh, I had never done such a thing. But he was so handsome. Blonde, brooding—he wasn't really reading the newspaper, I could tell. And my friends just kept teasing me. Egging me on, you might say. So—I asked him for directions back to Astley Cross. It was the only thing I could think of." Viviane laughed merrily. "Of course he had no idea. He told me he'd just come to Bewdley to see Tickenhill. Just visiting. An American. We invited him to join us at our table, and later when we went along to the pub." She winked. "I had the telephone number of the hotel he was staying before the afternoon was out. His home address before he left. We corresponded, and he stopped in to visit when he returned the next year."

"How long did it take?"

"Three years." Viviane shook her head. "But it was well worth it. By the time he finally proposed, he knew what he was getting in me. And I worked very hard to make him happy." She sighed and looked beyond the garden into the trees. "I loved that man beyond measure." She blinked her dark eyes several times and cleared her throat. "We had good years, Nolan and I. Sometimes he was broody and would go off for a walk—he'd collect worry stones and bring them back to me: I keep them all on the kitchen window sill. Perhaps you've noticed them?"

I had.

"And then we had Katti." Viviane blinked and turned her frank gaze on me. "She's a blessing, my daughter. So like him, even though the poor girl got my looks and not his." The smile was back. "That's why I'm so glad she's found someone she can love like I loved her father."

I was silent. I gazed at my hands, folded in my lap, the left ring finger pinched and slightly paler where the wedding ring had been for so long. The wedding ring that I'd taken off and hurled into the Delaware River.

"And you, my dear?" Viviane's voice was soft. "Have you found that someone?"

My smile was bitter. "I thought I had. I was married. For eleven years. And then I wasn't anymore."

"Your choice?"

"His."

"And you haven't found anyone else."

"No." But I felt my face grow hot and balled my fingers together in my lap. "Maybe there isn't anyone else." I blinked. *You two were made for each other.* Eleanor's voice. The words, now, infuriated me. Eleanor, who had had such a love, and who had thrown it away. What the hell had she known about anything? How could she have presumed to make a judgment about me, and about Carwyn? Even thinking of his name hurt, in a strange sort of way I hadn't expected.

"I'm sorry. I shouldn't pry. It isn't nice." Viviane stood, then bent to pick up the pitcher of flowers. With her free hand she patted my shoulder gently, the same sort of touch Katti had used that first time, at the castle. "Come. We'll fix dinner for the girls."

31

"LET'S GO FOR a walk," Katti suggested, pushing away from the table. "I need to work some of this off." She grinned at her mother. "You know how to keep your child well-fed, Mum."

"You girls go along," Viviane said. "I'll clean up here."

We protested, but Viviane would not be swayed. "Go watch the sunset. I'm sure after all that traveling, you need to stretch your legs, Helen. And you've been helping enough today, Emily—go on out and relax."

We left the house and strolled leisurely between the banks, up toward the common. The evening air was redolent with the scent of flowers I could not identify, and raucous with birdsong I could not identify, either. Helen and Katti entwined their fingers and swung their arms between them, a companionable gait of a relationship of long standing. At first none of us spoke, and the silence was surprisingly comfortable. I sighed contentedly.

"I wish," I said at last, "that I'd met you all sooner."

Katti smiled. "I do, too."

"Families," Helen said. "Why do they have to be so difficult?"

Katti leaned into her fiancée for a moment, a reassuring, perhaps comforting movement. "Helen's people," she said by way of explanation. "Not—how shall we say?—supportive?"

I glanced over at the pair, so happy in each other's company. "Not supportive?"

"I'm thirty-eight years old," Helen said. Exasperated, resentful. She flicked her blonde pageboy over her shoulders. "I know who I am. I know what I want. I've known since I was twelve. My parents, and my sister, are all about marriage—straight marriage—and children, and they don't allow me to forget that."

"I'm sorry," I commiserated. "My own mother is difficult as well. Not in that way, but difficult enough."

"Katti told me," Helen said.

"I hope you don't mind my talking about you," Katti broke in quickly. Her round cheeks had colored up. "I talk too much. I do. I'm sorry."

"Don't be—"

Before I could finish my thought, Helen put out a hand to stop us both on the dirt lane. Up ahead, in the fading light, a fox burst from the underbrush with a pronounced rustle. A brilliant orange flame tipped in black, it looked at us once and fled up the road a few yards before slipping into the bank opposite. The birds, who had fallen silent at its passing, gradually resumed their evening songs.

"Beautiful," I breathed. I couldn't remember when I'd ever seen a fox. If I'd ever seen a fox.

"The color of your hair," Helen said.

"You're a fox," Katti teased.

I pulled a strand of hair about and examined it. "Perhaps I should get black tips done. What do you think?"

"Oh, no, don't," Katti exclaimed. "It's lovely hair. Leave it alone." She smirked as they continued along the lane. "And you should do what your old auntie says."

"Katharine!" Helen laughed. "You're not old!"

Katti leaned again into Helen and turned to kiss her cheek. "You sound just like my dad when you use my full name."

"Is that a good thing? Or a bad thing? I need to know whether I should keep it up, or if it's a relationship breaker." Helen winked at me, inviting me in on the joke.

"It's good." Katti sighed. "I miss Dad." We had come out at the top of the rise, where the banks fell away, and the common opened before us, tall grass and scrub bushes dotted about here and there.

"I wish I'd known him," Helen said.

"I do, too," I added.

"He'd love you both. Because I do," Katti said stoutly.

"I think it's time for a group hug." Helen turned and threw her arms around both of us. I buried my face in the nearest shoulder and closed my eyes. It was nice. It was more than nice. I wrapped my arms around the other two and held on tightly.

The sun slipped further down the western sky, slicing beneath the clouds and painting the common around us in brilliant shades of russet and orange; the world around us suddenly blazed up.

"We should," Katti said slowly, "start to dance." She giggled gleefully. "To wind up the spell."

"What spell?" I asked.

"That's easy. A love spell. For you." She squeezed my arm. "Helen and I already have our love spell, so this one's for you."

"Widdershins!" Helen agreed. She nudged her hip into Katti's, and they began to move, shoving me along with them. "Because," she crowed, throwing her head back, "we are the Weird Sisters. And we are circle-dancing on the heath."

"It's not a heath," Katti objected, still laughing.

"We're still magic, though. At least Emily and I are, *Katharine.*" Helen made a face at her fiancée.

We circled, giggling like children. I couldn't remember when I had last felt like this: the spring evening air in my hair, the smell of June in my nose. The sun was fading beyond the edge of the common, slipping down behind the trees. All the worries which clung to my skin, my spirit, seemed to fall away into the long grass the faster we spun. I could almost see them flung away as we circle-danced, through the tears of laughter which streamed now from my eyes.

Then there was a sudden bark, and a golden retriever was leaping about us joyfully, threading between our legs so we nearly fell. Breathless, we three stumbled to a halt; I bent over at the waist, trying to catch my breath.

"Bella!" someone called, and reluctantly the dog peeled away.

Helen collapsed onto a stone and put her head between her knees. "Brilliant!" Her voice was still light with hilarity. "The three witches are taken down by a happy yellow dog."

Katti rested a hand on Helen's shoulder. "A yellow dog whose master no doubt thinks we're nuts."

"Well, we are," Helen said. She pulled Katti down and kissed her. "*Katharine.*"

It was not until we were nearly back to the house, coming down the darkened lane, that I finally worked up the courage to ask.

"Why Katharine?"

Katti looked over.

"I mean, Viviane said your father chose that name. She—and you—both say he was the only one who usually called you that. So—why Katharine?"

Up ahead on the left, the light over the porch door glowed warmly in welcome; in the big window I saw Viviane leaning forward, peering out to look for us.

Katti shrugged.

"He named me after Katharine of Aragon."

32

THE MORNING WAS dew-laden and a bit chilly, but I wiped off one of the cane chairs in the garden to settle with my first cup of coffee. It was early; the only company were the birds which trilled in the trees beyond the garden. In my other hand I held the rolled muslin I had kept so close since Eleanor's death. The rolled muslin that held the secret of my responsibility. If only I could figure out what that responsibility was.

I shivered in the cool dawn, despite the sweat, which still made itself felt along my hairline, down my spine. I had not felt this dizziness since the day at the castle, this sickness. I sighed, took a sip of the coffee, and set the cup aside. Then slowly I unrolled the cloth on my lap to gaze down at the small tapestry. With an unsteady finger, I touched the embroidered line in the corner. *Creavit ex Beatrice.*

The secret started with this tiny cherub, its narrow face, its golden-red hair. The first clue. The same golden-red as my own hair, tangled now in sweaty ringlets around my face and shoulders. It was a piece in the puzzle my grandmother meant me to put together, but what were the others?

The door snicked in its frame behind me, and I whirled.

"Only me." Helen wore a heavy sweatshirt over her pajamas, and clutched her own coffee cup in both hands. She yawned. Her blonde hair was tumbled and spiky from sleep. "Can I join you?" Without waiting for a reply, she slipped into the chair to my left, took another sip of coffee, and leaned her head back, eyes closed. "I always have trouble sleeping in, here at Viviane's. The mornings are so raucous. Damned birds." She chuckled.

I murmured in assent.

"What about you?" Helen asked. "Is this so different from where you come from?"

I really didn't know. "I've only been back to my hometown for a couple of months, since the divorce. I lived for years in Wilmington. A fairly large city. Not even vaguely rural." I took a deep breath. "I don't really know yet where I belong. I haven't figured out where I fit yet. So everything seems different and strange to me, one place as much as another."

"So it might be the birds waking you early, too."

"Yes."

Helen drained her coffee cup, then set it on the table next to mine. Her green gaze fell on the small tapestry across my knees. She started, her eyes widening, then slowly she looked up.

"My God, Emily—what have you got there?" she asked, her voice thick with excitement.

I chewed my lower lip, gazing down at the cherub my grandmother had entrusted to my care. For a long moment I said nothing, cursing myself silently for not rolling the tapestry back up before Helen's approach. It had been kept so secret, locked in the hidden compartment of the casket; Eleanor's secret, and I did not know to whom Eleanor had revealed it other than to myself, or if in fact she had ever shown the piece to anyone else. Under Helen's excited gaze, I squirmed uncomfortably.

"My grandmother left it to me," I said at last in a low voice.

"Good God, Emily," Helen breathed again. She stood, bent over my shoulder. She kept her hands jammed into the pocket of her sweatshirt, restraining herself from touching the weaving. For my part, I had to refrain from covering the small piece protectively with my hands. "Good God."

"What?"

Her eyes still on the weaving in my lap, Helen collapsed again into her chair. "How old is it?"

I too stared down at the tapestry, at the cherub, at the embroidered signature. "I don't know. Eleanor told me she inherited it from her mother, who inherited it from her mother. I don't know how long back it goes."

"Can I—" Helen's voice faded out, at the enormity of her request. "I mean, could I—see it?" She held out her hands, which were shaking slightly. "Could I *hold* it?"

Loath as I was to let the tapestry out of my hands, I could not see a reason to refuse; I'd already let the secret of its existence out, as it were.

"She kept it locked away," I said. "I don't know how many people knew she had it. Probably not many. Maybe not any."

Nevertheless, with Helen still waiting, I slipped my hands beneath the muslin, lifted it, and set it gently in Helen's outstretched palms. Helen grew perfectly still, seemed not even to take a breath, as she lay the cloth across her own lap. Still she did not touch it, but treated it with a designer's or historian's incredible respect.

"This is magnificent," she managed at last. "You keep it wrapped up in this?" She lifted the edge of the muslin with a finger. "Even this cloth wrapping is old. Really old."

I couldn't help but hover jealously. "Eleanor—she gave it to me—rolled in the cloth. She kept it in a wooden chest." *A chest which had disappeared.* Not for the first time was I grateful for the curiosity, and the larcenous impulse, which had made me take the rolled packet home. "I'm not sure if that's the way it came to her from her mother, or anything like that."

"She didn't tell you?"

"She died before she told me all the things she wanted to." *Because I'd taken so long to try to get to know her,* I thought bitterly. Then I thought, *because she fed me information a crumb at a time.* Until suddenly there was no time left. My skin prickled: the thought was disloyal.

Around us the bird chorus swelled and died away again. The sun had climbed into the tops of the trees to the east, the slanted light painting silver across the decking at our feet.

"This is really wonderful," Helen said. She seemed less interested in my story than in the piece of work on her lap. "It belongs in a museum somewhere. We shouldn't even be touching it. It needs the care of a preservationist." Her studious eyes roved over the strands of color, the figure, the border. "It's hundreds of years old. Perhaps Renaissance? I don't dare guess how old. Have you had it dated?" She examined the tiny signature. "I wonder who Beatrice could have been?" She frowned. "Most tapisers wove a signature shape or icon into the border, to identify their work. I've never seen an obvious signature like this before." Helen slumped back into her cane chair. "Hell, I've never seen a tapestry like this before. So small—it must have been done on a hand-loom. Perhaps by someone who was learning, an apprentice, though it really doesn't look like an apprentice's work." The frown deepened, lines carved between Helen's fine pale brows, as she thought aloud. "But so unusual, a woman tapiser." She looked up. "The guilds of Europe didn't allow women to weave during the Renaissance. Some women did anyway, of course, in secret. And the signature icon could disguise that. But this is right out there in the open, like she wanted everyone to know."

"Except that this piece was hidden."

"But was it *always* hidden?"

"I don't know."

Again Helen fell to a silent perusal. A fiber artist, Katti had explained, someone who had spent the past three weeks in Zurich, working on a costume production. A hum of excitement radiated from Helen; her breathing was uneven, as though her lungs were being squeezed. At last, though, and with an obvious reluctance, she lifted the muslin and set the weaving again in my lap. Slowly, without touching the tapestry itself. I rolled it loosely in its protective covering.

"Obviously, we have research to do," Helen said.

"But—"

"You'd like to keep it secret?"

"It's always been a secret." *The responsibility is yours.*

Helen turned her green frown on me. "I think there are questions I can ask and still maintain your anonymity. Will you let me?"

I gazed on the parcel in my lap. "I—don't know. I'm going to have to think about it." I coughed. "You caught me unawares. I hadn't made up my mind to show anyone this. It's still very much Eleanor's secret. I know she's dead, and she left it to me, but I'm still not sure what she intended I should do here."

"So you haven't shown this to Katti, or to Viviane," Helen said slowly. "Or told them about it, either?"

"No. I haven't."

And yet, now, I began to question why I had not. Despite the relatively short time of our acquaintance, I felt more comfortable with the women of this other branch of the family than I did with my own mother. I felt as though I was accepted, and that I belonged. But this was Eleanor's secret; she'd kept it from them in her life, so was I supposed to reveal it to them after her death?

"Will you?"

I raised my eyes to the windows beneath the eaves of the house. Up there, where Viviane and her daughter Katti still slept. Then I realized: the windows I was looking at, at this end of the house, were the ones of the room they had given me. *The small room—I hope you don't mind.* I didn't mind at all.

"Yes," I said slowly, "I think I will."

33

AS THE SUN climbed further into the morning sky, the air warmed, and the buzzing of the bees in the garden added a layer of harmony to the birdsong. Katti made breakfast—omelets and store-bought croissants—and we four women repasted in the sunshine.

"Who is Beatrice?" Viviane pondered. They'd all had examined the tapestry before I had rolled it up and taken it back to my room for safekeeping. Now Viviane buttered a bit of croissant and stared at it critically. "Who was she?"

"And how did her work come to be in Eleanor's possession?" Katti asked.

Helen had barely eaten anything. The excitement of earlier still radiated from her. She played with her silverware, though without appearing to see either the fork nor spoon. "I'd like to hazard a guess," she said slowly.

We fell silent, looking across the table.

"What is your guess?" Viviane prodded.

"The floor is yours, my brilliant love," Katti said.

"Beatrice is your ancestor," Helen suggested, turning to me.

She said it so firmly, as though an established fact.

I tipped my head. "We don't know that. Though Eleanor believed it."

"We don't know anything," Helen countered. "Of course it's all conjecture. But it's logical. This is an artifact which has been passed down from mother to daughter for as long as you know—"

"As long as I know *isn't* very long," I interjected. "And besides—it came to me from my grandmother, *not* from my mother. It apparently skipped over her entirely."

"Which does nothing to negate the theory. You said," Katti mused, "that they didn't have the best of relationships. And you're the youngest generation, anyway."

I surprised myself with a deep shuddering breath. Viviane cast me a concerned look, which slowly segued into calculation. I looked away quickly, feeling the blood rush into my face.

Helen ran a thoughtful finger along her lower lip, her brow still creased. "I think Katti has a point. And I think your mother might know more than she's letting on."

"Let's not talk about my mother," I countered quickly. The thought of Elaine was a dark cloud on the horizon of this gorgeous morning.

I ignored the glances between the others and fell instead to eating the omelet.

"Further," Helen continued after an uncomfortable few moments, "it's an amazing portrait, created by someone feeling an enormous amount of love, and possible feeling very protective. Perhaps it's a mother's love. I would suggest that our Beatrice is a relative of our Emily primarily because of that cherub."

Katti nodded, settling aside her fork and lifting her coffee cup to her lips.

"You saw it, too?" Viviane said. "I wasn't going to mention it. I thought perhaps it was just an old woman's fancy."

"The hair?" I made a face. "There are lots of people with red hair. Red curly hair, even." I tossed my own over my shoulders dismissively.

"It's not just the hair," Helen said patiently, as though speaking to a purposely obtuse person.

"Of course you can't see it, dear," Viviane said, patting me on the arm. "But the child in the tapestry looks exactly like you. Exactly."

34

"WE COULD TAKE a ramble up there," Katti suggested, looking at the Tickenhill Manor information in the museum. "Mum, you might come. It's not raining."

But Viviane demurred. "I'll just wander about the museum a bit more, shall I? If we could get into the Manor gardens and imagine, that might be one thing. But as they're closed to the public and we can't—"

"Mum has a hard time imagining from the pavement," Katti said confidentially. "Her signal's weak."

Viviane flapped a hand in mock impatience. "Get along with you, you naughty child." Then she smiled. "I'll meet you in the Shambles Café in an hour, then. You girls go along."

We three set off along Load Street, Katti and I falling in line behind Helen's purposeful march. The afternoon was bright, the pavement sparkling ahead of us in the sun, a few cars whispering past on the way down to the bridge over the Severn. We headed uphill.

"It's not much to look at," Katti warned and called ahead to Helen. "Even if we can see the house. Georgian rebuilding, all brick. Not much of the Tudor palace left—except, I understand, in the cellars."

Helen tossed a dismissive hand over her shoulder. Her words floated back to us. "We're here for the atmosphere, Katharine. Your namesake lived here for a bit." She paused in the street, looking up at the trees that separated them from the lodge. "I wonder if we could sneak in and just take a look."

Katti put her hands on her hips. "You want to get arrested for trespass, you go on ahead. I'll wait here for you."

I shook my head. "If *I* get arrested, they'll probably just deport me and be done with it."

"You two are not fun." Helen turned resolutely away from them and continued along Park Lane. "I should have brought Viviane. She's more adventurous than both of you combined." She peered up through the trees, frowned, then walked further.

Katti looked at me and shrugged. "I'm not getting atmosphere. Are you getting atmosphere? I'm trying to imagine Katharine of Aragon, and the gardens, and the deer park—and I'm just not getting anything." She sighed. "But I'm not the sensitive one. *You're* the sensitive one."

I threw up my hands. It was difficult keeping up with Helen's determined and manic pace, and my ears were ringing. The sweat was beading on my forehead and I wiped it away. "I'm not named after a queen. A queen who actually lived in this house. Or anything like that."

Katti narrowed her eyes. "I feel cheated. Dad wanted something, when he named me this, but I haven't got the slightest idea what that was. And he would always laugh at me, at how practical he said I was." She sighed, slowing, allowing Helen to stay on ahead. "I always thought he was relieved at how practical I turned out to be—but I don't know." She stared at my face. "You make me question everything."

I stopped, putting out a hand to a street sign to steady myself. My heart was pounding in my chest. "Sorry."

"Are you okay?"

Then suddenly Katti's hand was on my shoulder, the wide face with the wide brown eyes staring into mine. It might have been the first afternoon we met.

"You don't look so good all of a sudden," Katti said. "Are you feeling something?"

It wasn't that. I looked up into the trees that separated us from the hill on which Tickenhill Palace had stood.

"No," I said, trying to focus my eyes. "I don't sense anything. I'm sick. I'm feeling sick."

"*Helen!*" Katti called over her shoulder. But Helen, realizing she had left us behind, had already started back down the pavement toward us.

VIVIANE, WHEN WE returned to the café, was not alone.

By now I was feeling a bit self-conscious, with my bodyguards on either side, solicitous, having helped me down Load Street once again. The moment of dizziness had passed, leaving me feeling cold. But I was upright, and mobile. "I'm fine," I'd told them as they'd hustled me in the direction of tea, and a seat. "Fine."

Helen had only frowned, and Katti had said in her good-natured way, "We'll be the judge of that, thanks."

Still, when we entered, and Viviane's companion stood and turned, I felt the dizziness like a faraway memory, all the way down into the pit of my stomach.

Carwyn.

He didn't smile. Beside him, Viviane lifted her teacup delicately and took a sip, her eyes watchful over the rim.

"Hello," he said. At the sound of his voice, which I had not heard since I had left him, sleeping the sleep of the just, on my futon the morning after, I shivered.

"The amusing part," Viviane said neutrally, refilling their teacups and signaling the waitress for three more, "is that I'm always picking up handsome men in Bewdley tea rooms."

35

"YOU'RE ALWAYS PICKING up handsome men in Bewdley tea rooms," I said bitterly, "who are fleeing from Eleanor."

Viviane tipped her head and looked at me speculatively. A half-smile played about her lips. "Oh, Emily," she murmured, as though disappointed in a small child. "These things are much more complex than that, aren't they? Always." In the dimness of the sitting room, I could just make out the frame Viviane held in her lap. "And I fear that you Ludlow women make them even more complicated. Yes, even you, Emily."

I held myself still, my own palms pressed together. "I don't know what you mean," I whispered.

"I think you do," Viviane said gently. She seemed to be gazing at the photograph, though what she could see in the near-darkness was hard to tell. She laughed a little bit. "Nolan used to tell me that I was a relief. He always knew what was going on with me, because I kept no secrets. It's true, really. Keeping secrets always complicates things so."

"Eleanor kept a lot of secrets." I recalled my grandmother's excitement in sharing the contents of the hidden compartment of the small chest. "A lot of secrets."

"Yes. Her secretiveness made Nolan very unhappy."

Was there a hint of question in her words? I remained resolutely silent.

She sighed. "You keep secrets, too, Emily."

The night was so quiet that the sound of the mantle clock ticking grew enormous around us. Minutes passed. Time. Hundreds of years.

"I showed you," I protested weakly. "I showed you all the tapestry."

Then, instinctively, I knew. *That* was the passion that drove Eleanor, though the full flower of the reason was all still shrouded in mystery. Not dancing. Not choreography. The tapestry. *Creavit ex Beatrice.* The tapiser. The child so cleverly disguised as an angel, wings spread. The child who looked like me.

"That might be Eleanor's secret," Viviane said in the darkness as though reading my mind. "But that's not your secret. That's not the one you keep." She took a deep breath, and when she let it escape again, the rush of air was the rush of sorrow. "Don't do that to yourself, Emily. And don't do that to that boy."

There it was, the bomb dropped between us in the night. My first instinct was to leave the room—but to go where? Upstairs, to the bedroom I was using as a guest in this woman's house? "I don't want to talk about Carwyn," I said dully.

"He came all this way to find you," Viviane said. "He wasn't running from your grandmother. He was running after you. And you, for whatever reason, are running from him."

"No. I came to find you."

Viviane smiled. "I don't mind being your excuse."

So much love in the tone of voice. So much understanding. I lowered my head. I felt the burning in my eyes, the first tear tracing its way alongside my nose. Perhaps if I made no move to wipe it away, she wouldn't notice? On the shelf above the wood burner, the clock ticked away.

"She kept saying we were made for each other," I whispered at last.

"Carwyn and you? Eleanor said that?"

I nodded once. Another tear fell, this time onto the back of my hand. It glittered in the dim light. I blinked and stared at it.

In a confused rush, the words came. "I felt like I wasn't being given a choice. I felt like I'd lost control. I felt like—it *wasn't me.*"

Another long pause.

"Oh, dear," Viviane murmured. She sat very still in her wing-backed chair, her wedding photograph still cradled in her hands. She made no move to touch me, almost as though she recognized I would not welcome the familiarity. The mantle clock rang twice, and the sound seemed to echo in the sleeping house. "Oh, my dear." A long sigh. "What do you do now?"

I sniffed, and, like a child, wiped a sleeve across my cheeks. "I don't know."

Viviane nodded. Slowly she stood to cross the room to the breakfront, where she replaced the framed photograph. "Come to bed, then, you poor child," she said kindly, pausing at the doorway. "You need sleep. And tomorrow—" Her voice became more determined. "Tomorrow, you need to get a pregnancy test."

36

I WOKE LATE and found the package with my name on it beside the sink in the bathroom. Hands shaking, I opened the box, and read the directions. *Instant,* the insert read. And almost instantly I knew. My suspicions confirmed.

Three sets of eyes turned to me as I entered the kitchen.

"Come sit, my dear," Viviane said.

I sank gingerly into the proffered chair. My whole body felt different, foreign.

"I hope you don't mind my enlisting the girls' help in this. They were the ones who were worried about yesterday's lightheadedness and brought it to my attention."

I nodded. Under normal circumstances, I might have resented the interference, the curiosity. But these were not normal circumstances.

Helen poured a glass of orange juice and pushed it across the table. Wordlessly I took it up. I had forgotten how thin the orange juice here seemed, and grimaced, but drank half of it down. I hoped it would stay down.

Katti's hand was on my arm, that firm, reassuring touch. "So I take it you're going to have to make a decision."

I nodded. I had lain awake in the night considering the options, because, at Viviane's words, I had finally admitted it to myself: the pregnancy test was only a confirmation, really. In the total darkness of the bedroom, I had stared up at the sloping ceiling and remembered the sound that had not been a sound but a feeling. The tiny ping of the faraway bell. *Goal met.* The afternoon and night in which I had seduced Carwyn.

I had seduced Carwyn.

And yet, what I had said to Viviane in the middle of the night had been the truth. Even as I had seduced him, it had been as though I was not myself. Dissociation? I had heard of it, but now I knew what it meant. Someone else, *something else*, had been in control. Something—and I sucked in a breath now, not quite understanding what I was thinking—that smacked of destiny. Eleanor's word.

"Eleanor kept saying we were meant for each other," I repeated thickly. "Carwyn. And me." I looked up to meet the three pairs of eyes, two dark, one green. All three sympathetic.

"Are you?" Katti asked. "Would you like to be?"

"I don't know." And I didn't. I lifted my hands and dropped them again helplessly. "But I don't want to feel that, if I decide to sleep with a man, that it's somehow *preordained*. I don't want to fall into a relationship because it's *fated*. And I sure as hell don't want to partner up with some guy my grandmother has chosen for me, just because she chose him."

"Into free will, are you?" Helen asked, raising a pale eyebrow.

Viviane sighed. "Helen, darling, you are the life of the party with your ironic wit, but I fear it's not helping here."

Helen winked at Emily. "Levity, my friends. Or we shall all go mad."

I gulped the rest of the watery orange juice. "Helen's right. I've been thinking for a while now that I *am* going mad. So many things—so many odd things—all of them somehow related to Eleanor . . . and I just don't know what to do with this information."

"I think," Katti interrupted in her practical voice, "that we can put those odd things aside for right now. We have to deal with the immediate problem." She raised her eyebrows quizzically. "If it is a problem?"

For lack of anything other to do, I refilled my juice glass, but then dropped my hands again and splayed my fingers over my abdomen.

"I don't know. I don't *know*." I looked up; it was hard to meet their eyes. "I haven't really thought about having a child, especially since the divorce." I shook my head, trying to clear it. "Rob kept saying there was plenty of time, and I just went along with it. But now I'm alone. I don't know whether I'm up to the task of being a single parent. I don't know if I can do it."

"You don't *have* to do it alone," Viviane pointed out.

"There *is* a sperm donor in the picture," Katti agreed.

"If she wants him to be," Helen countered. "Remember that part."

I cast her a grateful look.

"You don't even have to do it at all," Helen said. "You don't have to have this child."

Viviane smiled gently and touched my hand lightly. "The decision is yours, my dear, and we will help you with whatever you decide. You know that, don't you?"

The tears were threatening again, and I leaned my head on Viviane's narrow shoulder. "I know. Thank you."

37

THERE WAS A message from Carwyn when I checked my phone.
We need to talk.

I sat on the edge of the bed and stared at the screen. The words blurred and sharpened, and I realized my chest was tight. We did need to talk, but I felt talked out. As though I had run a marathon: muscles weak, breath short, head spinning. So many things. *So many things.* I saw him again in my mind's eye, rising from the table in the café and turning, his blue eyes on my face, level and questioning and angry, before I had turned and fled to the ladies' room. I felt again my gorge rising, the cold of the porcelain of the toilet as I knelt before it, turning myself inside out. How Katti had bustled me out of the café and back to the car, how I'd stumbled into this very bed and slept until the middle of the night.

We need to talk.

What was I supposed to even say? That seeing him at the table with Viviane had made me sick? That wasn't the truth of the matter, of course, but to explain the alternative—that I was pregnant and hormonal and dizzy and nauseated—was beyond me. Just too much. *I'm pregnant with your child.* I laughed bitterly, my head spinning. That would sure go over well.

Did I want a child?

Did I want *his* child?

From the depths of my memory I heard Eleanor's voice—Eleanor, whom I blamed for all of this mess, all of it. *I needed to have a child. I didn't need to be married.* I squeezed my head between my palms, trying to stop the whirling. There was something cold in those words, in that assessment. That my grandmother had simply used my grandfather, then cast him aside. Sperm donor. Katti's words. But I resisted that with everything I had. Hadn't Eleanor told me that Nolan was the only man she had ever loved?

And hadn't Elaine countered that Eleanor had never truly loved him, or anyone, but had only used people in the service of her grand passion?

Whatever that grand passion, related somehow to the tiny tapestry, was. Not for the first time did I wish, violently, that I had had the presence of mind to ask Eleanor about all the little clues she had let drop in the past several weeks. The secrets. *Why the hell didn't you just come out and tell me what you wanted me to know?* I demanded now. Helplessly. Uselessly.

In my hands the cell phone vibrated again.

Please.

38

"YOU DON'T HAVE to go," Helen said as I opened the car door.

"You don't have to go *today,*" Katti added.

"I know." I gathered my purse from the back seat and closed the door, patting it twice, then watched as the two drove off, disappearing around the corner on the way to the car park. I slipped down the narrow passage indicating the way to the church with a sign high on the brick wall; below it leaned a blue sign informing the world that the gift shop was open today. The walls crowded so close on either side that I could spread out my arms and touch them both. Ahead, rails sprouted, holding up yet another blue sign, in case anyone missed the church dead ahead. I felt a drop of rain on my skin, then another, and glanced up at the threatening sky, punctuated by the tower. Against the wall to the left, a boy with a ponytail leaned, strumming a guitar, oblivious to the pending rain. I slowed for a moment, listening to his arpeggio runs on the strings, then smiled awkwardly when he glanced up to catch my eye. I stuffed my hands into my pockets, hunched my shoulders, and moved toward the door.

Carwyn was waiting. He unfolded himself from the shelter of the doorway and stepped forward.

"You came," he said. He too had his hands stuffed into his pockets, and made no move to touch me, for which I was grateful. His blonde hair was dull in the darkening afternoon, and his eyes were shadowed.

"Yes."

He laughed a little, turning his head to look off toward College Street. "I didn't know if you would. Since the last time you saw me, the sight of me made you sick."

"It wasn't that," I protested weakly. "I've had a bug. I was dizzy out in the street, and Katti made me come in. She was worried about me."

"Katti. Your aunt?"

It was still odd to think of her as that. "Elaine's half-sister. Yes."

The rain was picking up, speckling the pavement around our feet. Drops glistened on the shoulders of Carwyn's jacket, then soaked into the material. I shivered. "Can we go inside?"

Wordlessly, Carwyn turned and led the way; he held the door and stood back. Inside, our footsteps echoed hollowly in the nave. The air was cold, like a cellar or tomb, with an occasional movement that caressed my skin and made me shiver more; it smelled heavily of lilies. I almost wished to be back out in the rain, away from the cloying air inside. I turned up the nave and walked slowly along its length; Carwyn followed slightly behind, and I could feel his eyes on me, felt the concentration of his attention. I paused at the crossing and looked up into the dizzying heights of the lantern. As I did, the bells rang the hour. The sound seemed to come from all directions, and from inside my chest. I reached out a hand blindly.

Carwyn caught it.

"Easy," he said.

I felt an electric jolt at his touch and jerked my hand away.

I moved forward quickly, toward the chancel, the high altar backed by stone figures and topped by a soaring set of stained glass panels, and sat on a bench to the side. Across the way, tombs of lords and ladies in stone sleep ignored me.

Carwyn sat as well, careful not to touch. He was silent, his eyes on the carvings.

"Palmers," he said.

I took a deep breath. "You said we needed to talk. So talk."

More footsteps, echoing. Far away, as if in a dream, there was a low roll of thunder.

Carwyn laughed, bitterly, and the sound was lonely and hollow in the chancel. "It's suddenly very difficult. Maybe not one of my best ideas, to talk about sex in a church."

I found myself shivering again, though my skin did not feel cold. I pressed my eyes closed, opened them. If only I could convince myself that it had been only sex. *Only sex.* Instinctively I crossed my arms over my abdomen. Protection.

You don't have to tell him, Helen had reiterated.

I thrust that thought aside. That was a decision for a different time.

"It was," Carwyn said, and there was question and confusion in his voice, "the most—breathtaking —night of my life."

I bit my lower lip and looked away resolutely, at the stained glass where the colors all bled together.

"And then you were gone."

Again I said nothing.

A couple wandered past, the man with a brochure clutched in one hand, the woman holding her cell phone camera before her like a shield. They dipped their heads together, murmuring, the man pointing upward, then toward the floor.

Even after the couple left us alone, Carwyn seemed to be waiting. When I was not forthcoming, he threw up his hands in despair.

"I don't even know what to say to you. I thought we needed to talk, but now you're here, I can't even think of the words to use." He kept his voice pitched low, but there was an urgency to it, the fury of his confusion. "Your face—it's so hard, the profile, the stone of those statues. As sharp as the profiles in that stained glass back there." He coughed. "I can't read you, Emily. I feel like you gave me something—that night—something really important—and now you've taken it back. You regret it."

"I don't regret it," I said dully.

"So tell me what happened," he shot back. "Tell me what I did."

The anguish in his voice now was what made me turn. Slowly, willing myself to be calm. Next to me, he leaned forward in exhaustion, his chin in his hands. I waited until he raised his eyes to my face and steeled myself to meet them. I owed him that. Just that.

"You won't understand," I said.

Two teenaged girls in hoodies wandered almost aimlessly toward the altar, their eyes roving over the statues, the misericords; not finding what they were looking for, they wandered desultorily away again.

"Try me."

I bit my lip, then took the plunge.

"Eleanor," I said.

Carwyn sat up. "What about her? What does she have to do with anything?" He took a deep breath. "God help us, Emily. She was dead."

"Yes." How to say it?

"You're not going to tell me I was some sort of solace?" He shook his head, and a stray shaft of light fell across his hair, burnishing it. "It didn't feel like that, Emily. It didn't feel like you needed comforting."

"No. That wasn't it at all." My shoulders lifted and fell in my frustration. "I told you you wouldn't understand."

He put up his hands. "Sorry. Sorry. Go on. Tell me."

I wiped my hand across my brow. Another faraway roll of thunder, and then from somewhere, organ music. A multi-colored flash through the stained glass above us. "She wanted us together, you know. She kept saying that."

I felt Carwyn flinch, but when I looked at him, he merely held up his hands again.

"And that afternoon, when you came to the apartment—" *Don't cry. Don't cry.* "I wasn't—myself."

A quick suck of indrawn breath.

"It sounds like you're talking about," and he paused, swallowed, "a kind of possession."

But I shook my head. Fiercely. He didn't get it. "No. Not that." I lifted my chin, blinking at the blearing colors of the stained glass. "I wasn't myself. But I wasn't anyone else, either."

With a jerky movement, Carwyn stood and crossed to stare down at the stone floor beyond the step. He clenched his fists and relaxed them at his sides, clenched and relaxed. "I don't understand." His voice was as far away as the receding thunderstorm, almost drowned by the organ from back toward the crossing. His face was discolored by the vague light falling from the windows above.

"It wasn't possession," I said. Struggling. "It was more like compulsion."

He turned.

"I was not myself. I was not in control. What I wanted—what I didn't want—none of that entered into it." I stood, too, and my legs felt unsteady, as though they would not hold my weight. I placed one foot in front of the other, crossed to his side to look up into his strained face. "Carwyn. I slept with you because I had to. I can't expect you to understand that, because I can't understand it myself. I might have been a puppet. *I had no free will.*"

The words burned as they left my mouth. I could almost see their flames before me.

For a long time we stared at one another, me willing him to understand—it suddenly seemed vital that he understand—and he searching my face with his shadowed eyes.

"I know what it sounds like," she whispered at last. "Believe me, Carwyn, *I know.* Some sort of dissociative disorder. Some sort of mental illness. I know, Carwyn. But there's no other way to explain it."

"But why? Why would you be compelled?"

"I wish I knew."

"And why *me?*" His mouth worked. "I feel used, somehow."

I shook my head. "I know. I do, too. And at the same time, I was the one who did it." I blinked the tears that were so perilously close, no matter how hard I tried to hold them at bay. "Can you imagine how that feels? How I feel? Can you understand—why I ran away?"

Can you imagine how dirty I feel? How guilty? How I was both the victim and the victimizer?

Carwyn held up a hand which was not quite steady in the sepulchral dimness. "Emily, I—" He took a deep breath, started again. "I don't know, Emily. I have to think. I have to figure this out."

I nodded and turned away. Then my eyes fell on the ruddy stone of the monument in the floor.

ARTHUR
PRINCE OF WALES
DIED AT LUDLOW CASTLE
2ND APRIL 1502
AGED 15 YEARS 7 MONTHS
HIS HEART WAS BURIED NEAR THIS PLACE

The wash of sadness, profound, which I had felt emanating from the stones at Ludlow Castle was back, and I was flooded in it. One hand pressed to my heart, I threw out the other as a drowning person might, for help, for rescue, and clutched wildly at Carwyn's arm, a single small cry escaping me.

39

CARWYN TOOK MY arm in his to steady me and guided me back through the nave to the heavy double doors.

"I'm sorry," I whispered, over and over. "I'm sorry."

Overhead the faces of the noble dead of St. Laurence's Church looked down upon us impassively from the great west window, some praying. Arthur Tudor, kneeling with his sword by his side, held his hands slightly apart as though in appeal, his red hair cascading over his shoulders, his face surprisingly feminine.

"I'm sorry," I said again, perhaps to him.

Outside, the passage was wet and glistening in the weak sunlight, the rain having stopped and the thunder having moved on.

WE MET THEM in a pub.

"My mother feels," Katti said slowly, sinking into a chair after finishing her telephone call to Viviane, "as though she's become the foster parent for a litter of orphaned puppies. She wants you all to know this."

Helen laughed delightedly. "I'm a puppy!"

Carwyn deposited four pints on the scarred table. "I am not a puppy. I'm a big dog." He slid the glasses toward the others. His joking seemed an effort.

Katti threw me a quick glance. "You still look like death warmed over. You don't need a pint, you need a cuppa. With lots of sugar." She pushed away from the table, but Carwyn waved her down and headed back to the bar.

"Did you tell him?" Helen whispered urgently, edging forward, glancing over her shoulder. "I don't want to put my foot in it here."

"I told him I'd had a bug," I said.

I watched Carwyn lean forward for a word with the woman wiping down the optics. She eyed him up and down appreciatively. Tall. He was tall, but I knew that, just as I knew the breadth of his shoulders beneath his denim jacket, the length of his legs. The touch of his hands. I blinked, looked away.

"And then, as if to prove it, I had a—spell." I grimaced.

"Jesus," Helen said.

"No," I answered wryly. Despite our having chosen a table near the hearth, I still felt cold, and hunched with my arms wrapped around me. "Arthur Tudor."

Katti had been in the middle of a sip from her pint glass, but now she set it back on the coaster. "Arthur? What about him?"

"She nearly passed out on his heart," Carwyn said, rejoining us. "I had to bundle her out of there." He sat, shrugging his way out of his jacket. He nodded toward the bar. "She'll bring the tea as soon as it's up."

Katti and Helen's eyes met over the table; they might have been semaphoring, they were so obvious.

"What is it?" Carwyn demanded.

I looked down at my hands.

"I'd forgotten," Katti said slowly, her face reddening, "that his heart was in St. Laurence's. Arthur's."

"*Heart.*" Carwyn's lips twisted. "A euphemism. Most of his entrails."

"Such a romantic," Helen shot back.

"I'm a historian." Carwyn put up his hands in defense. "This kind of stuff is right up my alley." He took a drink from his pint. "Guy probably didn't even have a heart," he added darkly.

Katti narrowed her eyes. "Not many people know about Arthur's heart or entrails or anything like that."

Carwyn seemed to sense her mild antagonism, but he met her gaze squarely. "I was coming here. I looked it up. Like I said: I'm a historian."

Why was he coming here?

The tea arrived, the woman carrying a tray with pot, mug, milk, and sugar. I poured myself a cup and breathed in the steam.

"Sugar it," Katti ordered sternly.

"I don't like sugar."

Had there been room, Katti might have put her hands on her hips. As it was, she had to settle for glaring. "You've had a shock. Sugar it, or I will."

"Don't cross her," Helen warned. "I did once. It didn't end well."

I reluctantly dropped a cube of demerara sugar into the cup and stirred.

"You'll thank me for this," Katti said. "Drink up."

"You're more of a mother to me than my own mother," I said. But I sipped at the mug of hot tea like a dutiful child. "Are you sure you're *not* my mother?"

"I would have had to start really early," Katti reminded me. "At fifteen years old, in case you need help with the maths." She shook her dark curly hair back over her shoulders. "I'm just a young thing, and don't you forget that."

"Shock?" Carwyn broke in. "What do you mean by shock? I thought you said you'd been sick."

"I have been," I said. *Morning sickness.* But I was not yet prepared to drop that bomb. Not yet.

"She has been," both Helen and Katti echoed, with one voice.

Carwyn stared across the table at me, his eyes hard. He looked as though he was going to speak, but thought better of it, and drained his pint instead. Then he set the glass down on the coaster.

"I'm tired," he said slowly, "of being lied to."

"I have never," I ground out, "lied to you."

"Not with words. But there are other ways to lie, Emily." Carwyn stood up quickly, gathered his glass, and went to the bar.

"Oh, dear," Helen said.

"To hell with him," Katti said. She patted my arm. "Drink your tea."

40

WHEN WE RETURNED to the house, I left them to walk up to the common by myself. The sun had returned, but weakly; the air was still heavy with unfallen rain. *I'm fine,* I'd told them. *I need to think.* Katti had looked as though she wanted to argue, but Helen had tucked a hand beneath her elbow and guided her firmly into the house. When the door had closed, I sighed with something akin to relief.

The afternoon had been a cock-up. There was no other word for it.

Carwyn was so angry. An anger, I knew, born of hurt. And I knew only too well that I had been the cause of it. As I headed up between the trees, I put a hand to my abdomen and choked back a sob.

How could I tell him what—what had *happened*—had led to?

I *had* told him the truth. Just not all of it.

I *had* felt used. Compelled. Something *not me* had made me seduce him. And now I was pregnant.

It didn't make sense.

The worst part was that I had thought I might feel some attraction for him. But *this thing* had run roughshod over whatever real feelings I might have had, and now I couldn't trust myself. I didn't want him *because* I was supposed to want him. The more I tried to extract the strands of confusion from one another, the more tangled they became.

I thought of my mother, my father long dead. I had been a fatherless child. I thought of *her* mother, Nolan long banished from Eleanor's life; Elaine, too, had been a fatherless child. Would this child be another?

I heard the rustle in the bushes and looked up quickly, hoping to see the fox, the orange plume of its tail. But I saw nothing. Dropping my eyes to the track once again, I trudged uphill toward the place where the banks fell away on the sides of the lane, and the common opened out before me. Back in the days of squatters on the common, Katti had said, if a family could have a roof and a chimney able to vent a household fire by morning, they were allowed to keep the house and remain in it. *That's how Mum's house got built,* she'd said. I looked out over the common, at the clumps of bushes and scrub trees, and wondered how one built a house that quickly. How one built anything that quickly. I turned slowly around in the fading light—not even close to as dramatic as the evening I'd first come up with Katti and Helen—and looked back down the lane. I couldn't see the house; I doubted I'd be able to see the smoke from the woodburner and the chimney if in fact there had been a fire.

I headed slowly back down toward the house, nothing resolved, and the rustling startled me again. This time the fox stepped out onto the road, leisurely, unafraid. It lifted its sharp nose, and, smelling me on the air, turned its head slowly to look at me. I froze and stared back.

The fox had a black face and a black tip to its tail. Between the face and tail, however, it was a blazing red-yellow that glowed even in the sullen light. As we stood regarding each other, there was another rustle, and then a tiny kit stepped out of the protection of the bank to stand by its mother. The vixen looked down, nudged the kit with her nose, and then crossed the lane without hurry. She gave me one last glance before leading her offspring back into the bracken.

41

"YOU LOOK AS though you might have come to a decision," Viviane said, smiling gently over her shoulder. She bent to the oven and withdrew a casserole dish. The table beside the big window was set. The flowers in the vase had shed a few petals, and I paused to wipe them from the tablecloth. "Why don't you freshen up and you can tell us about it." Viviane chose a slotted serving spoon from the drawer to her right.

When I returned, having splashed water on my face and run my fingers through my hair, the other three were seated about the table, steaming dishes before them. I slid into my place, marveling again that a particular chair was now designated as mine. In the wide bowl before me were chicken, green beans, baby mushrooms, and tiny new potatoes in a cream sauce. I dipped my spoon in, blew on it, and tasted: rich, and warming. The room was filled with the quiet sound of silver against dish. The others seemed to be waiting for me to open the conversation. I hesitated, spooned up a morsel of chicken.

Katti nudged the bread basket closer to my elbow.

"How was your walk?" Katti asked, once I had broken and buttered a hunk of bread.

I ate some vegetables. "It was good. What I needed. The fox was out again, up the lane. She had a kit with her."

"Just one?"

"Just one."

We ate some more, the others waiting on me.

"I think," I said at last, looking at my own reflection in the big window; my face was a white moon, my eyes big and surprisingly dark. My hair, the color of the vixen, threw off sparks. "I think this child is a girl."

Now that I had said that, I wasn't sure how I'd come to that conclusion But the sex of the child I was carrying had burgeoned into certainty in my mind.

"Girls are good," Helen said. She broke a piece of bread from the ravaged loaf. Katti wordlessly handed her the butter plate. "We like them."

Viviane set her spoon beside her dish and folded her lined hands together. "Early days yet. You can't be sure."

"But I am," I replied. I scraped the last of the sauce up with my spoon, chasing the remaining half of potato around until I caught it.

When I too had set aside my silver, Katti took both my bowl and her mother's to the stove and ladled more into them. "Helen, love? More for you?"

Helen held up a hand to decline.

Katti returned to the table. "Mum's right, you know," she said, setting the bowls down before settling back into her chair. "You can't be sure. It's so early, more than likely the baby isn't even sure what it is yet."

Another spoonful of the rich and satisfying cream sauce. I wondered momentarily about the underlying mushroom taste. "My mother had the one child, me, a girl. Her mother before her: one child, a girl. My great-grandmother had a single child, a girl."

"Coincidence?" Katti suggested.

But I shook my head. "I don't think so. *Maybe* it is—I mean, how could it really be anything else? But I don't think so."

"Don't forget," Katti pointed out. "Men determine the sex."

"But what determines the men?"

There was a pause.

"You're suggesting some vaguely unnatural stuff here," Helen objected at last.

"Yes." I nodded. "I know it sounds strange. But I think if you go further back, even beyond Eleanor's mother, you'll find the pattern continuing."

"You don't know that," Katti said quickly. She was frowning.

Strangely, I was as certain of this as I was of the sex of the child I was carrying. Of course it was nuts; I knew it was nuts. But I couldn't shake the conviction. This child would be a daughter in a long line of daughters. This child would be an only child. The thought was unnerving, bordering as it did so closely on my fears of fate and the lack of free will in my life recently. Again I felt the sureness that somehow, all of this was beyond my control.

Destiny.

Viviane's gaze on my face was probing.

"You're a sensitive," she said quietly. "We know you're a sensitive. You don't understand it—and quite frankly, the three of us, practical lights that we are, understand it even less."

"Is that what it is?" I asked bitterly. But I knew the answer.

"I'm inclined to think that if you know these things," Vivian continued, "then you *know* them, and they are true."

"I wish I didn't *know* these things."

Helen held up a hand. "Wait a minute. Just wait a minute." She took a deep breath, her frown mirroring Katti's. "You said you think this pattern, as you call it, of only daughters of only daughters of only daughters, goes back beyond your grandmother, and her mother. How far back do you think it goes?"

The answer, I realized, was obvious. Helen just wanted me to say it.

"To Beatrice," I said, glancing from one to the next. "I am *creavit ex Beatrice.*"

42

I AWOKE IN the middle of the night and listened to the sleeping house. If I strained, I could hear the ticking of the mantle clock in the front room below. As my eyes grew accustomed to the darkness, I saw the slight fluttering of the curtain at the window, left open a crack. I heard the trees around the house breathing the night air, a gentle movement, more comforting than alarming. In the distance, a bark. The vixen, I though, calling to her kit.

Who was probably a daughter.

Just one?

Just one.

Then I remembered Helen's words as the ate the dessert, a lovely panna cotta, Viviane had concocted while we had been in town. "It's not enough to know. You need proof."

I rolled onto my side and found the phone on the bedside table. The screen glowed in the dark room, and it took a moment for my eyes to get used to the light. Then I bit my lip and typed in the text.

I'm sorry.

I hit send before I could change my mind.

Then, *I need your help.*

The clock on the cell phone gave me the time: 1:14 a.m. I did not expect an answer right away; if Carwyn felt like answering at all, his reply wouldn't come before morning. He was angry, so angry, or at least had been when we had parted company in Ludlow. So many questions I still had. How had he found me? Why had he even come? But there had been no chance to ask before everything had further degenerated between us. I sighed, rolling back over. And was so surprised at the vibration of the phone that I dropped it on the floor and had to scramble for it.

I'm sorry, too. What do you need?

Now I had to figure out how to ask. I typed in several starts and deleted them all before settling on *Research. Historical.*

This time the answer was longer in coming. I imagined him in his hotel room—I didn't even know what hotel he was staying at—trying to decide whether he wanted to even listen to my request, let alone fulfill it. I imagined him lying in a darkened room, just as I was, the only illumination that of his cell phone screen.

What's the problem?

Autocorrect did not want me to type *Genealogy.* Finally I was able to override it.

Whose?

Mine.

Which side? Or both?

Eleanor's.

Another longish pause. I heard a door open along the hallway, and another close: someone making use of the toilet in the middle of the night. Outside the window an owl hooted.

I've never done much with family trees.

Me, neither. And I should have. Except that my mother and I had never discussed family or origins, and I had had sporadic contact with my grandmother growing up. No father nor grandfather to speak of. A dysfunctional family of the first water. Carwyn, always Eleanor's favorite, probably knew more about the family tree than I did. I grimaced in the darkness. *You know how to research. You know where to look.*

After another few moments: *All right. Call me in the morning.*

I stared at the words. Gulped. *Are you sure?* I typed, half-regretting my impulse. *Call me.*

43

I HITCHED A ride into Ludlow with Katti, who needed to be to work at the castle. She kept slewing sideways glances in my direction, jaw hard with disapproval. We parted at the car park, Katti still looking unhappy.

"I love that you care," I whispered into her ear, giving her a quick impulsive hug.

"Of course I do," Katti said stiffly, stalking away.

I went the other way, past the market, to the corner of Broad Street. I saw Carwyn before he noticed me, and for a moment I quailed. I could turn; I could walk away. I could call a taxi and be back in the welcoming warmth of Viviane's house within the hour. But I steeled my spine. I had called him. I had requested his help. His expertise. And the answers he might find seemed suddenly so important.

Carwyn was looking down the street toward the river, his face in profile. As I approached, I examined his slightly long nose, the way his blonde hair curled back from his high forehead. He really was very handsome; but again I found my assessment overshadowed by Eleanor's. *You two were made for each other.* No. I couldn't trust my own judgment.

He turned when he heard my footsteps. "Good," he said without smiling. "I've got a car down here at the hotel's car park." He seemed to have compacted himself further since the previous afternoon; every movement was economical. He led the way along the pavement.

"Car?" I asked. His legs were much longer than mine; it was a struggle to keep up.

"Rented."

"You *drive* here?"

He laughed shortly. "I drive everywhere."

He turned into the drive behind a brick-faced hotel and led the way to the lot in the rear. Only a couple of cars were scattered between the lines; he unlocked the doors of a small blue Renault and waited for me to slip into the passenger seat before he climbed behind the wheel.

We were out on the road before I called up the nerve to speak again. "Where are we going?"

"Worcester," Carwyn said.

I frowned, peering out the window at the cloud-covered countryside. It looked like I felt. "I thought—" My voice failed me, and I fell silent.

"You thought what?" He sounded almost belligerent.

I dropped my eyes to my hands, my fingers gripped tightly together. "I don't know. I just thought you might have your laptop here with you. That you might be able to—look somethings up, to find out about Eleanor's forebears." I blew out a breath. My chest hurt. "I didn't mean that this should be a major production for you."

"This is not a major production." He slowed the car, leaned forward to check for traffic, then spun the wheel to turn right. "I just need to make a run to Worcester. There's one other thing I need to check out."

We fell silent again. The miles sailed past my window, and I watched them without seeing them. The wind of the previous night had long since died away, and it did not look as though there'd be rain this morning, though the clouds remained low. I wished inanely that I had thought to check the weather forecast. Were the clouds overhead breaking up? I couldn't really tell, though I saw one or two hopeful patches of blue sky. I sighed. When the weather cooperated, there was nothing quite as blue as the English sky, but as with anything else I loved, it very rarely cooperated.

I caught my breath.

I had not thought that. *I had not.* But I had, hadn't I?

I stole a glance at Carwyn. He had taken a pair of sunglasses from the console, and now he put them on. I fumbled in my purse for my own pair, and donned them, hoping he would not notice my eyes upon him. I needed to think. But every time I approached the thought of Carwyn, of us together, my mind shied away as though from a blazing hot torch.

"What have you found so far?" I asked, desperately seeking cover. "Anything?" Even that was a stupid question. I had asked him to look not even ten hours ago. "Sorry. I should give you more time. I don't even know why it suddenly occurred to me that this was important." I pressed a hand to my lips, attempting to stop my own embarrassing babbling.

He was slow in answering. We were approaching Worcester, the city appearing to float in the green countryside. We entered a roundabout, then another. The car was a standard shift, and I wondered fleetingly how he managed to shift down to slow, and then back up, all the while driving on the wrong side of the road. I watched his hand, the golden hairs on his arm above the black band of his watch.

"I think I've found some things to interest you," he said.

"Did you even sleep?"

He turned his dark sunglasses on me for a moment, then returned his attention to the road. "Not well."

"I'm sorry."

At my abject tone, he seemed to deflate like a balloon. The grim line of his mouth softened. "Don't be. I haven't slept well in a long time. But it gives me time to think, time to work. So yeah. I found some things for you. It isn't really difficult online, if you know what you're looking for."

"And you do."

That might have been the smallest of rueful grins. "I'm a historian. It's my job."

44

WE LEFT THE car on a side street and walked up toward the guild hall, with its ornamented front. With the warming of the day and the scattering of the clouds, people were swarming, in and out of shops and banks, carrying bags, briefcases. I felt the sun on my hair, on my cheeks—which meant there'd be sunburn—but I didn't care, and welcomed the warmth. I might have been someone just released from prison, at first seeing the light of day. I followed Carwyn as he turned to the left and headed up toward the tower of Worcester Cathedral.

"I really am sorry," I said, attempting once again to match his stride. "About everything. I said it last night in the text, and I meant it."

He nodded. His glasses still hid his eyes. But then, mine did, too.

"I don't know why we can't ever seem to be friends. Ever." I sighed. "Since the time we were kids. When you were Nick. We have never seemed to be able to rub along the right way."

"No," he said. "We never have."

He still didn't look at me, but his pace slowed slightly.

I swallowed, put a hesitant hand on his arm. "I'm sorry about that, Carwyn." The words came hard. My throat felt closed. "But I want to change that. Can we change that? Or is it too late?"

Now, at last, he stopped. We had entered the cathedral yard, the great doors straight ahead. Carwyn looked up to the tower, square and gray, a few stray clouds scudding past it. I waited, hand still on his sleeve. After a moment he lowered his chin and took off his sunglasses. His blue eyes fell on my hand, then rose to my face.

"Slowly," he said. "I'm still feeling a bit battered here, Emily. I'm still not sure I understand what the hell is going on."

You and me both, I thought, but I did not say it aloud. Rather, I had a flash to when we'd first met again, just a couple of months ago, when everything had seemed a game to him. When everything I'd said or done, no matter how prickly I'd been, seemed to delight him. He was well past that now. I nodded once.

"Slowly," I agreed.

ANOTHER CHURCH. WELL, cathedral, actually; church on a larger scale. Larger, and colder. I was glad for the slight chill of the morning which had prompted me to wear a sweater under my jacket. Still, beneath the high airy recesses of the nave, I still shivered. Jewels of light from the stained glass fell about us, prisms of red and blue and green. Footsteps echoed. Carwyn cast me a quick look.

"What do you need in here?" I asked.

Voices seemed to carry, though I could not make out words of others' conversations; nevertheless, I pitched my voice low and glanced around. A few other people were in evidence, wandering about, reading memorial inscriptions, examining carved tombs.

Carwyn paused, lifting his eyes to the soaring arches. He hitched his backpack further up his shoulder. "There's a tearoom. In the chapter house—which I think is this way." He pointed.

I nearly objected, but had no idea why, and bit back the words before they escaped. *Slowly.* Perhaps Carwyn needed tea, or a muffin: sustenance. And this was his show. He was, after all, doing me a favor.

"I'm following you," I said instead.

The chapter house was domed, round; I thought of the Round Table, made that way to ensure that no one person took precedence. The monks obviously had had the same idea. Tables were scattered about, and along the far wall, a few women of a certain age, all wearing sprigged aprons, were dishing up from covered cake stands and teapots. Carwyn and I selected our cakes—I felt suddenly ravenous—and took our mismatched cups and saucers to a table near the center of the round room. Beside us, a stone pillar rose to the ceiling, a tiny bit of electronics belted around it above our heads.

"What's that?" I asked.

He too looked up. "Sensor of some kind." He studied it for a moment, then raised his eyes to the curved ceiling. "To see if the building is moving, I'd think. Measuring it." He frowned. "Same principle as a Geiger counter, but I bet far more sensitive."

"The building is *moving?*"

He laughed. "It's more than six hundred years old. Even much younger buildings settle. I'd say this one is doing quite well."

As I forked up my spice cake, however, I couldn't keep my eyes from the sensor. Not that it would help, of course; if the chapter house decided to collapse anytime in the next twenty minutes or half an hour, Carwyn and I and the aproned ladies and the man across the way reading the newspaper—we'd all be crushed to death, and that would be the end of the story.

And there was more to the story.

Across the table, Carwyn shoved his now-empty cake plate to the side and lifted his backpack into his lap. He unzipped it and withdrew a sheaf of paper, which he spread out on the table between us. Then he selected one page and slid it across the tablecloth to me.

"Stop looking at that sensor," he suggested, "and look at this instead."

I felt my face warm slightly and took the page from him. The printed marks organized themselves, once I had turned it right-side-up, into a family tree. I found myself, married to Rob—and then divorced again—at the bottom. I glanced up quickly.

Carwyn shrugged. "What I found last night. Plugged it in on a family tree app."

"You carry a printer around with you? When visiting foreign countries?"

He raised a blonde eyebrow. "I print everywhere."

I stared at him. Maybe my jaw dropped.

He laughed and held up a hand. "No, really. The hotel had a printer. They only charged some strange amount per page."

"I'll pay you back," I said quickly.

Carwyn leaned back in his chair. "Don't be foolish. It's fine."

Slowly. It was so difficult.

I lowered my eyes again to the page, tracing the tree branches backward. My mother, Elaine, but a blank where my father's name should have been. I had expected that. Mitch, she had called him, on those few occasions she'd mentioned him, her voice rife with disappointment with him for having died. She was an only child, as I knew. Then Eleanor, and Nolan, who had not married. Before her, Eleanor's mother and father, and again, the only child. In the next generation, I looked at Eleanor's mother: also an only child. And *her* mother, an only child before that. The tree ran off the edge of the sheet. Reading my mind, Carwyn handed me another page. I traced the generations, took the third sheet of paper, continued the line.

"It gets a bit hazy on the last page," Carwyn said, holding one final sheet. There was no room left for it on the table, where I had laid each page in a line all the way to the edge. He set it on top of the others. "Early 1500s. That's about the outer limit of modern genealogical studies—at least with any accuracy." Sensing my frustration, he collected the empty cake plates and silver and brought them back to the ladies at the tables to the rear. When he returned, I looked up to him, my finger on the last page.

"Do you see it?" I asked on a long drawn-out breath. "It's just as I thought it would be. Right here on all your pages. Look."

Carwyn tilted his head, lowering himself back into his seat.

I ran my finger once again from my own name, then back and back and back, shifting the final page, some five hundred years. "Look at them."

"The matrilineal line?"

"The line of only children," I corrected. "That is—if you found everything?"

"I found what was there."

"And you found no sisters or brothers in this line." I leaned forward eagerly. "Especially *no brothers.*"

He too leaned forward, his eyes scanning the sheets of paper between us. "It is unusual," he agreed slowly, his voice non-committal.

"It's what I thought there would be."

"Why? Had Eleanor said something about it to you?"

I shook my head, pinching my lips together. "No. Though I have no doubt she knew." I rubbed my face. "She knew a lot more than she chose to tell me."

Carwyn tented his fingers. "In her defense, she didn't know she was going to die."

I glared at him. "Maybe she didn't know she was going to die *that day.* But, Carwyn—" I took a deep breath. "She was nearly ninety years old. She kept reminding me she was an old woman."

He didn't answer, but I thought I saw his gaze cloud a bit.

"She played me." I gathered the pages up into a small pile and tapped their edges together. "She fed me a bit of information at a time, so I'd keep coming back for more. She kept secrets, and she liked it. It was a game she was playing with me."

"That's kind of a harsh judgment."

I shrugged. "Maybe. But you—you keep defending her."

"She was always kind to me," he protested.

He didn't see it. Hell, I couldn't see it *all*—what I sensed was there as through the proverbial glass darkly. Bits of information, hints from my grandmother. But our truce right now was so tenuous, and his affection for Eleanor so strong, that to try to force the point with him was sure to tear down our white flag and grind it into the dust. Again I bit my lip.

"She used to dance," Carwyn broke out suddenly, blinking quickly, and then looking up to the sensor on the column, as though it might have some answers. There was the smallest hint of a sad smile about his mouth. "When I was a kid. When she used to let me hang around for tea when I'd finished her yard work."

"When you were *Nick.*"

The smile broadened, and then faded away, like a wave against the seashore.

He was so different now, and yet, he carried the teenaged Nick in him still. The boy I'd been so envious of, the one who heard the stories my grandmother had never told me. I carried that memory, hard like a stone, of coming upon them on one of the rare times when Eleanor had been home: he seated on one of her high-backed chairs, she pirouetting in the space between the tall windows. I had fled, frightened of the strangeness of the scene. My grandmother had employed him to cut grass, to prune trees, to do those things she was too busy to do. Nick. His name had been Nick then, but now he was Carwyn.

"She never danced for me," I managed thickly.

"She wanted to," he answered.

He was watching me now, his eyes blue and intent. Instead of being comforted by his words, I felt the familiar wash of resentment: that this boy, now this man, knew more of my grandmother than I did. Except he didn't. He couldn't.

"It felt like you had replaced me," I said sadly.

Again he cocked his head. "If you think that's true, you are more wrong than I can tell you."

After a moment, he let his fingers rest on the back of my hand. I looked at his fingers and thought of lying together, thought of my grandmother's forcing us together, thought of the girl child I knew I was carrying and he didn't. It was all I could do to keep from jerking my hand away.

"She loved you, Emily. You should know that."

She had one passion. Elaine's words. *She didn't love anyone.*

Another thing I couldn't repeat to him.

Instead I let my eyes fall to the top page. The last page, piled in reverse order. The one with the single name I had known would appear, but now with a date. *Beatrice.*

And then Elisabeth, born 1502.

Creavit ex Beatrice.

45

"I DON'T UNDERSTAND why we had to come all the way here for you to show me these pages," I said, as Carwyn slid them back into the backpack.

His jaw worked slightly, and his eyes went one more time to the sensor on the column.

"Unless it was to live dangerously between a centuries-old ceiling which may or may not kill us yet." I pushed my chair in, wiped some crumbs from the tabletop. As he zipped the backpack closed, I collected the teacups and brought them to the bus tray. I lifted a hand and smiled to the tea ladies.

Carwyn was waiting, the backpack returned to its accustomed place on his shoulder. "There was something I needed to look at." He sounded evasive, but maybe I was just being paranoid. *Sensitive,* Viviane had said.

We left the chapter house and turned right along the cloisters to return to the south transept. My eyes were drawn upward, toward the heights of the tower. The shower of jeweled lights from the windows seemed more intense, and the nave to my left seemed more crowded than before—but that wasn't saying much. Still, I was startled by the sound of my own footsteps, and Carwyn's, and all the others.

He turned right again, angling a bit until we approached an ornate sarcophagus, inlaid with coats of arms, on which lay a crowned figure with flowing hair and an unsheathed sword. At either shoulder a smaller figure was carved. To the left, a sign indicated that this was the tomb of King John, he of the Magna Carta. I read the information on the sign, then turned to examine the figure. His eyes were open; I decided that was rather creepy. His left foot was turned out: why? All in all, he looked rather benign; I wondered whether it was a true representation of a king I had learned, somewhere in the misty past, had been a usurper and a despot and probably a wife-beater.

"He doesn't look all that bad," I said, puzzled.

"He doesn't," Carwyn agreed.

I glanced over to find his eyes on my face.

"Almost harmless," he added, still looking at me intently, in a way that made me nervous.

"Was he? Give me your expert opinion."

Carwyn's eyes flickered. "Not my time period. Not my area of expertise. But someone hired to carve his likeness, for the royals, for installation in a cathedral, is hardly going to make him look particularly evil, I don't think."

"You have a point."

We gazed on the dead king for a bit longer. I was still puzzled, and Carwyn seemed preoccupied. Each time I skewed my eyes toward him, his glance skimmed away and back to the effigy. At last he indicated we should move on.

"One more I want to look at," he said. "Over this way."

I was beginning to like the hollowness of our steps as we moved along the south choir; to the side was a gorgeous carved stone screen. I followed him into the chantry, high windows to one side, the other three walls covered with statues of saints, hundreds of saints, many of them defaced. In the center of the chantry, when I turned, was another tomb, this one with a plain but gleaming marble top.

I caught my breath. I stumbled backward.

The sadness.

"No," I said. Or thought I said. I wasn't sure. "Please. No."

After everything. Not this.

I couldn't look. I turned back into the choir quickly, found a seat, leaned forward with my head between my knees, my brain swimming.

"YOU SET ME UP," I hissed.

I could taste fury like metal at the back of my tongue, now that I could at last speak. We had driven out of Worcester; it had begun to rain, fitfully, angrily. I stared resolutely out the streaked window. I had been so careful—*so careful*—all day to keep away from things that would upset the delicate balance between us.

"You were angry yesterday about lying—'there are other ways to lie, Emily'—and then you set me up."

"I needed to see what would happen," Carwyn said. Despite the rain, he had his sunglasses back on.

"Oh, so I was an experiment, then," I spat. "Isn't that just fine."

He steered the car over onto the verge and pulled the handbrake. "Emily—"

"Don't you dare," I ground out. "Don't you even dare."

The tears were part shock, part fury, and they were hot as they spilled over and ran down my cheeks. I felt them alongside my nose, tasted them on my lips, warm and salty. I pulled as far away from him on the seat as I could manage. In my peripheral vision, I saw him holding out a handkerchief, but I refused to acknowledge it. I was shaking with a hideous cold, and I ignored him when he turned up the heat at the console.

It was too much. I wrenched my way out of the seatbelt and kicked the door open. Then I was off along the verge, where the hedge grew close. I had no idea where we were; this was not the main road we had driven in on. I heard him calling after me, but did not turn.

I don't know how far away I was from the car before Carwyn grabbed my arm. The rain was streaming down my face, my hair clinging damply to my cheeks. I shrugged his grip away. I could feel him behind me, following along the side of the road. A car passed, tires hissing on the wet tar, then another.

"Emily, get back in the car. I'll take you home."

I whirled so quickly he nearly ran into me, but I shoved him back with both hands. "Don't. Don't pretend you even care after what you've done."

"I didn't know you'd have this reaction."

"Again. *Again.* You didn't know I'd have this reaction again." My face felt stiff, the rain mixing with the tears. My head was pounding. "But you suspected."

"All right. Yes."

"And you went ahead and did it anyway. You watched me yesterday in St. Laurence's, and you decided to see if it would happen again today."

"Yes."

"Even though you *saw* me. You *saw* how St. Laurence's affected me."

This time Carwyn didn't answer.

I pushed him again. "It's physical, Carwyn. I get dizzy and sick and I can't stand up—and I can't stand it. It's pain." I sucked in a breath that became a furious sob. "You saw it happen yesterday, and you weren't just content to let it happen again today: you manipulated me into a situation where it *would* happen." I balled my hands into fists and pounded them against my thighs. "Why don't you just hit me, then? Why don't you just haul off and punch me? Because isn't this the same? *Isn't it?*"

Again no answer.

"God damn it," I shouted. "Did you enjoy that?"

He slammed away from me and took a few steps back toward the car, where it was idling on the grass. Then he stripped away the sunglasses and hurled them off into the hedge. His chest was heaving.

"I'm sorry," he said. "Let's just stop this. Can we stop this?"

I blinked away tears and rain, wracked by the deep sobs that shook my shoulders. I couldn't bring myself to look at him and turned away, one hand over my face, the other wrapped around my stomach. Betrayed. I had been betrayed, by everyone. I was shattered and scattered: by my mother, my grandmother, Carwyn—Nick—whoever the hell he was now. I was alone, pregnant, and dreadfully unhappy. And frightened, I realized. So frightened. I felt incredibly young, in a horrifyingly big world where it was dangerous to trust anyone.

Then he was back by my side. "I'm sorry, Emily," he whispered roughly. He pulled me toward him and turned me to face him. I was too weak to resist, to fight him off, and so I covered my face with both hands. His hands were on my shoulders, but he left the space between us. Still I cried, even when he pushed my streaming hair away from my cheeks with a shaking hand.

"I'm such an ass," he said. "I'm such an ass."

47

"IT'S A GOOD thing Katti's not home yet," Helen said as the settled in the sitting room. She looked at Carwyn with a kind of evaluation. "She'd probably kill you. She takes this whole aunt role seriously, you know."

"Good to know."

"She'll be home soon, however, so you'd better come up with some sort of cover."

Carwyn's grin was half-hearted and lopsided.

We'd returned to the house and dried off; I'd changed my clothes, and Helen had insisted upon wrapping me in a blanket before the woodburner.

"We told you," Viviane said reproachfully. "Our Emily is a sensitive. And from the looks of it, she's growing more sensitive all the time."

"Put your feet up," Helen suggested to me. She swept a hand toward the unoccupied end of the sofa.

I rebelled weakly. "I'm not dead yet. I'm not some fainting Victorian heroine."

"Still, you've had a shock," Viviane said, shaking her head. "Another shock. And that's not good for you." Her eyes flickered over the others and back. "It's not good for anyone." She pressed her lips together. "Really, young man. What made you think it was a good idea to take her to the Cathedral? What on earth were you doing?"

Carwyn looked down, his hands clasped between his knees.

"You're as bad as your daughter, Viviane," Helen said, her voice and expression full of affection. "Looking out for the underdog."

"I'm not the underdog," I protested again.

Each of them looked uncomfortable, not meeting each other's eyes. I found it easier just to close mine.

"I can't deal with your bickering," I said at last. "Because I'm tired. Exhausted. Confused. Please don't make it worse by fighting with one another."

"Who's fighting?"

Katti banged her way into the house, then into the sitting room, looking at us spread out over the room, different armed camps. Her brown eyes fell on Carwyn, still slump-shouldered, still with his hands clasped between his knees, and her jaw hardened.

"Oh," she said. The single syllable dropped like a stone into water.

Carwyn unfolded himself and stood. "Katti."

"Katti, I love you. Don't start." I held up a hand.

"She's had a shock," Viviane repeated.

"I'll go fix tea," Helen said, with a hint of a knowing glint in her eye. She kissed her fiancée on the cheek and slipped out of the sitting room.

"You're marrying a wise girl," Carwyn said.

"I knew it was a mistake, her going with you. I don't know why she would even want to. I don't know why I didn't just put my foot down."

"Because I'm an adult," I broke in. "Because I asked for a favor. Because Carwyn's research has taken us straight to Beatrice."

Katti crossed to the back of the sofa and placed her hands on it. Still she glared at Carwyn, who stood awkwardly. She seemed to recognize that he would remain standing until she sat, and was unwilling to give him that satisfaction.

"I don't like this," she said.

"I think," Carwyn said, "that it's about time you all told me about this Beatrice."

Now all eyes turned to me; the decision was mine. Slowly I stood, clutching the blanket around my shoulders. "Stay here. All of you." I looked from Katti to Carwyn and back again. "And for God's sake, sit down already."

When I returned from the bedroom, I saw with some relief that they were in fact seated, though they had left the sofa empty for me. Katti and Carwyn still glared at one another, while Helen appeared mildly amused, and Viviane poured and handed tea cheerfully and almost obliviously. I held the rolled bit of tapestry, in its muslin wrapping, in both hands to my breast under the cloak of the blanket, as though I myself was nursing the cherub-child depicted within it.

Elisabeth, I thought as I resumed my seat on the sofa, tucking my feet up beneath me.

"I wish you'd wear gloves or something when you hold that," Helen murmured peevishly. "I wish you'd let me take that to London and have it dated."

"I wish you'd let me see what you have there," Carwyn interjected.

Again I carefully unrolled the muslin to reveal the square of tapestry. The colors, as always, struck me with their brilliance, but now I stared at the face of the cherub.

"Elisabeth," I said aloud, though my voice was low. The finely woven face smiled up at me beatifically, happy to be, after all this time, addressed by its name.

With a soft intake of breath, Carwyn set his cup and saucer aside on a low table and fell to his knees beside me, the better to examine the weaving. He lifted his hands as though drawn to touch the tapestry, but then pressed them to his chest. Carefully, I turned the small square, touching only the muslin, so that he might see it right-side-up. I saw his eyes rove over the cherub hungrily, and he seemed to be examining each small strand of color separately, his throat working, his expression escalating from interest through curiosity to awe.

"My God," he said at last, his voice barely more than a whisper. "My God, Emily."

"What do you think, as a historian?" Viviane asked, lifting her tea cup delicately to her lips.

Carwyn shook his head as though his thoughts were unimportant before the very existence of this artifact. "I can't really speak to this—this *piece*. I'm not a fabric or a textile historian. I've seen larger tapestries, of course—with depictions of cherubs—in museums, in art books. Is this—is it Renaissance?" He looked up to Helen. "You work in textiles. What do you know of textile history? Anything?"

"I work in theater textiles," Helen corrected. "I'm not an expert, really I'm not. But the style—the subject—I think Renaissance might be a good guess." She held out her hands, palms out. "That's why I don't want to touch it—that's why I don't want anyone to touch it."

"I think we can date it now," I broke in, sliding the cloth onto the coffee table. Helen hurried to clear cups and saucers to a side table. "Thanks to the genealogical work Carwyn's done. He's found Beatrice for us. And her daughter. Elisabeth."

"Who *is* Beatrice? Aside from your grandmother, twenty generations removed?" Carwyn asked.

With a single finger, I pointed to the signature worked in black, careful not to touch.

Carwyn stared. Mesmerized.

"And how did you find her?" Viviane asked. "If I might be so bold."

Slowly Carwyn got to his feet, his eyes still on the tapestry. "Let me get my backpack from the car. If you'll excuse me?" He was gone only a few moments, and once he returned, he quickly dug the sheaf of papers from the pack. These he handed to Viviane, who lifted her reading glasses, worn on a chain around her neck. She examined the pages slowly and carefully, passing each one on to Katti when she was done with it. Helen leaned over Katti's chair for a better look.

"I asked Carwyn for this. Last night." It felt like a hundred years ago. I shoved my drying hair, curling and tangled, away from my face. "Because he's a historian. I thought he might know how to research it better than I."

"And this is what you came up with." Viviane looked over the rims of her glasses at him, holding up the last sheet of paper.

"All of this?" Katti demanded skeptically. "All of this last night?"

Carwyn flushed. "No."

Alarms went off. Again. I sat up straighter on the sofa. "No? What do you mean, *no*?"

"Not all of it," he said.

"I'm not following," I said sharply.

"'There are other ways to lie.' I believe that's a quote." Katti handed the papers to Helen and crossed her arms in challenge.

"Katharine!" her mother admonished.

"Please don't, Katti," I said. I turned back to Carwyn and narrowed my eyes. "Let's hear what he has to say."

He held up his hands. "Not much, okay? Katti's right. I should have told you." He paused, inhaled deeply. "I started this research for Eleanor. She asked. Weeks ago. And then—" He blinked, flexed his fingers before closing his hands into fists. "And then she died. I stopped. I didn't start looking again until Emily texted last night." He seemed to be studying the patterns of the carpet below his feet. "Since I couldn't sleep, I went back as far as I could find."

"For Eleanor." There it was again: the prickly feeling along the back of my neck. I had thought he was doing me a favor; but it was really Eleanor's favor. Had I been compelled, last night, to text him? Was I somehow *supposed* to have prodded him to finish this piece of research? I tried to convince myself I was being ridiculous and paranoid. I had wanted to know. I had wanted to satisfy my curiosity about the matrilineal line. And now I knew.

"Never mind that, Katti," I said, forcing myself to focus. "Look at the line. Daughters, all of it. I come from a line of daughters who are only children."

Katti took the pages again from Helen and flipped through them.

"It's like we suspected," I repeated. "All daughters. All only children."

Helen nodded, still leaning over her fiancée's shoulder. "And spotty attendance by the fathers here, I might add." She reached down to trace a line. "Dead, dead, dead. They don't seem to fare well."

"Good thing Dad got out of it, then," Katti said dryly.

"Katharine!" Viviane exclaimed again. "You are certainly something else this evening, aren't you?" She reached for her cup of tea, which was no longer steaming. She took a sip, grimaced slightly, and poured a bit more from the pot wrapped in its cozy.

"A bit feisty," Helen agreed. "I like a feisty girl."

"Get a room," I said.

"We've got one," Helen shot back and made a face.

Katti was frowning, turning from one sheet to another.

"But you're wrong," she said at last. Slowly, puzzled. She shot a quick glance at Carwyn. "Or—someone is."

"What is it?" I asked quickly. I struggled to my feet to look over Katti's other shoulder. "What do you mean?"

"Right here." Katti put her finger on one of the top lines on a sheet. "Beatrice. Daughter of Arnaud and Mathilde ver Vloet." She looked around at the others, her eyes resting longest on my face. "And her sister. Elisabeth."

I snatched the page from her hand and stared at the line, the placement of names. Beatrice, and her *sister* Elisabeth. I looked up again, to Carwyn. The line started with Elisabeth, then, not with Beatrice. And Beatrice was not an only daughter.

"Why didn't I see this morning?"

Carwyn shook his head. "Too much to think about this morning."

"Perhaps, my dear," Viviane said calmly, "you saw what you wanted to see this morning."

"But it does hold—the only child daughter of only child daughters—all the way back until this Elisabeth," Helen said. "You're not entirely wrong. Just a generation off."

Sheet of paper in hand, I returned to the sofa and sat down, feeling the frown between my eyes. "I was so sure."

"Perhaps I made a mistake," Carwyn offered.

But I knew he hadn't made a mistake.

The female line descended, straight as a rule, from Elisabeth. Beatrice was a sideline.

"But *Beatrice made this,*" I whispered.

Helen sat beside me on the sofa, sliding the muslin holding the tapestry onto her lap, careful not to touch the tapestry itself. "You're reading far too much into it, then. Beatrice made *this*. She made the tapestry—probably the first one she ever completed, probably on a hand loom. Probably an exercise her father set for her, if he was a weaver. Could we find out more about that? About him?" She looked to Carwyn, who shrugged and nodded. Then she returned her thoughtful gaze to the cherub. "Beatrice needn't have had to have made this *child*."

"I was so sure," I breathed again. A knot of anxiety and disappointment had formed in my chest. I had set my heart on this, and had had it stripped away.

"You need food," Katti suggested sympathetically. "You've had a shock, my mother says, and now you've had another one, from the looks of it." She smiled at me and got to her feet. "And I'm hungry."

"Let's call down to the pub. A pizza or something." Viviane smiled ruefully. "I had a plan for dinner, but this afternoon has thrown it all off."

"I'll go down and get it," Carwyn offered.

"It's the least you can do," Katti said. But her voice had lost its rancor.

"WHAT WAS THE shock?" Katti asked when he had gone.

"My darling, you are such a hedgehog," Helen said fondly. She handed her a glass of Scotch, then passed another to Viviane. "What would you like, Emily?"

I shook my head. "Nothing for me, thanks."

Katti took a sip from her drink. "And the shock?"

I shivered from the remembered cold. "We went to Worcester Cathedral."

"You're a sensitive," Viviane said. "Something there bothered you? We only got part of the story."

"The place is absolutely crawling with tombs." Helen sat. "You didn't go into the catacombs, did you? That's probably not the safest place for someone like you."

"Not the catacombs," I reassured her. "First we had a look at King John."

"Bastard," Helen snarled. "He would have upset me, and I'm not a sensitive."

Waving her to silence, Katti leaned forward. "Nothing there, though, for you, was there?" Her expression was calculating.

"Nothing." I shook my head. "But I guess, for Carwyn, that was just a test run. Or a control tomb. He wanted to see my reaction there, and I didn't have any."

"But . . . ?"

"Arthur Tudor."

Katti sat back, nodding.

"What happened, my dear?" Viviane asked. She sipped her Scotch, gazing levelly at me over the rim of her glass. "If it doesn't upset you too much to tell us about it."

"I couldn't stay in the chantry."

I found suddenly that I did need a drink after all, my mouth had gone so dry. I excused myself and slipped to the kitchen for a glass of water. I drank that one down quickly at the sink, then filled the glass a second time before returning to the others. They were waiting, watching.

"I couldn't stay," I said again. "I felt the cold, and I felt the sadness. I had to get out of there. It was—visceral."

Katti nodded. "Four times now. Four times this has happened to you, in four places."

"And all four connected to Arthur Tudor." Her drink finished, Viviane set the glass aside and folded her hands. "Which I think tells us something interesting."

"Ludlow Castle, Bewdley, St. Laurence's, Worcester Cathedral. The places where he lived and died," Katti mused. "And the places where his heart and body are buried."

"But Bewdley—" I interrupted quickly. "That felt different. Like morning sickness."

"In the afternoon," Katti pointed out.

"It happens, darling," her mother shushed with a hand on her arm.

"I wonder," Helen said, tapping a finger against her chin as she formulated her thoughts. "I wonder if you'd have the same reaction at the place he was born. Where was that? Here? Maybe we could find out if you did."

"No, he was born in Winchester," Katti corrected. "But you make this sound like an experiment. The kind, apparently, that Carwyn was conducting." She glared. "An experiment, but on a *person*. I saw how badly Emily reacted in a couple of places. I *saw* that. Tricking her into going to Arthur's tomb was cruel."

"I wouldn't *trick* her," Helen protested. "I wouldn't do that."

"And I didn't mean to be cruel," Carwyn said, sticking his head through from the entryway. His hands were filled with packages. He took a step further in. "I guess I didn't really understand"—His eyes fell on me and stayed—"what I was seeing in St. Laurence's. I mean, you told me you were suffering the after-effects of a bug of some sort. I didn't really understand it was a dead king you were reacting to."

"Not a dead king. A dead prince." Katti snorted. "And you call yourself a historian."

"I know." He hung his head. "A failure. As a human being, *and* as a historian."

Despite myself, I found I was close to smiling. I glanced at Katti and saw a slight quirk play about her lips.

Viviane stood. "Let's take this discussion into the kitchen. I suspect we all need sustenance at this point." She held out a hand, and we all followed Carwyn through to the other end of the house and to dinner.

48

THERE WERE TWO pizzas, one cheese, one pepperoni, in their boxes opened on the countertop. We brought our plates to the table, and squeezed around it when Carwyn brought an extra chair in from the sitting room.

"I never have this many people at my table," Viviane said with some satisfaction. "It's crowded, but it's rather nice."

"Here's to the company," Carwyn said, lifting his glass for the toast. "If they don't decide to gang up on me and kill me."

"It depends entirely on whether you have any more secrets to drop on us," I said. Though I really meant on *me*.

"I think I've confessed them all," he replied. "Except maybe one, and that's just going to have to wait."

"Is it a good one, or another bad one?" Helen asked, pulling up her chair. She had refilled her drink, as well as those of the others.

"Could go either way," Carwyn answered. He flipped open his napkin and placed it on his lap. He did not meet anyone's eyes.

I considered challenging him, but I had my own last secret and decided keeping quiet was best at this point. We ate in silence for a few moments, a silence only punctuated by the sound of silver on plates. I drank my water, vaguely envying the others their Scotch. As the smell of tomato sauce filled my nose, I found I was ravenous. Had I really eaten nothing since the spice cake of the ladies' cathedral guild in the late morning? I plucked a slice of pepperoni from my plate—it had slid off the pizza—and devoured it hungrily.

"Ver Vloet," Helen broke in after a bit. "Of the stream, by the stream, something like that."

"Dutch?" Katti asked.

Helen frowned. "Flemish, I think. Northern Belgium. Bruges was a hub of weaving activity in the fifteenth century."

"I'll look into it," Carwyn said. "Once I get back to my computer."

"You can use mine. After dinner. It's just upstairs." Helen finished off her slice of pizza, then stood to help herself to more. She held the pie server up, and when no one responded, served herself and returned. "If this Arnaud ver Vloet was in fact a weaver, a member of a guild, perhaps, he should be relatively easy to track."

"But it puzzles me," I said, taking another bite and chewing it slowly before continuing. "I always had the idea that Eleanor's family was an English one— maybe it was something she said when I was a kid or something. Or maybe it was something Elaine said." I glanced across the table at Carwyn. I shoved aside my resentment, realizing his closeness to my grandmother was something we might be able to use. "What about you? What's your sense of her background? Did she ever mention anything to you about it?"

He leaned back in his chair and studied the beams crossing the plaster ceiling. "I'm not sure," he said after a moment. "I've got the same sense as you do, Emily, that hers was an English background, or maybe Welsh—"

"We *are* in the Marcher country," Viviane reminded him gently. She delicately cut a small piece from her slice of cheese pizza and ate it with her fork, then wiped her lips with her napkin. "The Marcher lords at times warred with one another, but the English and the Welsh have found this border to be remarkably porous."

Carwyn nodded. He was still studying the ceiling, his brow furrowed as he tried to remember. "Yes. But, if you'll pardon me, the point I think I'm trying to make is that Eleanor's family references—and my recollections of them are somewhat vague—all seemed to be of the English or Welsh variety."

"And she chose her name—Nora Ludlow," I pointed out. "She didn't choose to be Nora Bruges, for crying out loud. That has to tell us something."

"Yes," Carwyn agreed. "And I have to admit that, when I came upon Arnaud ver Vloet in the research, I was as confused and surprised as you seem to be, Emily. I didn't expect the Flemish."

"And that was as far as you got in your research?" Viviane asked.

He made a face. "In the time allowed. And from my laptop in the hotel room." He glanced around. "There are other resources, some of them not online, but it's a pretty standard understanding in historical and genealogical circles that the early 1500s, late 1400s, are the outer limit for research of this nature—unless you're looking at royal families. And we're not doing that."

"Unless you're looking at me," Katti said.

"You're not royal, darling," Viviane replied. "Don't be silly."

Katti splayed her fingers over her breast. "I am named after Katharine of Aragon. Don't any of you be forgetting that."

"I always thought he was joking, your father," Viviane said slowly. "About that. But now—I'm not so sure. It's beginning to look as though that's just another piece in a puzzle that's coming together far far too slowly."

"I don't understand," I said.

"Sadly, my dear," Viviane replied, "neither do I. You told us your grandmother was a good woman for keeping secrets. It's beginning to look as though your grandfather was keeping secrets of his own."

"THE SPELLING, THOUGH," Helen said thoughtfully. She glanced at Carwyn. "I take it you copied this directly from your source?"

"Of course." He looked mildly taken aback. "I'm a historian."

"It's his job," I tacked on.

"Then the name 'Beatrice' is, I think, Anglicized." Helen frowned. "The Flemish would usually spell it *B-E-A-T-R-Y-S* or something similar to that."

"Maybe she had English blood."

"Not with parents named Arnaud and Mathilde. And a sister named Elisabeth with an 's.'" Helen rested her chin in her fisted hands, still frowning. "Something's wrong here. Something's off kilter."

Katti pointed at Carwyn. "You, Mr. Historian, have more work to do." She stood and began clearing plates. "Helen will lend you her computer."

"I'll do the dishes," I offered quickly.

"If you young people don't mind," Viviane interrupted, "it's getting a bit late for these old bones, so I think I'll bid you goodnight."

Carwyn slid back his chair, looking to the clock over the stove top. "I should go. I didn't realize it was getting so late."

"You can't go," Katti said. She was still pointing. "You've got work to do."

Viviane held up a hand. "The four of you can do whatever you wish. I, however, am an old woman who needs her beauty sleep." She circled the table, kissing each of us women in turn, and patting Carwyn on the shoulder on the way by. She leaned forward to stage-whisper into his ear, her gaze flitting between us. "Don't let them bully you. You might be a fool, but you're an inherently good boy."

Carwyn laughed, placing his hand on hers where it rested on his shoulder. "I'll try to be strong."

Then Viviane kissed his cheek as well. "You really are a good boy." Then she straightened and waved an airy hand. "Goodnight. Goodnight, all. Be good to one another."

Helen jogged upstairs and returned almost immediately with her laptop.

"Your mother likes me, Katti," Carwyn threw over his shoulder as he followed Helen into the sitting room.

She put her hands on her hips and made a face at me where I was filling the washbasin in the sink. "I guess that means I'm going to have to try to like him, too," she said, and sighed mightily.

49

I WOKE ON the sofa, a blanket tucked up around me, a pillow under my head. At first I couldn't orient myself: the clock ticked closer than I was used to, a sound which I had trouble recognizing. Rain battered at the windows to the front of the room, and in their dim light, I could just barely make out the lanky form on the floor on the other side of the coffee table, also covered in blankets. I held myself perfectly still, listening to his even breathing. I had heard that breathing before, in any case, in the middle of the night. The thought of that particular night was, as always, uncomfortable, and I shifted uneasily on the sofa.

There were papers on the coffee table, white against the dark background. Beside them, Helen's laptop, closed down for the night. The last thing I remembered before I'd fallen asleep was the sound of their bickering—Carwyn, Katti, Helen. I could not remember the words. I didn't think it had been rancorous, however, and for that I was grateful. Katti and Helen must have gone up to bed. I turned my head toward the mantle-clock, but could not make out the time in the darkness.

Slowly I sat up, clutching the blanket around my shoulders. I tested everything out, gingerly, for aches, for nausea. Other than a bit of kink in my neck—no doubt from the couch—I felt intact, and was relieved. I reached for the papers on the table. Print-outs. I wondered if I could make it to the kitchen and examine them under a light without disturbing Carwyn where he slept.

Except he was awake. "What are you doing?" he asked in the darkness. "Go back to sleep."

"I didn't want to wake you."

"Well, you did." He, too, struggled to a sitting position. "Actually, I haven't been sleeping well here at all." He snorted. "I'm too old to be camping out on a floor."

"Why didn't you take the guest room upstairs?"

His laugh was short, a bark. "A bit presumptuous, don't you think? You fall asleep on the couch, so I climb into your bed?" He shook his head, a moving shadow, black against black. "I probably could have gone back to the hotel, but after all the single-malt—your step-grandmother has really good taste in Scotch, by the way—I didn't feel confident enough to drive on the wrong side of the road."

I felt his grin in the dark and was reassured. Perhaps we might be getting back to that brief—very brief—period of getting along. *Slowly,* he had said. *Slowly.*

"I fell asleep. I'm sorry." I held up the new sheaf of papers. "What did you three find?"

"Arnaud ver Vloet," he answered. "He wasn't that difficult to track down."

"Tell me."

In the dimness he clambered to his feet, pushing the blankets aside. He crossed to a standing lamp and flicked it on.

"He and his brother had a fairly successful weaving workshop in Bruges in the late 1400s. He was primarily a cartoonist, and his brother, Pieter, a weaver—though there's some conjecture that Arnaud worked on tapestries in the workshop as well." He held out a hand for the pages, shuffled through them, and pulled one out. Skirting the coffee table, he slid onto the sofa next to me. "Here." He indicated a paragraph midway down the page. "According to this website, Arnaud ver Vloet and his workshop did some cartoons, and then some weaving for Henry VII: some tapestry work for the Palace of Placentia, and then for Ludlow Castle when Prince Arthur took up residence there as the Lord Warden of the Marches."

I half-turned. "He did work for Ludlow."

"Tapestries of any size, as wall hangings, frequently traveled with the household—so it's likely that tapestries went back and forth with the Prince's household between Ludlow and Bewdley."

"Are there—any surviving?" My voice sounded far away, weak. I couldn't take any air into my lungs.

Carwyn flipped through his pages. "There's one in the collection at Hever Castle—one that's a suspected product of the ver Vloet workshop."

"How do they tell?"

Another flip of the page. "Tapisers would typically weave a signature into the border of a piece—a specially colored leaf, for example. Or a single letter. The ver Vloets' signature was a two-arched bridge, for two brothers next to the river, I expect." There was an illustration of the signature bridge on the page, the arches of which Carwyn traced with his index finger.

"So there's one out there, one left for me to look at," I breathed. "I have to go to Hever Castle, then. To see this thing made by my grandfather fifteen times removed."

"Or perhaps your great-uncle," Carwyn reminded me.

"Perhaps."

He set the pages down on the table before them. "What do you think you'll find there?"

I shook my head. It was still difficult to get a breath. "I don't know. But I'm a sensitive, right? We've already determined that. Maybe I'll feel something."

"From what I've witnessed, your *feeling something* tends not to be a good thing."

I wiped the back of my wrist across my forehead. "It hasn't proved terribly healthy so far, no." Again I looked at him, at the shadow growth along his jaw. Did I want to run my hand over it, or did the something outside me want me to do it? I couldn't be sure, so I pressed my hands together between my knees. "But it's a chance to—meet—my ancestor, isn't it? I need to go to Hever. I'll risk the reaction."

"You can't go alone," he protested.

"Are you offering?"

Carwyn shifted uncomfortably on the cushion next to me. "If you like. Or you could take your aunt, and Helen, or Viviane. Just don't go alone."

I felt a moment's disappointment at his lack of enthusiasm, but I pushed it aside sternly. I slowly went back through the pages again. "And what about the workshop? In Bruges? Does it still exist? Do you know?"

Carwyn shook his head. "I couldn't find out where exactly it was located."

I sighed. "Probably even if it had survived up until the last century, it would have been destroyed in World War I or II."

Now Carwyn straightened. "Early twentieth-century Europe *is* my area of expertise. And just so you know, Bruges was one of the few European cities that managed to escape relatively unscathed in either war. Still, it's unlikely that the workshop—a relatively small family operation like that, as opposed to, say, the Gobelins in Paris—would have survived over the past five hundred years. If you're looking for your fifteenth great-grandfather, you're probably better off looking at Hever."

The clock struck. I leaned my head back into the sofa cushions, thinking of Beatrice's tiny scrap of weaving, safely returned to my room upstairs. The cherub, the child, who might be nor now might not be Elisabeth, Beatrice's younger sister.

"I was so sure," I murmured again. "About Beatrice."

Carwyn leaned back as well, his face turned toward her, shadowed in the lamplight. "That's what happens when you conjecture before the facts. Any historian can tell you that."

"But any scientist will tell you to form your hypothesis first," I answered tartly, "and then see how the facts support it or refute it."

"You're not a scientist. You're a librarian."

"You don't even know," I said scathingly. "I'm a Master of Library *Science*. So back off, already."

He laughed, the sound I remembered from before things got so complicated. Quickly I lay a hand on his arm to shush him, pointing to the bedrooms overhead. Carwyn covered his mouth and bit back on the laughter.

"I'm just a bit disappointed in the refutation," I continued. "I wanted to be one of the things that Beatrice made."

"Even that, though," Carwyn protested. "Fifteen generations is a long time. You might have the matrilineal DNA, but all those fathers in there have diluted the mix."

"It's a weird family, though, isn't it?" I felt a prickle at the back of my neck and tried to rub it away, before placing my splayed fingers on my abdomen. "All the fathers cheerfully provide their sperm and then seem to disappear from the world. Through death, or in Nolan's case, removal from the picture."

"From the continent, even," Carwyn added, cocking his head.

"*The only man she ever loved.*"

"He seemed to have made out all right in the end, though. Viviane is charming, and Katti is great." Carwyn slewed me a look. "Maybe someday she'll even like me a little bit."

It was my turn to smile in the semi-darkness. "She *is* fiercely loyal."

"And protective. And motherly."

"And motherly. From the first moment I met her." My lips twisted. "Unlike some other mothers we might know."

Carwyn reached across the space between us to touch my hand, then withdrew his fingers quickly. "I understand. I mean, my mother was fine in her way, but after the first seven kids, I think she was just plain tired out. Eleanor—she wasn't exactly motherly to me, but she gave me the place I felt I belonged. I didn't really think, back when we were kids, that she might be expending more energy on me than on you." He smiled apologetically. "Really. I was lonely and self-involved enough that I was just grateful to her. I loved her for the attention she gave me."

"A bit of hero worship there? Heroine worship?"

He raised his eyebrows, shrugging. "Probably. But she gave me what I needed—what every kid needs—that sense of self-worth. Encouragement."

"My mother—Elaine—says that Eleanor didn't love any of us. That there was always some sort of ulterior motive."

"Elaine is bitter."

"Elaine *is* bitter. But I'm beginning to think she wasn't all that far wrong about Eleanor." I closed my eyes, rubbed them with the balls of my hands. "At the same time, I feel rather guilty for saying that. I mean, my relationship with my mother has never been the smoothest. And I never saw Eleanor all that much when I was growing up—she was always off somewhere, involved in some production or other—and I resented the attention she gave you; I guess I *did* think that was attention that was supposed to be mine. Then, these past couple of months, when I had been feeling pretty beat up by my divorce and having to move back home from a big house to a one-room apartment, and not finding a full-time job . . . she was a constant, and I started to feel *important* to her. Does that make sense? I started to feel like we were establishing a real relationship at last."

"It makes sense," Carwyn said reassuringly. "Perfect sense."

"But now, I'm not sure. Because of all the secrets I'm discovering. Things she knew and never said."

"There wasn't much time," he protested.

"There was enough," I countered. "But Eleanor, as I told you before, liked feeding me enough information to play me on a line like a fish. Case in point: I'm here. Outside Ludlow. Staying in the home of family I never knew I had, falling in love with people who should have been in my life all along. *All she had to do was tell me.*"

Carwyn threw up his hands. "I don't know. I guess I can only speak to my experience with her, just as you can only speak to yours."

"And Elaine to hers." It seemed so difficult, at two in the morning, in the semi-darkness. But then, all vaguely philosophical arguments seemed difficult. I rubbed my eyes some more. They felt gritty. "And then, by extension, only Eleanor can speak to her experience, and I know nothing of her relationship with her mother, and nothing really of her relationship to Nolan. Except that he's my mother's father, and allegedly the only man Eleanor ever loved."

"But couldn't bring herself to marry."

"She told me she needed a child, but she didn't need a husband."

Carwyn looked taken aback. "She said that to you? Those were her words?"

"Yes."

"That sounds . . . rather like she was shopping for a sperm donor. A bit calculating." He sounded uneasy.

"Yes. That's exactly what Katti and Helen called it."

Uncomfortable myself, I stood to cross to the breakfront, where I collected the wedding photograph of Viviane and Nolan in its silver frame. I brought it back to Carwyn, who leaned forward into the circle of light, the better to examine it.

Nolan would have been about twenty years older than Viviane, and I fancied, looking at their faces again, that he looked somewhat tired, but relieved. Perhaps at finding someone so loving and accepting and relatively uncomplicated as

Viviane. Because the more I learned, the more I realized: even up until her end, Eleanor had been exhausting. Demanding, energy-wise. There was quite a bit of work to be done to survive a relationship with her.

"Katti looks just like her, doesn't she? Just as you look very much like your mother."

"Yes. Yes, to both. Very much. Almost as though poor Nolan left no DNA trace." I sat again, my shoulder touching Carwyn's, and touched Nolan's face under the glass. "I mean, look at him, Carwyn. Just look at the man."

"What do you mean?"

I had thought about this from the moment Viviane had first shown me the photograph. Even in his late forties, Nolan Harris had been a handsome man, all blonde good looks.

"Who does he remind you of?"

Maybe I was making things up. Maybe the searching and the discoveries of the past few weeks were making me paranoid. But maybe not.

"I don't know," Carwyn answered slowly, his pale eyebrows drawing together in a frown. "What am I supposed to see? Someone famous? A young Robert Redford or something?"

"He's tall—much taller than she is. He's blonde. He's blue-eyed."

"So?"

"Carwyn, I'm describing you."

He jerked away quickly, stood the frame up on the table, and looked at it as though on a poisonous snake. "I don't know what you're saying." Abruptly he stood and left the room. I could hear the water running in the kitchen. He was stalling, getting a drink of water for himself; I recognized my own avoidance mechanism in him. After a few moment he returned with two glasses, which he set on coasters before resuming his seat, with a pronounced distance between us on the sofa. I took up my glass; the water was cold and somehow soothing, the drink I hadn't really known I needed. I downed half of it before setting the glass by again.

"I don't know what you're saying." Carwyn stared at the photograph, his eyes—blue eyes—roving over Nolan Harris's face. Was that the tiniest note of panic in his voice. "We don't look that much alike. Not really."

"Not like you are related, no," I reassured him. "But superficially, yes. You are the same type of build, the same hair color, the same eye color."

He sat back. "All right," he said, still uneasily.

"It's like the woman in my branch of the family have the same taste in men." I felt my face flush and reached again for the water glass.

"And treat them the same way?" he shot.

I sucked in a sharp breath.

"Wow," I managed at last.

The mantle clock rang the quarter hour.

Carwyn shook his head. "Sorry. I'm sorry. I shouldn't have said that."

"But it's true." I lowered my head. "And I'm sorry, too."

Again the silence. I drank the rest of my water, then went to the kitchen for some more. The big window over the table was beginning to lighten up; dawn would be coming soon. After a moment, I turned to the sound of Carwyn's footsteps.

"If I smoked, now would be a good time to step outside and light up," he said dryly.

I nodded. Everything in the kitchen was grey in the odd pre-dawn light, the collection of stones on the window sill grey shadows. "Out here," I suggested, leading the way to the side door to the deck. I grabbed one of Katti's roomy coats from the peg on the way by and shrugged my way into it.

The air was damp, dew glistening darkly on leaves, on grass.

"There was a fox out here, up the lane," I said quietly. "The other evening, and the evening before. With a single kit."

I felt him close by, imagined how his mouth would be twisted up at the corner in that wry smile.

"Just the mother and the daughter," he said.

"Could have been a sign," I agreed. "Could have been a male kit, too, and I'm giving it too much meaning."

With the advancing morning, the birdsong became more pronounced in the cool air.

"*The smale fowle*," I observed.

"*That slepen al the nycht with open eye*," Carwyn finished. "Must be time to wake up and sing."

"For some of us, anyway." I pulled Katti's coat more tightly about me; there was plenty of overlap. The wooden decking under my bare feet was damp from dew, and cold.

"You should go back to bed," Carwyn suggested, seeing my shiver and yawn.

I let out a quiet laugh. "Back? What's this back?"

"If you go up to your room, I might be able to fold up and fit on that sofa. Or I could just head back to the hotel in Ludlow." He lifted his eyes to look up at the fading stars in the slowly lightening sky. "I don't even know what time it is."

"It hardly matters, I guess." I shifted my cold feet. "Stay here, at least until breakfast. I expect we've got to have one more group-think, the bunch of us." I glanced at him where he still stood gazing at the stars. "About Hever."

"Yes," he said, looking quickly at me, then back up at the sky. "But before we go in, tell me this. What did your father look like?"

My father. I felt the familiar hole.

"I don't remember him," I said sadly. "He died before I even registered his existence."

"But you've seen pictures."

I closed my eyes, and the birdsong grew louder. One picture, the one on Elaine's dresser in her bedroom, the one she had snatched from my hands the one time I'd picked it up to have a hungry look at it. So many years ago.

"*A* picture." I squeezed my eyes more tightly shut, trying to remember. "Blonde. I don't know about the eyes."

"Your mother has green eyes," he said.

I bit my lower lip. "Yep. And so do I. So he'd have to have some sort of genetic material that allowed me the green eyes."

"I'm betting his were blue," Carwyn said.

50

"PARK HERE," VIVIANE instructed, pointing.

Awkwardly, I bumped Katti's car onto the verge, stomping on the clutch just before it jerked to a stall. I pulled on the handbrake, then turned the key with relief.

"Thank God that's over," I groaned, resting my forehead against the steering wheel.

Viviane patted my knee. "You'll still have to drive us home, my dear," she warned.

"You are not making me feel better."

Smiling benignly, Viviane opened the door and stepped out of the car. She picked her way along the path to the lych gate and waited for me to join her. Together we entered the churchyard, Viviane leading the way beyond a weeping willow toward the far wall. The grass was tall, with tiny blue-eyed flowers interspersed among the green. As we walked the path worn by many feet—a path of desire, Carwyn would have called it—butterflies lifted up before us, darted about, and settled a bit further away. The path forked, and we kept to the right, turning away from the church itself.

Viviane stopped at a low plaque in the tall grass, beside which lay a number of smooth stones. "Your grandfather," she said, sadly, but still smiling. "It's a shame you have to meet him this way."

Nolan Aaron Harris. 1922-1983.

"Too young," I said. "Too soon."

Viviane took her hand, cocking her head. "You were born when? 1984? 1985?"

"1985."

A light squeeze. "Just missed him, then. He would have loved you, Emily. He would have found you to be such a delight. As we do."

Gazing down on the marker, scrubbed free of dirt and moss—I imagined, fleetingly, Katti on her hands and knees with a scrub brush—I was grateful for the warmth of Viviane's hand in mine. "I feel as though"—I choked up, but pushed on anyway—"as though I've missed out on so much."

"Oh, my dear," Viviane murmured sympathetically. "Oh, Emily."

"And I'm angry," I broke out. "So angry, Viviane! So much I could have had—except for these stupid games my mother and grandmother had to play all my life."

"Don't let it weigh you down, my darling," Viviane advised. She tucked my arm through her own, still holding my hand. "It's done. Don't carry it around with you."

Not for the first time did I wonder about the great equanimity of this woman. "It's hard. I'd like to be philosophical about it, like you, but I'm not there yet. Not even close. All of this is so new to me."

"Of course it is. Of course it is." She turned slightly. "There's a bench over here. Near the willow. Come sit. I need a rest."

I suspected the rest was not for her, but acquiesced. The bench was weathered and worn, but Viviane settled onto it familiarly and comfortably. She obviously came here often.

"You miss him."

"For more than thirty years I've missed that man. He was mine for fifteen years, and those were by far the most wonderful fifteen years of my life."

I found myself close to tears. "That might possibly be the most lovely characterization of a marriage I've ever heard."

"Your own experience hasn't gone well."

"That's putting it kindly," I said wryly. "But you're right. I hate to say it, though, but Eleanor warned me against marrying Rob. She said he was all wrong for me. And she turned out to be right."

Viviane shook her head. "That was cruel for her to say, however. She shouldn't have done that."

"It was more cruel, though, for Eleanor to insist that Carwyn and I were made for each other. Because now—every time I think I'd like to maybe get close to him—I feel her looking over my shoulder. I feel her pushing me toward him. Manipulating. And I second-guess myself."

"Ah." Again Viviane nodded; again she patted my hand. She gazed toward the place where her husband lay. "Ah. Well, that brings me to the one thing I really wanted to speak to you about, before you leave."

Her tone had changed, had become more serious, more urgent. I felt myself stiffen slightly and stared at the dappled shadows of the willow leaves, moving gently in the morning air.

"If it's about Carwyn—"

"It *is* about Carwyn," Viviane interrupted. "And I want you to know that I've thought long and hard about speaking to you about this matter—it's your business, and your relationship, and your decision."

"Yes. It is."

Viviane sighed. "Oh, I was worried I'd do this all wrong." She shook her head. "Katti always tells me I have no tact, as though she has the corner on the market." A rueful smile played about her lips. "It's a good thing I never told her what I wanted to speak to you about."

"I really don't want to talk about him," I said, softening at Viviane's contrite tone. "Please, Viviane."

Another breath of wind moved the fronds of the willow and caressed my warm cheeks. Beyond the protective circle of the tree, the butterflies rose from the waving grass and fluttered down again. I watched a pale yellow one flit toward us, then away again.

"I know you don't want to," Viviane said gently. "So don't talk. I'll talk." She cleared her throat delicately. "I want to tell you a story, and it's not nice. It's about your grandfather. Your grandfather, who had no idea that he even had a child until that child was nearly ten years old."

I stared at her.

"What—" It was unfathomable. "What do you mean?"

Viviane held both hands out before her. She might have been reaching for Nolan, for courage from him. For something.

"Eleanor did not tell Nolan about Elaine for years. Years, Emily." For the first time since we'd met, I sensed a real anger in Viviane. "She deprived him of his daughter for that long. And by then, your mother was so wounded that no matter how hard Nolan tried, they couldn't bond." Her jaw was hard, her eyes dark and furious, her lipsticked mouth drawn into a thin line. "And he tried. Oh, how he tried."

"Years?"

"Yes. Something awful, close to ten years. And he really tried hard to connect with Elaine, so hard. So hard." Viviane's eyes glittered, but they were tears of fury. "Can you imagine how that hurt him? To have something so enormous hidden from him, something so important, by a woman he loved, and who claimed to love him. And for what reason? None that he could ever understand." She turned, and this time gripped my hand fiercely, angrily. Convulsively. "You have to understand, that Nolan was a good man. And a good father: I know this, because he was the father of my own daughter, a child whom he loved twice as hard, since he wasn't allowed to love his first-born, except from a distance."

"But—Elaine—"

"She thought Nolan didn't want her, for most of her childhood. She thought her own father didn't want her. Can you imagine what that does to a *child*? It's no wonder she couldn't trust him when they finally met. She'd been taught not to.

By her mother. Eleanor did this, Emily. *Eleanor did this.* To Nolan and to your mother."

Now the angry tears spilled from Viviane's dark eyes, and for the first time, she looked old to me. Old, tired, and angry. She snapped open her purse and withdrew a tiny handkerchief, with which she wiped furiously at her wrinkled cheeks.

The ripples in the pond were suddenly obvious. Eleanor had done this. And now concentric circles of pain and anger were flowing outward, from Elaine, to me. My mother had been a terrible mother, but what a model she had had. No wonder our relationship was fraught. The new burst of sympathy for Elaine surprised me. I quickly patted my pockets for my own handkerchief, a search I knew would be fruitless. Again Viviane snapped open the purse, and this time withdrew a small packet of tissues, which she handed to me.

"If there's anything I've never been able to forgive anyone for, it's this. I cannot forgive your grandmother for the damage she did to my husband. And to Elaine." *And to you.* The words were unspoken, but I read volumes in Viviane's gaze.

"I wish I had known him," I said thickly. "Nolan. Granddad."

"I wish your grandmother had not made that impossible—I think he would have lived longer had that unhappiness not weighed him down." Viviane's tone was bitter. Again she wiped at her tears, then blew her nose, and tucked the handkerchief back in her purse: she would not be needing that again, her actions indicated. She stood and looked down on me. "And I hope you do nothing to make that impossible for your daughter and her father. The choice is yours, Emily. Make the right one."

Then she turned on her heel and made her way back to Nolan's grave marker, her spine straight, her shoulders squared. I watched her progress without moving from the bench. I understood that this last conversation before we left the churchyard was between Viviane and her husband, and I had no place in it; I understood that I had been given advice I seriously needed to consider.

51

WE HEADED SOUTHEAST in the early morning in Carwyn's rental car.

"I've known them for days. Not even two weeks." I sniffed, watching the villages give way to long stretches of motorway out the passenger window. I clutched the packet of tissues Viviane had given me in the cemetery, not daring to use them for the irrational fear of using them all. In my pocket was one of Nolan's worry stones, the one Viviane had given me from the kitchen windowsill. *Hold it close,* Viviane had said, *and know we are thinking about you.* Laughing, Katti had kissed it and handed it back, saying *hold it against your cheek, and that's your old auntie kissing you there.*

Damned cold kiss, Helen had muttered.

Carwyn peered over his shoulder, then flicked on the blinker and pulled out to pass a lorry. "Only days? You four carry on like you've been playing in the sandbox together for all your lives."

I sighed, then wiped the resulting mist from the window with the side of my fist. "Not even two weeks. But this was the family I was supposed to be born into."

"Far more demonstrative than Elaine."

"Far more demonstrative than Eleanor, too."

Carwyn didn't answer. He was wearing a new pair of sunglasses, though the day couldn't quite seem to decide yet if it was going to be sunny or cloudy. I couldn't read his expression.

"You don't agree?" I demanded.

"I can't agree," he corrected, returning to the left-hand lane. "I told you. I only know my experience. I didn't live yours."

"I wish—" I wished so many things, many of them nebulous, without a form defined by any words I could think of. "If I had known what kind of reception I was going to get from them, I would have planned a longer trip, a longer stay. Or purchased an open-ended ticket or something."

"Wait. You didn't tell them you were coming?"

"I didn't even know my grandfather had another daughter until I met her." Then I laughed. "Until *after* I met her. I only knew about his wife, and set out on a blind quest to meet her."

"What, just showed up at her house?"

My face grew warm. "Well, yeah. Just showed up. And even though it was the first time we'd met, Viviane still behaved as though she'd expected me all along. Welcomed me. See, I didn't know anything about her until a couple of months ago, but she'd known all about me. Because Nolan—my grandfather—kept an eye on my mother, even from a distance. Even though he knew his interest wasn't welcomed."

"Really?" Carwyn sounded shocked. A service plaza loomed up on the left; he put on the blinker and slowed.

"I was born a couple of years after he died. But Viviane knew I was out there, and she thought, in her strangely logical way, that I'd come looking for information before long."

I smiled at the thought of Viviane, and then it hit me with a jolt. *I know what you want me to do, Viviane.* It was like a sucker punch, and I caught my breath. I slewed a glance to Carwyn's face as he found a parking spot and slotted the rental car into it. *And I will do it. I will. For Nolan. But not yet. Not here. This is not the time.*

"Wait," I said. "I knew to look for Viviane outside Ludlow. But how did you know where to find me?"

"Same," Carwyn said. "Ludlow. Eleanor once told me all the answers were there. I didn't know then what she meant. But I went there for answers."

"And found more questions."

"Maybe."

WE CIRCLED LONDON and continued south to Hever.

"It's not the Boleyns you want." The lane was narrow, and he slowed as he took the blind corner around the Henry VIII pub. A bit further to the car park, where a boy in a brilliant yellow vest directed us to the left. It was a bit after noon, and the uncertain morning had brightened into brilliance.

"Just the ver Vloets." We locked the car, crossed the lane, and headed up the drive to the entrance kiosk, also manned by a boy in a yellow vest. I dug in my purse for some notes to pay for admission.

"I've got this," Carwyn said, waving my money away.

"You're unemployed," I countered, "and thanks to my divorce settlement and Eleanor's will, I've just come into more money than anyone deserves. Don't be silly."

"Don't remind me," he said with surprising bitterness. "I feel my lack of worth every moment, thank you very much."

I stopped. "Sorry." I looked up into his face. "I didn't mean to hit a sore spot. But this is all free money, mostly from Eleanor, and you know she'd want you to use it."

This only made his expression grow more fierce. "I was not her friend for money. I never took any once I'd grown up, and I won't start now."

I threw up my hands in exasperation. "For God's sake. Have I ever said anything about your friendship being mercenary? Have I? Did I imply it? No. I only meant that I've got this money. And you have driven me all this way when you didn't have to, and you've paid for gas. Let me pay for the admission. It's not like I'm buying your soul. It's not like you're prostituting yourself."

For a long moment we glared at each other, until a busload of tourists from the car park washed around and past us, parting like the Red Sea. Taking our place in line at the kiosk behind them, we did not speak.

Finally, Carwyn mumbled, "Sorry."

"We still can't get along." I was surprised by how sad that made me feel. "Not even about little things."

"That's because we've already fought about the big things," he said ruefully.

"Not all of them."

"What?"

"Nothing." I shook my head, and my smile felt forced and tight on my cheeks. "Apology accepted. As long as I pay for the tickets."

"All right—as long as I buy lunch."

52

WE JOINED THE line, still short, threading through the gatehouse, the small square courtyard, and into the castle itself, where a woman took our tickets and directed us to the right. It was, I was impatient to discover, a path dictated by red velvet ropes: no paths of desire here. We found the first tapestry in the library—formerly the Great Hall, I read in the guide book I'd purchased on the way in; impossible to get close to. We edged our way upstairs, along to what was known as the Book of Hours room, where another tapestry hung, this one depicting the wedding of Henry VIII's sister Margaret; we were able to get closer to it, even close enough to examine the repairs that had been made to the lower border. In front of both, I felt Carwyn's eyes on me, watching for a reaction. He frowned the entire time.

"None of these are making you feel strange," he said, sounding puzzled.

I shook my head. "None of them."

Nothing. Yet we hadn't found the ver Vloet piece: nothing at all labeled as coming from Bruges.

"I'll ask," Carwyn offered and slipped away to accost one of the attendants stationed near a doorway the better to scan the rooms on either side. He was back momentarily. "This way."

I followed him around a corner into a small room to the right. A knot of people were moving slowly ahead of us, and I felt an irrational urge to elbow them aside. They seemed to be directionless, unless it was to move into our path, regardless of which way we turned. At last we were able to reach the far wall, and there it was, waiting for us, the one tapestry we were really looking for. I approached it warily, looking into the wild eyes of a fawn, and the resolute face of a woman who stood between it and the huntsmen, suggested in the lower corner by raised weaponry above the backs of heads. The colors were more vibrant than anything that old had a right to be.

"It's recently undergone some preservation work," Carwyn said from a few steps behind, his voice echoing slightly, either in the room or in my head. "The website I was reading up on said that if we'd come only a couple of months ago, it wouldn't have been hanging here."

I barely registered his words. The colors drew me: the brilliant blues especially, in the woman's cloak. The same blue as the eyes of the cherub? I stepped closer, my hands clenched behind my back. Looking. Desperately wanting to touch. Examining my own reactions. Curiosity, mostly. Awe. And something else I couldn't name.

"Where is the signature?" I asked, scanning the borders, as far up the sides as I could make out. This border, a stylized repeating pattern, was perhaps three inches in width. "The icon, or whatever you called it?"

Carwyn stood close enough that our shoulders touched. He looked from my face to the tapestry and back again. "I don't know," he said slowly. He too leaned a bit closer. "Probably your Helen would know."

"She's not *my* Helen."

"Yes, but when she marries your aunt, she'll be your aunt."

"Is there a question I can help you with?"

We both whirled, startled. This particular attendant was an older man, peering at us over the rims of his glasses. Suspiciously, as though he saw us as reprobates attempting to vandalize or steal the tapestry.

"Ver Vloet," I managed, fighting back the feeling of being caught red-handed in the commission of a crime, or perhaps an act of public indecency. "We were looking for the two-arched bridge."

Apparently that was exactly the right thing to say, because the man drew nearer, his round red face breaking into a delighted smile. "You're certainly up on your knowledge," he said approvingly. "Most people look, some people marvel, but so very few actually *know*."

Carwyn held up a hand. "We don't know much. Not much—but we've been doing some research."

The man's name tag read *Tom*. He came to stand beside me, taking his reading glasses off and tucking them into his breast pocket. "I can't see with these, and I can't see without them. But I don't want to get too close to the tapestry." He cast a warning glance toward either of us.

"Of course."

"What makes you interested in the ver Vloet?" he asked.

"I am a ver Vloet descendent," I told him. "I only recently discovered this."

"Ah, genealogy." He sighed. He turned his bright eyes upon me; we were close to the same height. "There were brothers, you know."

"Two," I said.

"And from which are you descended?"

It was like a test.

"Arnaud."

The attendant nodded. I'd passed. "Ah. The cartoonist. Are you an artist, too?"

I laughed. "I'm afraid all the artistic talent has syphoned away after fifteen generations." I shook my head. "I'm a librarian."

"And you?" The man turned his bright gaze on Carwyn.

"A historian. Sorry."

Tom shrugged. "Never mind. I was a hospice nurse before I retired and got taken on part-time here. At least you're coming round." He winked. "But you wanted to know where the signature is, did you? The bridge?"

He leaned forward, squinting, toward the lower left-hand side of the stylized border. Then he grunted and pointed, keeping his finger a careful few inches away.

I leaned forward, too. The spot to which Tom was pointing was in the repeating pattern, green tricked out with a shadow of darker green fading to black, in an attempt to give the illusion of a three-dimensional frame.

"I can't see it," I said, frustrated, at the same moment Carwyn let out a slight gasp.

"There," he said, his point, from my other side, at the same spot as Tom's, a kind of triangulation. "On the dark green horizontal line. In black. You'd mistake it for shadow, except for the undersides of the arches."

"Brilliant, isn't it?"

The two men glanced over my head in mutual congratulations, almost as though they'd created the symbol, rather than just looked at it. I fought back the urge to smack their heads together. Instead, I leaned just a fraction closer, clutching at Carwyn's arm for balance. Dark green, horizontal, black. I concentrated—and saw the light beneath the two arches first. Slowly the tiny black bridge resolved itself before my eyes, and I wondered how I could ever have missed it.

Two arches. Two brothers. A bridge over a five-hundred-year-old river.

"It *is* brilliant," I breathed.

Now Tom was chuckling. "I don't think I've ever had people come in— who weren't textile historians—who were more interested in the border than the subject of the tapestry." He turned his eyes on me once more. "I call her 'Beauty,' this girl in the tapestry, because I don't know her name. She's got your hair."

She did, too, the woman shielding the fawn from the hunters with her imperious gaze. The same red-gold, in fact, of the cherub in my own small tapestry. But the woman's face was not like the baby's in either shape or expression. This woman had a fuller face, rounder, and her expression was fierce and determined. None of those hunters would harm the fawn behind her while she stood against them.

"What is the story?" I asked. "Is it symbolic? Mythological?"

Tom now looked disappointed. "I can't tell you. So many of the tapestries *are* mythological—the Diana and Actaeon downstairs, for example. Or historical, like the wedding of Mary Rose Tudor. But this one—no one seems to know. It was no doubt commissioned by someone, but many of the newly rich who commissioned these works had little classical education, and the cartoonist, like your grandfather Arnaud, might just come up with a design someone liked, and that client would go along with it."

"This tapestry is not original to Hever, then?" Carwyn asked.

The attendant shook his head. "Oh, no. Nearly everything here was purchased and placed by the Astors. Mr. Astor collected pieces he thought would fit, and since the castle became a museum, we've kept them all here on display." He looked as though he had more to say, but the radio at his hip squawked into life. "Excuse me, but duty calls. Enjoy the rest of your visit." He drifted away with a wave, speaking into his radio.

Another group of visitors wound their way into the small room, swirled around us, wandered desultorily out again. We stood before the tapestry for a few more moments, considering. I scanned the face of the woman, and barely thinking, I wound a finger in a strand of my own hair. Definitely the same hair, but not the same face. A piece to the puzzle, but not one I could fit into the crazy collection I already had before me.

"How does it feel?" Carwyn turned away from the hanging and looked down at me. "Here?"

I held myself very still, listening to my own breathing, feeling the beating of my own heart. I let my eyes fall again to the two-arched bridge, which absolutely jumped out at me now I knew where to look. I felt wonder, and curiosity. When I raised my eyes again to the figure with her flowing red-gold hair and her flowing deep blue gown, I felt admiration, maybe even something warmer, like love. I felt the young woman's protection.

"No sadness," I said. Wonderingly. I looked to Carwyn in question. "It's not like the other places."

He studied my face intently. "No. It isn't, is it?"

I turned away, to the exit. When I turned back, one hand on the doorframe, I saw he was still standing before the tapestry, the red-haired woman towering above him. *Beauty,* as Tom had called her, was looking toward the hunters, but Carwyn's eyes were still on her.

"Let's find somewhere private to sit," I said. "I have something important to tell you, Carwyn."

53

WE WALKED THE length of the arbor without speaking, without looking. Finally, at the Italian Loggia, I told him.

"How long have you known?"

"Viviane made me take a test. It was positive. I haven't seen a doctor yet."

"So it wasn't a bug."

"No."

"But how could this even *happen?*"

I looked away, down the length of the lake to what the map said was a Japanese tea house.

"I had a sinus infection—you remember? Right when Eleanor died. The antibiotics must have interfered with the pill."

"So you were protected."

"Of course I was." Sudden fury. I glared. "I'm not an idiot."

Deep breath. "Sorry. Sorry."

"I didn't plan any of this," I said. "I didn't know this would happen. Hell, I don't even know why I threw myself at you like that."

"Thanks for that, anyway."

I threw up my hands. "I told you. It was as though there was some outside force. I didn't have control that night."

"Neither did I," he said wryly.

We fell silent.

Again I thought of the faraway *ping.* More of a feeling than a noise.

"I suspected it had happened, though," I confessed, feeling the confusion rise again. I forced myself to look him full in the face. "I don't know how. I don't know why. It was as though"—and I felt cold again, used—"as though a goal had been reached." I tried to explain the sound, the feeling; I saw my own confusion mirrored on his face.

"You were *supposed* to get pregnant," he said slowly. His voice sounded hollow.

I nodded. "There was an—inevitability—about it. And the more I learn, the more I'm sure of that—though I still don't know why."

Now he laughed, and it was an ugly sound. "So I *was* the sperm donor. Like Nolan."

"Like my father, who provided his, then died. And like Eleanor's father."

"It's like you women are black widow spiders."

Now it was my turn to laugh bitterly. The waves on the lake before us were kicking up in a wind, and the sky had darkened. The sky always seemed to darken.

"I'm not going to kill you." I looked away quickly.

"What?"

"But . . . what you said. About being the sperm donor." I shied away from the thought; it was too horrifying to consider. But I couldn't get past it. "Eleanor kept saying, over and over, that you and I were made for each other. Like she had selected you."

"Don't say that. *Don't say that.*"

"Like she had groomed you. From an early age."

"Don't say that!" Carwyn spun away, shoving his hands into his pockets, hunching his shoulders against the attack.

I watched him reel away, his back to the lake and to me. He stumbled toward the statuary and the pool. I thought I saw his shoulders shake, and I turned my face, unwilling to bear witness to his agony.

"But—*why?*" he choked over his shoulder.

"I don't know!" I scrubbed at my face: I would not cry. *I would not cry.* How many times had I repeated that mantra, and to what end?

I forced myself to take a step toward him, and another. There were voices from the loggia above us, and I saw a couple look down, saw the woman's pitying expression as she indicated she and her partner should move on. Obviously she suspected they'd stumbled upon a break-up, but it was much worse than that. Much worse.

"Do you understand why I ran? Do you understand how I couldn't face you? I did a horrible thing to you, Carwyn, and I wasn't alone in that. I realized that straight away. When you and I were together, it wasn't just us." I drew in a ragged breath. "Do you see?"

Carwyn slumped down on the stone lip of the pool and lowered his head, his hands between his knees.

"I thought," he coughed, "she loved me."

"Love doesn't mean the same thing in this family as it does to everyone else."

"I thought she was being kind to me."

"Kindness doesn't mean the same thing, either."

I too sat, but not too close, and returned my gaze to the rough grey water. There was a hire boat out there now, propelled hurriedly toward the dock down the lake to the right. Three people hunched against the freshening wind, laughing: man, woman, child. An uncomplicated family. Then I shook my head; I didn't really know that about them. There was no way I could know that. I could only know that they looked, even from this distance, even beneath the darkening sky, to be having a nice, uncomplicated boat ride. And maybe that was enough. I sighed and looked down at my hands, clasped between my knees, mirroring Carwyn's.

"What I thought," I said at last, "was that you were kind to me. I thought I was no longer jealous of you. I thought we might be friends." I took a deep breath, and it hurt in my chest. "I thought you were someone I *might* think about dating, might think about entering into a relationship with. And then this happened and ruined it all." I sniffed, then opened my purse to root for the packet of tissues. "I don't know whether it's me feeling anymore, or something else forcing me to feel. I just don't know what's *real.*" I blew my nose, shoved the tissue into my jeans pocket.

"And now you're going to bear my child."

"Yes."

"You don't have to."

"I know."

54

"ONE MORE THING to look at," Carwyn said, determined, as we headed back toward the castle along the other side of the Italian gardens. He looked pale and strained behind his dark glasses, and his hands, at his sides, were squeezed so tightly into fists that his knuckles showed white. He slowed his steps slightly. "You're not too tired?"

"I'm fine," I said. To our right, alcove after alcove displaying statues, one of a couple in the midst of intercourse; I looked away quickly.

There were more people at the castle, crossing the drawbridge, lined up in the tiny courtyard.

"What's the one more thing?"

"A portrait. One more experiment." He took a deep breath. "Are you okay with that?"

I nodded.

"You won't be alone," he said.

"I'll be fine." I could not, however, inject the reassurance I wanted into my voice. I wished I could be certain of my own reaction.

"One face. Then we'll go."

I nodded.

"This way."

He took my arm impersonally, bypassing the parlor, the library, breaking the proscribed order of the lines. Paths of desire indeed—more like paths of desperation, of determination. He consulted the map in the guide book, then touched my elbow to indicate the way toward the stairs.

"Do you know how to get everywhere?"

"I know how to research," he reminded me. "It's my job. Or would be my job, if I had one."

I followed him around a corner and through the Book of Hours room once again. He looked neither left nor right. However, at the next door, he slowed and reached for my arm.

"One face," he repeated, looking down at me. He removed the glasses, and his expression now was one of concern—and a bit of uncertainty. "Are you sure you're all right?"

I took a deep breath and blew it out again. A couple pushed past us impatiently. "I guess I won't know until I see it. So we'd better just have a look, hadn't we?"

Carwyn tucked my arm through his and led me into the room. A glass case reposed along the left-hand wall; he steered us through the crowds toward it. Inside, a small panel of a boy with a narrow face, a sharply-carved nose, and reddish hair beneath a black hat. In his long delicate fingers he held a pinkish flower.

"Look at this, and tell me what you feel."

It was immediate, and not even a surprise now.

Arthur, I thought.

And was wracked with the sadness. The sadness. My fingers scrabbled to find Carwyn's.

55

"SO *IT IS* Arthur Tudor," Carwyn said.

He had given me his jacket, and I huddled in it as we sped toward Heathrow.

"He died in 1502," I said dismissively. "I'm not crying for him."

"Someone is," Carwyn countered. "You're a sensitive, and you're picking up on an intense feeling that someone had about him. In 1502."

"That's just nuts."

Carwyn's laugh was a bark, short and sharp. "I would have thought so, too. Until recently. When *everything* became 'just nuts.'" He glanced down at the speedometer, and let up on the gas with a grimace. "It's all nuts, Emily, and this is just part of it. Remember: every single time you've had this feeling—this intense sadness that's so close to grief that you can hardly bear it—you've been near Arthur. His grave, the place his heart is buried, his home in Bewdley, Ludlow Castle, and now, standing in front of the one portrait that was supposed to have been painted during his lifetime. There is something obvious there that you're refusing to pick up."

"You're assuming all of this is real. That I'm not crazy."

"You're not, though. Are you?"

"I don't even know anymore," I said weakly. I wrapped my arms more protectively around myself.

Carwyn sighed, checked the GPS on his telephone. "I do. I don't think you're crazy, and I think, weird though this all may be, that it's *real,* to use your word. And besides, remember that 1502 is an important date."

"Because Arthur died then?"

"Because Elisabeth ver Vloet was born then."

I sucked in a ragged breath, shaking my head so vigorously that my hair fell across my face and I had to shove it back. "Coincidence. I'm sure lots of people were born in 1502. Not just someone we found in my family tree."

"Not people whose lives and impressions converge at a single point: you. You're like the vanishing point in perspective, without vanishing."

"You sound so sure."

"As sure as you sound when you tell me our child will be a girl."

"Not just any girl," I reminded him. "A girl with red-yellow hair and green eyes. Because she has my DNA, and yours."

"So she'll look like you."

"And my mother. And her mother. And, I'm willing to wager, her mother before her. I rather think that has been the plan all along."

"Whose plan?"

I shook my head again. "Damned if I know. I'm just a pawn in this strange and frightening historical game of chess."

"And my DNA?"

"In case you haven't figured it out yet, you're blond and blue-eyed. You're the king of recessive genes. As was my father, and Nolan, and Eleanor's father— again, I'm willing to bet the house on that."

"The House of Tudor?" Carwyn blew out a breath so forcefully that he whistled. "This is so weird. This is so freaking weird."

The signs on the motorway began to appear for Heathrow terminals, the traffic slowing to a crawl. Carwyn checked the GPS on his phone again, frowning.

"The question is why? Why am I supposed to have this daughter? Why are you supposed to supply your recessive genes? Who the hell is controlling my universe? Yeah, you're damn right. This entire situation is freaking weird."

We turned into the rental car lot and rolled to a stop in front of the building.

"Come on," Carwyn said, turning off the engine. "Let's get rid of this car, then get some dinner. I don't know about you, but after today, I think I could have a couple of drinks and sleep for a few years."

"I'm with you," I said, collecting my purse from the back seat. "Except for the drinks."

"MY CAR IS in long-term at the airport back home," Carwyn said after we'd checked our bags at the counter and gone through security screening the next morning. "My flight'll be in an hour or so after yours. Wait for me, and I'll drive you home."

"You don't have to," I protested. I took my shoes to a nearby bench and sat to put them back on.

He shook his head as he sat next to me, his own shoes in hand. "You'd rather take the bus." He made a face. "That's ridiculous."

"I know." I looked around for the departures board, finding my flight number, reassuring myself about the gate number, even though I'd read that information when we'd entered Terminal 5. Sneakers tied, I stood and collected my purse and carry-on. "Everything is pretty crazy, myself included." I glanced along the concourse. "Let's find the Costa's and get a cup of coffee. We've got time."

"So you'll wait for me?"

In the terminal, the sea of people parted to swirl around us, reforming once it had passed. The morning light from the great windows facing the runways fell across Carwyn's hair, turning it to spun gold. He really was handsome. And he really was kind. Wasn't he? I looked away in confusion.

"I'll wait for you," I said. It seemed an enormous concession, but somehow, it also felt right to make it.

Carwyn's smile was slow-dawning, but grew bright enough to light up his entire face. It was infectious. I smiled back.

Slowly.

"Let's get that coffee," he said.

Interlude

IT HAD BEEN so sudden.

Beatrice had not expected to find anyone in the garden at this hour, least of all him.

He caught her hand before she was aware of his presence, and she started like a wild animal, tried to jerk away, a tiny shriek escaping from her lips, her shawl falling away to the damp grass.

"Hush," he whispered hoarsely. "You'll have the whole house down on us."

She felt herself relax at the sound of the familiar voice, and as her eyes grew used to the dimness of the alcove between the trellises, she saw the angle of his jaw and the glint of his eyes.

"Whatever are you doing out here?" She looked to the sky, to the position of the stars and the sickle moon, trying to ascertain the time. Past midnight, she was sure of that much. Then she remembered, and dropped low. "Your Highness."

"Sleep escapes me," he said. He had not released her hand. "You, mistress?"

She shook her head. "Same. But I must not disturb you." Abashed, and suddenly chilled in her nightdress, her shawl at her feet, she attempted once again to pull away. "I must away to bed, by your leave."

But he did not let her go. "Stay. A few moments." When she did not acquiesce, he repeated, "A few."

She felt the smile play about her lips, glancing up at his silhouette. "You could command me, your Grace."

But the small joke immediately went wrong.

"I do not wish to do that. I wish you to sit with me"—he took a deep breath—"of your own accord."

When she ceased tugging at her hand, he finally released his grip. Then he bent to gather her shawl and, draped it gently about her shoulders, held it under her chin. He was so close she could feel the movement of his breath against her forehead.

"Rise, Beatrice," he said. "We leave for London shortly."

She nodded.

"For my marriage."

"It has long been awaited." And carried forward by proxy, she might have added, thinking of the Spanish ambassador symbolically half-climbing into the bed at Tickenhill.

Suddenly he released his hold on her shawl and threw himself back onto the bench beside the bank of flowers, which still cast their sweet scent upon the night air.

"I don't wish to go forth," he whispered.

She stood looking at his bent head, imagining him in his wedding finery, a circlet crowning his fiery hair. Something in that made her unimaginably sad. Hesitantly she took a step forward and lowered herself onto the stone bench beside him. It was cold, damp, through the thin cloth of her nightclothes. She shivered slightly and clutched the shawl about her more tightly.

"What is it," she asked slowly, surprised at her own forwardness, "that you do wish?"

He did not look at her. "I wish to go on like this. In this summer. In this garden." There was a long pause. "With you."

She held her breath. It seemed as though someone should come crashing through the garden after them at this point, someone shouting. Her guardian, or another of the ladies. One of his knights. Someone. But the night was still. Far off, a single bird sang a short, lonely song, and then left off. She felt the slightest touch on her cheek as a petal fluttered to the ground. She closed her eyes.

The touch now on her cheek was not a petal, but his finger. She felt his lips against hers.

"I wish to go on like this," he whispered again, against her mouth.

"Go on," she said.

BEATRICE STARED AT the cartoon and knew what was missing.

Her hands shook as she took up the scrap of charcoal, shook as they had not since the first day Master Arnaud had handed it to her. With the side of her hand she smudged out the lines of the cherub's cheeks, chin—then she attempted them again, finer, and with a tiny dimple. It took her several tries, and still she was less than satisfied. The hair, the wings—those did not matter. Only the face, the face. She clenched her cold hands and tried again. In the depths of her roiling stomach, she knew that was what mattered. She knew it, as she knew the danger of what she did. Master Arnaud would not care, though his dark eyes, she knew, would flicker over the changes, then to her face and back. Master Arnaud, she was convinced, knew far more than he let on. The secret, and no doubt he would guess it, would be safe with him.

She worked until the candle had burned low in its dish, and then she rolled the cartoon carefully and hid it at the bottom of her chest. It would not do for any of the other girls to find it, the other girls who could not keep a secret to save their own—or anyone else's—life.

Part Three
Bloodlines

56

FACETIME ME WHEN you get home, Katti had messaged; she had included Helen in a group chat.

What if it's really late?

Just do it, Helen broke in. *We'll be waiting.*

The rush of belonging which washed over me far outstripped the sense of dislocation as I unlocked the apartment door and let myself in. I had expected a mess—I had fled early that morning in such a precipitous manner—and was shocked to find that, beyond the staleness of unoccupied space, the room was surprisingly neat. I stood paralyzed in the doorway. The futon was closed back up, the blankets folded neatly and piled at one end. The dishes were put away. When I finally made it to the bathroom, I found the towels hung over the rack— more than dry now—and the bath rug draped over the top of the shower stall.

The story the neatened apartment told was an obvious one, and I gulped, the knot of guilt stuck in my throat. The last time I had left the apartment, I was fleeing; I'd jammed clothes into my tiny suitcase, grabbed my passport, and run. Away from Carwyn, sleeping the sleep of the just, tangled in the blankets. He hadn't known what I was doing, what I had done; and not understanding, he'd cleaned up the mess we'd made between us in the midst of our passionate frenzy, waiting for my return. Waiting. And I had not returned.

So he had come to find me. Trusting blindly in Eleanor's words. And he had appeared.

I stumbled to the futon, sat, and pulled my laptop from its case. The computer took a moment to boot up, took another moment to connect to my landlord's wireless. At last I was able to click on the icon and call Katti's computer.

"You're home. Safe?" Her round cheerful face split into a delighted grin. "You look tired." She was, I realized, wearing her pajamas. I looked to the time in the corner of the screen. 7:12. Past midnight in the cottage.

"It's about time." Helen, in the familiar room thousands of miles away, drew a chair forward to sit directly behind Katti's shoulder.

"Hello, my dear," Viviane said from outside the limits of the screen.

"What's the matter?" Helen asked. She leaned forward, her chin on Katti's shoulder, frowning. "It's more than tired. You look, as they say, as though you've been kicked by a horse."

"It wasn't Carwyn, was it?" Katti demanded darkly. "He didn't say anything, did he? He didn't treat you badly?"

I opened my mouth to defend him, but I couldn't think of the words. "No," I gasped at last. "Not that."

"Then what?"

"I think—I think he loves me."

From off screen, Viviane laughed. "Oh, my silly darling Emily. Of course he does. You've just figured that out?"

57

IN THE LIBRARY, I couldn't help but glance over my shoulder to the bank of computers. Force of habit. Of course Carwyn wasn't there. I continued on to the circulation desk and back into the office, where Madeline was at her desk, thumbing through catalogues over a cup of Dunkin' Donuts coffee.

"You're back," my boss said, looking up over her reading glasses. "How was England?"

"English."

"Ha." Madeline swung around in her desk chair. "Pubs? Handsome British men?"

"I'm sure there were some," I said evasively. "Listen. I've come to check on the schedule—about when you'll be needing me to pick up more hours."

Madeline took off her glasses and set them aside on the desk. "Not until August. End of August, probably. Once the students start coming back for the fall semester." She shook her head. "You know we took some cuts in state funding in this year's budget. I was hoping, when I hired you on originally, that there'd be enough to have you go full-time eventually, but it's not looking really good for this fiscal year."

I nodded, my stomach clenching. "I'd heard. And I'd kind of expected it." Despite the words, I couldn't help but feel a bit disappointed. Full time meant health insurance, and it looked as though health insurance was going to come in a bit handy in the coming year. Years, I corrected: babies took years and demanded care all that time. I sighed. How had Eleanor done it? How had Elaine? I'd have to ask my mother. When I broke the news.

Madeline's expression was vaguely uncomfortable. "Besides, didn't you just come into some grand inheritance or something? Why would you want to keep working?" She leaned in conspiratorially. "You know I buy a lottery ticket every week. If I won, I'd be out of here like a shot."

"I work here for the books." I shrugged. "And it gets me out of the house."

"And keeps you off the streets."

"At least half the time."

But I was still knocked up, I thought sarcastically, as I left Madeline to the distributors' catalogues.

Carwyn was at the computers on my way back through, but back to the terminals, swinging side to side in the chair. He caught my eye and winked before standing.

"Let me take you out for a cup of coffee," he suggested. "Maybe we can Mulligan this entire relationship."

Hardly, at this point. "Okay," I said, and couldn't help but feel marginally better. "Slowly."

"Slowly," he agreed, and held the door for me.

"HAVE YOU TALKED to your mother yet?"

I shook my head, feeling suddenly panicked, and pressed my hands to my face. "I called her to let her know I was home, but it went straight to voice mail. I've face-timed with Viviane, Katti, and Helen, though, the other night. Well, *talked* to Viviane—she stayed off-camera. Then she waved when she went up to bed."

Carwyn grinned, his chin on his fist.

"What?"

"The difference in your expression when you talk of your mother, then of those three."

I shrugged, lifted the cup of decaf to my lips without enthusiasm. *Decaf?* He'd asked incredulously at the counter. *Better for pregnant people,* I'd answered. It had better be true.

Pregnant people. The panic was back. I really should have told Madeline about the pregnancy; once I was back to work, I'd have to take time off for maternity leave. Yet somehow, it seemed wrong to make a public announcement—a public admission—before telling my own mother. At this jumble of thoughts, my stress level rose, and I broke out into a sweat. Unless that was hormones.

"I'm trying," I said slowly, thinking aloud, "to understand Elaine. Or at least where she's coming from. I know, on an intellectual level, that she never set out at the beginning of my life to be a crap mother, but I still feel all sorts of resentment about our relationship—especially now, especially living for a week with Viviane and Katti, who have the kind of mother-daughter relationship I'd always imagined and never had." I sighed. The coffee was distinctly unsatisfying, and not helping at all. "I always just wanted my mother to like me. That's all."

"But now you know what she had for a model growing up. She was just repeating history."

This was, I knew, a hard-fought understanding for Carwyn, and an even harder admission, he who had lived most of his life admiring Eleanor. When he reached out to touch my hand in sympathy, I turned my own hand palm-up beneath his. He looked down at our hands, surprised.

"Thank you," I said.

"For?"

"For not discounting me out of hand. For not, God help me, discounting my mother. I know how much you loved my grandmother."

His brow creased. "*Love* her. Still do." He looked out through the window into the plantings of the border, the rhododendrons long past flowers, and now all glossy leaves. "But you're right. I'm not having an easy time of this. I feel *betrayed.*"

And he had a lot of reason to feel that way. "By me?" I asked in a small voice.

He examined my face for a long time, the frown still darkening his expression. "At first, yes. You know that. But—" He looked down to our hands again; he twined his fingers through mine, and I did not resist. "I'm starting to understand. And you're right about this, too. I'm not discounting you."

It was my turn to work up my courage to speak, to ask what had to be asked. "And this baby?"

The silence stretched to the point where I regretted speaking. He cupped our hands in his other palm, turned mine over, and examined my fingers, my nails, measuring them against his.

"It's still a shock," he said.

I swallowed. It wasn't, I discovered, the answer I wanted.

"What would you like me to do?" I asked quietly.

Now he reached for my other hand.

"That is entirely your decision." He looked up, and his smile was small, lop-sided. "Thank you, though, for asking me."

58

OUTSIDE, I CALLED Elaine's cell phone number again, and was sent straight to voice mail once more. I hung up without leaving a message and slumped back into the car seat, fidgeting with the keys. It was Friday afternoon, and though it was possible my mother could still be at the office, it was unlikely that she'd not have her phone, that she'd turn off the ringer. And as for forgetting to pay her bill—something I'd be likely to do—the idea was downright laughable. She forgot nothing.

Curious—and slightly anxious—I started the car and headed up toward the condominium. As I cruised through the narrow parking lot, I looked for Elaine's car and found it in her numbered spot, backed in as usual. Next to it, in the space reserved for visitors, the blue Malibu I'd seen before. The *friend's* car. I found a free spot in the visitors' lot beyond the last building, but when I climbed out of the car and shaded my eyes to look to the door, I had a sudden stab of worry. I hadn't planned for this, not well enough. Then I snorted and grabbed my purse before locking the car. Not that there was any real way to plan well enough for the moment you told your mother that you were pregnant, a year after your husband had left and filed for divorce. And not that there was any real way to tell your mother you seemed to be fulfilling the family destiny. I tucked the keys into my purse and squared my shoulders. There was no good time, and no good way.

I rang the bell and waited. I had the key, grudgingly given to me, but I didn't feel comfortable using it. Still, when after a minute or two there was no answer, the anxiety returned. I turned to look at the Malibu, which presented its smug grill to me. Four in the afternoon on a Friday seemed an odd time for my mother to be home; perhaps she was sick? Fishing the keys back out again, I unlocked the door and let myself in.

"Mom?" I called. "Elaine?"

I moved from the entryway into the kitchen: empty. I turned back to the living room, which was also empty, white and echoing like a room in *House Beautiful*. I was halfway up the stairs when the bedroom door opened and Elaine appeared, clutching her robe at the throat. Her red-gold hair was tousled around her face, and she kept trying to tuck it behind her ear.

"Mom?" I stopped, hand on the rail. "Are you all right? Are you sick?"

"Jesus, Emily," Elaine gasped. "Couldn't you call first?"

"I *did* call. A couple of times. Check your voice mail."

"I was sleeping," my mother said. She glanced over her shoulder, then pulled the bedroom door shut behind her.

We stared at each other for a moment marked by the ticking of a clock somewhere. Then finally I got it. And smiled. "Oh, for God's sake, Mom." I half-turned on the steps. "I'm going downstairs to get a drink. Get dressed. I'll meet you there when you're decent."

"Jesus, Emily," Elaine said again, and this time the annoyance was heavy.

I waved a hand over my shoulder. "Bring him with you. It's about time he and I met, I think. Your *friend.*"

"Emily, I don't want—"

But the door opened again, and a silver-haired man looked out. The same man, unless I was mistaken, whom I had seen driving away from the condominium the afternoon of our funeral-planning.

"I agree, Emily," he said. "I'll meet you down in the kitchen."

ELAINE DRANK GIN and tonics, so I mixed two, hoping the stranger shared that taste, and set them on cocktail napkins on the counter. For myself, I drew a glass of water and plopped a few ice cubes in before pulling up a stool. I was flipping through last week's copy of *The New Yorker,* looking for an Anthony Lane film review, when the man appeared.

"Hi," he said awkwardly, hesitant in the kitchen doorway. He wore khakis and a blue Oxford shirt; his feet were bare.

"Hi." I indicated the drinks. "I didn't know what you like, so I made you one of Mom's. I'm Emily."

He laughed and stepped forward to shake my hand, which he might have held for a fraction of a second too long before releasing it. "You look so much like Elaine that only a blind man would not know you were her daughter." He looked at the drink, rueful, his blue eyes watchful. "I don't drink at all." He reached into his pocket and brought out a token.

"Oh, God, I'm sorry." I sprang up and took the glass.

"I'll have one of your glasses of water, though, if you don't mind."

I filled a glass, put in ice. We sat across from one another at the counter.

"Howard, by the way," he said. He raised his glass, the outside sweating condensation. "Cheers."

We clinked glasses.

"This is rather weird," I said after a sip. "Are you and Elaine—are you her boyfriend? I'm not sure what to call you."

"Howard's good enough." He too took a drink. "I'd *like* to be your mother's boyfriend. If that's not a foolish word to apply to a man of my age." He chuckled. "I've been trying to convince Elaine that I'd be a great boyfriend for—oh, I don't know"—and he looked mildly uncomfortable—"twenty-five years? Thirty?" He shrugged. "But things just got in the way."

"As they do." *Things*. I traced a finger around the damp ring my glass had left on the cocktail napkin. Then I smiled at him. "If you're here, you're already pretty convincing, I imagine. My mother hasn't been in a steady relationship since—my father." I frowned, cocking my head with the weight of the sudden realization. Why had I never really thought about that? "Wow. Since my father."

"Your father—"

But before Howard could finish the thought, Elaine appeared at the doorway.

"What about her father?" she asked. She came forward and, spying the gin and tonic, lifted it to her lips. She grimaced slightly. "A little lighter on the tonic, I think, next time."

"*Thanks* would have sufficed, Mom," I said tartly.

"Don't start. I don't have the patience for this."

Howard held up his hands, in mock need of protection. He wore a wedding band, I noticed with a jolt—but on his right hand, not his left. "Wow, you two. Prickly."

Elaine settled on the stool next to Howard, but seemed to take care not to touch him. "Emily has been the most prickly of daughters. Since the time she was a child. Since she could first speak."

"I would have liked to have heard that," Howard said.

I ignored him, and glared at my mother. "Yeah? Well, Elaine has been the most prickly of mothers. Since the time I was a child. Since I could first understand speech."

"Jesus, Emily," Elaine said.

That seemed to be her mantra this afternoon. She picked up her glass again and circled around the counter for the bottle of Tanqueray No. 10. She poured another hefty dollop into her drink, tasted it, then re-capped the bottle. I wondered at the blindness that made her drink in front of her lover, wondered at his power of will before her drinking.

"Oh, dear," Howard said, his pale eyes flitting from one to the other. "You two really do spark off each other like flint, don't you?"

Neither of us answered.

"Can you pretend to get along?" he suggested after a silence rife with antagonism. "Just pretend? For the sake of a guest?" He smiled at each of us in turn, and I noticed that he had a single dimple to the left of his mouth, which made his smile endearingly lopsided.

I felt a twinge of guilt. "Sorry." I returned my attention to the wet ring on the napkin; every time I set the tumbler down, it made a new, somewhat interlocking circle. Like the Olympic rings, I thought nonsensically. It was an Olympic sport, sometimes, trying to converse with my mother.

Out of the corner of my eye, I saw Elaine touch Howard's hand lightly in apology and then pull away again. An apology to her lover, but none to her daughter. I returned my attention to my water. The ice had melted; I stood to get more.

You need to talk to your mother. That was Viviane's voice in my head, eminently sensible and kind. *You need to be patient with your mother. She drew the short straw as a child.*

"Mom," I said, sitting back down. I reached across the counter and took my mother's cold hand in mine, pretending I didn't see the shocked expression on her face. "I'm sorry. Really. I am."

Elaine frowned. "To quote Howard, *wow.*" She pulled her hand away, much to my great disappointment—though I knew I should have expected the reaction. Elaine had never liked to be touched. By me, anyway.

"I'm serious."

My mother lifted her finely sculpted eyebrows. "The visit to Ludlow seems to have done wonders for your disposition."

I would not respond in kind. I would not respond in kind. I took a deep breath. "I learned a lot there," I offered slowly, presenting an opening. I waited, but Elaine did not seem at all inclined to take the opportunity.

Howard shifted on his stool, his eyes flitting between us as though he were watching a tennis match. "I'll bite," he said, when it appeared Elaine would not. "What kind of things did you learn in Ludlow?"

I turned my own gaze to Howard, who had, I decided inconsequentially, a very nice face. A kind face. With that quirky dimple. "I learned that my grandfather, Elaine's father, had another family there. I met his wife."

"The woman he left Eleanor for," Elaine said bitterly.

But I was armed. "You know they met and married more than ten years after you were born. Your chronology is off."

Elaine didn't answer, but looked away, toward the window. Her lips pressed together tightly.

"I saw his grave," I continued.

No answer from Elaine, but her green eyes had darkened.

"And I met his other daughter," I said. "Your half-sister, Mom. Katti. Katharine. Who is fifteen years younger than you are, more or less."

Now Elaine's tears started, spilling over onto her pale cheeks. She wiped them away, furiously, brushing her gold hair—only a bit duller than my own—back behind her ears. Still she did not look at me.

"Like old home week for you, then, wasn't it?" She spat with sudden fury. "Well, I hope you enjoyed your visit with your new family. It sounds as though you like them better than your old family."

"Mom—"

But Elaine had fled the kitchen.

I stared, open-mouthed, after her. Moments passed, then I turned to Howard. "I just can't say anything," I whispered. "I just can't say anything at all to her." I lowered my head into my hands. "I just wish she didn't think everything I say is an attack. I just wish she—even *liked* me."

Howard looked sadly at me. "Oh, she likes you. Don't be confused about that. She just doesn't know how to show it. And this—it's insecurity, Emily. She has always felt that her father replaced her with his English family, even though I'm sure that impression had more to do with what Eleanor told her than with anything else. Still, you can't reason with an emotional child, and she first felt that as a child. You need to be patient with her." His words echoed Viviane's. The look he threw toward the hall door, even as they heard Elaine slam the bedroom door upstairs, was sad, and loving.

His meaning sank in slowly.

"Wait," I said. "How do you know this? How do you know any of this?"

Howard turned his sad smile back on me. "Because I love her, Emily. I've loved her for nearly my entire life."

59

THE SUSPICION WAS a niggling shadow, but I could not shake it.

I set about sorting bills and writing materials into the cubby-holes of Eleanor's desk. I decided to put my passport, the cover of which I petted nostalgically, into the top middle drawer. In passing, I opened it to check the expiration date. December. I'd have to renew. I tried to remember where I'd put my birth certificate, and whether I needed it to get a new one.

"Come over," I suggested to Carwyn when he called. "It didn't go well at all. I've lost all my courage."

"Be there in a couple," he said.

I dug the file box out of the closet, and, kneeling, flicked through the folders. Marriage certificate. Divorce papers. Car title. I plucked out the folder with my birth certificate. Opening it, I felt the same disquiet I always had at the sight of the blank line for my father's name. But now the vague shadow was hovering, and I couldn't give it a name, but couldn't banish it either. I was still holding the pale blue sheet when I opened the door to Carwyn.

"What is it?" he asked immediately.

"It's blank," I said stupidly. I held the birth certificate out for his examination. "The line for my father's name. Elaine left it blank all those years ago. She told me it was because he died before I was born. Then she told me she didn't want to talk about it."

Carwyn took the heavy paper to the window above the sink and unfolded it.

"Her name is listed here as Harris."

"Yes."

"Her maiden name."

"Her father's name, anyway. Nolan's. I'm starting to think that names are just a formality. The women in my family seem to just append them randomly." I sighed, closing the desk and sinking onto the futon. "I was Harris, too, until I married. Eleanor, who didn't want me to marry Rob, asked me if, as a true feminist, I wouldn't be more comfortable keeping my own name, rather than taking Rob's." I laughed shortly. "But I wanted his name. I wanted the marriedness of it. A lot of good it did me in the end, of course."

"And Elaine didn't even bother to put your father's name on this birth certificate." Carwyn, unable to get past that point, refolded the paper along the worn lines and tapped it against the fingers of his right hand. "Once again, rather like he was only a sperm donor."

"She told me, when I was old enough to ask, that it was because he died. And for a long time, when I was a kid, I thought that children whose fathers had died were all like me: with a blank line on the birth certificate. I didn't realize this wasn't the case for years, if you can believe that."

Carwyn was still tapping the heavy paper, repeatedly, rhythmically. "I can believe it. By now I can believe practically anything out of your family. I mean, when I was a kid, I thought your grandfather was just—dead—"

"He was, by then."

"Yeah, but I didn't know anything about your grandparents never marrying—I just thought they were, and he died, because Eleanor was old to me, and old people were frequently widowed, you know? I just dismissed the fact that there was no grandfather in your family. I just dismissed the fact that there was no *father* in your family." He looked down at the birth certificate in his hand, and then held it out to me. "I was so dumb, as a kid. I never thought."

"I don't think kids *do* think, really, before a certain age. Most of them, like me, just respond emotionally."

"Like me, too. I told you I loved Eleanor because she was kind to me." He pulled out a stool at the island and sat. Then he sighed. "I thought it was me she was interested in. I never considered that it might be something else."

The look I threw at him was appraising. "Oh, it was you, all right. Don't kid yourself about that."

"You know what I mean."

"I'm rather afraid I do."

I got up and crossed to the small desk—my grandmother's desk, the delivery of which had begun this whirlwind of craziness—and slipped the birth certificate into one of the cubby holes. When I turned back, Carwyn was holding out my purse.

"Here. Let's go out for pizza or Chinese or something. Something easy and uncomplicated." He turned to the door, then back again. "So what was your father's name? I mean, surely Elaine must have told you that much."

"Mitch. She called him Mitch. When she spoke of him at all, which she generally didn't do."

I grabbed my keys from the hook near the door. "And when I asked, in the way kids do, you know, like *Mom, what was Dad like?* She'd tell me it was too painful to talk about. So after a while I learned not to ask." I pulled the door closed behind us, then tested it to make sure it was locked. The evening was warm and smelled of flowers and exhaust, with an underlying trace of barbeque:

somewhere along the cul de sac, someone was having a cookout. Some normal family.

"Sad."

"Yes." I stopped suddenly, as a stray memory forced its way toward the front of my mind. Something I hadn't thought of in ages. "But she made a mistake once, my mother. Once—and so unlike her, that I've held onto the memory for years. She told me that my father loved me very much."

"But—he was dead when you were born."

I shrugged, letting Carwyn lead the way to the street and his car. "Then he must have loved me before I was born. That's something I've had to hold onto, see? That my father knew I was coming, and he was happy about that."

"Emily, that might be the saddest thing I've ever heard."

60

WHICH MADE IT all the more ironic when Elaine appeared at my door Sunday evening. The first time she'd ever visited the apartment. She glanced around in vague disapproval.

"I need to give this to you," she said, holding out an envelope. Plain, white, number ten.

I found myself looking at it much as I might have looked at a viper: gifts from my mother were few and far between, and very rarely innocuous. I raised my eyes slowly to her face. Elaine's jaw was hard, her lips pressed together in that straight line so familiar to me. Everything about her stance and expression implied iron control.

"What is it?" I asked cautiously. I backed up to the futon and sat. Fell. As I made no move to take the envelope from her, Elaine dropped it into my lap. Then she turned her back to me, to look out the window down into the road. The streetlight outside cast her face into shadow, a carved thing. A statue.

Slowly I slid my index finger beneath the unsealed flap. Inside, the heavy paper and blue color gave it away.

"A birth certificate?" I asked.

"It's yours," my mother said shortly.

"I've already got a copy." It was still in the desk, where I had left it after taking it from Carwyn. I reached up to turn on the lamp over my shoulder.

Elaine said nothing, only looked out into the street.

I drew out the paper, and set the envelope aside. I unfolded the birth certificate with the care of someone disarming a bomb.

My name: *Emily Elizabeth Harris.*

My birthdate: *October 21, 1985.*

I scanned the rest of the page, finding the familiar information. Then I realized what I was looking at, and froze.

My mother's name. And my father's.

The line was not blank.

Howard Mitchell.

Mitch.

And more than that. *Howard.*

I felt it like a punch in the solar plexus. I couldn't breathe. I resisted the urge to double over, to curl into a protective fetal position. Instead, trying to fill my lungs, I lifted my eyes to my mother's hard face.

"*What is this?*" I gasped.

"It's your amended birth certificate. I decided to add your father's name."

"You *decided?*"

"Don't be melodramatic, Emily." Elaine turned on the lamp next to the window, then pulled the front curtains. Night was falling. "I've known all the time what your father's name was. I thought it was about time I put it on the official paperwork." Her laugh was ugly. "Unless you envision me as one of those women who has no idea who impregnated her."

The room was spinning. "You told me he was dead. You told me he died before I was born. You called him *Mitch.*" I shook and shook my head. I suddenly realized that I was crushing the birth certificate between my hands, and I thrust it away. *Howard's good enough for now,* he had said, Friday evening, over the counter. *Howard.*

"I lied." Elaine moved her purse from one arm to the other, as though impatient to get the interview over, and to leave.

I reared back on the futon, staring at my mother. I opened my mouth, closed it again, having difficulty forming the shock into words. "Lied?" I repeated finally. "*Lied?*"

"Howard said this would happen," Elaine said.

"Yeah, well, we'll get to Howard in a minute, won't we?" My voice was acid. "Right now, I'd like to hear what you have to say about your telling me my father died. Telling me for years my father *was dead.* What's that all about, then?"

Elaine opened her purse and pulled out a handkerchief, then snapped the purse shut again. She made no use of the handkerchief, however. "He wasn't fit to be a parent then," she said, her voice low. "He was drinking. He wasn't capable of being a father when you were born." For the first time she turned her gaze fully on me. "I thought it was best."

"You could have let me decide that."

"When you were a baby? Don't be stupid. I made the best decision I could, for your health and wellbeing. It was better that way."

"And him? Howard? How did he feel about having no claim to me, to his child?" My voice rose in anger and frustration, and I could not control it. I leaned forward. "Or maybe you didn't tell him—just like your mother never bothered to tell your father about you, for ten years."

Elaine sucked in a breath. "Who told you that? One of Nolan's other family?"

"It hardly matters. What *does* matter here is that I have a father, and I've been deprived of him all my life. Did he know about me? Back then? And choose to stay away? Or was he totally ignorant of my existence?"

"He knew." Elaine's voice remained steady, as though she had rehearsed. "And he wasn't able to be a father. Howard is an alcoholic. He's sober now, but then, he wasn't. He couldn't care for himself. He sure as hell couldn't care for a daughter. Ad definitely not just any daughter—you."

My hands were shaking. My stomach was turning inside out. "Did he choose to stay out of my life, or did you force him to?"

"Emily, I know you think I'm some sort of monster," Elaine said wearily. "You have never cared for me, and all we've ever done is fight. But I want you to understand. I did the best I could for you. I had your grandmother on one side, and your—incapacitated—father on the other, and I did the best I could. Perhaps someday you'll understand that—hopefully before I'm dead. Perhaps someday you'll have a child of your own, and you'll end up facing some of the things I've faced, and you'll understand that *I've done the best I can.*" She sighed. "Someday, when you have a daughter of your own."

It was too much to bear. We locked eyes for a moment before I snatched up the amended birth certificate and stood to yank the door open, a clear invitation for Elaine to go. Then I whirled on her.

"We'll have to see, then, won't we?" I said. "Because that day's coming right up in about eight months."

"Emily—"

"Right, Elaine," I hissed. "I'm pregnant."

The steel seemed suddenly to go out of my mother. Her shoulders slumped, and at the door, she seemed to grow smaller and smaller.

"She's won, then," she said in that low voice. "Eleanor. She's won after all."

61

THE KNOCK ON the door startled me, where I lay on the futon, staring at the ceiling.

There was a shadow against the curtain over the window in the door.

I didn't want to see anyone. I didn't want to talk to anyone. I rolled over and pressed my face into the futon cushion.

The knock came again.

I lay perfectly still, perfectly silent, waiting for whoever it was to go away.

"I know you're in there, Emily."

A male voice. Not Carwyn's.

"Your car is out here. I know you're home. And I need to talk to you."

I did not move.

"All right. I'll just sit out here until you open the door." A pause. "I've outwaited your mother, and I can outwait you."

Slowly I struggled to my feet, feeling queasy and unsteady, as I had all day. I navigated my way to the sink, where I drew myself a glass of water, hoping it would settle my stomach. Then I crossed to open the door.

Howard was seated on the top step, and now he stood slowly. His gray hair was ruffled, his blue eyes shadowed. His glance fell to the glass I held in my hand.

"Water," I said.

"I could use some."

"What if I don't want to talk to you?"

He shrugged, his lips turning down. "I'll have to live with that. But I'll keep coming back. I need you to know that."

I leaned against the doorframe. "Yeah? Why now? Why after thirty-odd years?"

He pulled the token out of his pocket and let it lie on the flat of his palm while he studied it. "Because I'm in much better shape now than I was thirty-odd years ago. My hand is steady."

It was.

"More than thirty years I've been without a father."

"I'm sorry. There's a lot more I can say, but that's the most important part. I'm sorry, Emily." He closed his fingers around the token as though gripping it tightly might lend him some strength, then slipped the coin back into his pocket and lifted his eyes. "Can I come in?"

So much I didn't know. So much.

I stood away from the door.

He took a seat on one of the stools at the counter, and I fixed him a glass of ice water, then returned to the futon. I curled my feet up under me and pulled a throw blanket over my lap.

"Shoot," I said. "And make it worth the effort of listening to you."

Howard looked at the glass of water, sweating away on the counter, but did not touch it.

"Your mother's right about me," he said at last.

I made a noise deep in my throat.

He turned his eyes on me. "I'm a drinker. An alcoholic. I've been sober now for three thousand six hundred and twenty-two days."

"And you're in AA."

He nodded. "Yes. Because I need all the support I can get." He held out his hands. "But when you were born, I hadn't managed to stay on the wagon for any appreciable time ever. I didn't even admit I had a problem. When your mother told me she was pregnant, I went on one hell of a bender. There was a long stretch of time I don't even remember. That's how bad I was."

"Why? Because of a baby?" I nearly spat the words, they tasted so of bile. "People have babies all the time."

"Not in your family. There's something *strange* about your family, Emily, though I'm not sure of all the details. Being the father in your family was a responsibility"—Howard took a deep breath that seemed to cause him pain—"that I wasn't prepared to shoulder."

"So you walked away."

"No." Howard spoke the word with surprising violence. "No. I never walked away from you, Emily. I stayed away and tried to get sober for you, and for your mother."

"And let me believe you were dead."

"I know. It all sounds ludicrous when you put it into words. But I agreed to that. It seemed easiest."

"For you."

He met my furious gaze steadily. "You are right, there. It was easiest for me. I was sick and drunk and frightened and angry with your mother for how this all came about, and I did what was easiest for me. I could have fought Elaine about this. And I didn't. In that, I failed you. I might have allowed her to do what she thought was best, but I failed *you.*"

I wrapped my arms around my knees and stared at him critically. "So you stayed away and tried to get sober, and between the pair of you, decided it was best for me to believe I was fatherless." I shook my head, scoffing. "Brilliant plan, that. Did you ever stop to think of what you would do once you got sober? I mean, about telling me that you weren't dead after all. You know. That minor detail."

Again he spread his hands before him helplessly. "No. I was too drunk then to think I'd ever be sober, or to think what I'd do once I was. If I was." Howard's face was lined in the angle of the afternoon light. "I thought I was going to die. I was that bad. And then what your mother told you would have been true."

I laughed bitterly. "But here you are. 'Surprise, Emily! Here I am, your dad, risen from the dead like the second coming!'"

Howard was silent for a moment. He reached into his pocket for his token once more and turned it between his fingers, obviously a habit of long standing. "There was no right way to do this. I know that, Emily." He sighed. "But if you're familiar with the Twelve Steps, you know that number nine is about making amends to the people I've harmed. And I can't begin to do that for you until I admit how I wronged you. You, more than anyone else. So this is my beginning."

Slowly he stood, and for a moment it looked as though he might approach me; but then he seemed to think better of it. Instead he moved toward the door. "I told you the other day that I've always loved your mother. This is true, the truest thing I know. I've been trying to make amends to her, and I think she's coming to a place where she might forgive me. I know that I forgave her a long time ago."

I did not respond. I wrapped my arms more tightly around my legs, making myself small, a protective ball.

"Your mother and I are working toward something: the relationship we tried to destroy all that time ago. And you are integral to that, Emily. Your mother loves you."

Now I snorted.

Howard held up a hand. "I won't argue with you on this. But, your mother is wounded in ways that you might not understand. She has only her own mother for a model, and, judging from what you've said about your grandfather's other family, you are starting to discover that perhaps Eleanor was not the best model." His hand was on the doorknob now. "Elaine loves you, but she doesn't know how to make you understand that. Give her a chance. Hell, Emily—" He paused, choking up a bit. "Give *me* a chance. Your mother and I have screwed up royally with you, but we want to make it right. Give us a chance to make it right."

When I still said nothing, he nodded in farewell, then let himself out. He closed the door gently behind him.

62

"I'M GLAD YOU called," Carwyn said, even before I could say hello. "I've got an interview." He sounded breathless and excited.

"Where?"

"At the university." He dialed the excitement back a bit. "Adjunct work. But work. And all due to your help uploading documents to my online dossier."

"You never needed my help."

"That's our little secret."

"Right." I closed my eyes, realizing that calling him might not have been the wisest of ideas. But—and I opened my eyes again to squint at the clock on the stove—it was past midnight at the cottage, so talking to Viviane or Katti or Helen was out.

As if he sensed my misgivings, he demanded, "What is it, Emily?"

When I didn't answer straight away, he sucked in a breath.

"Are you all right?" he asked. "Is the baby all right?"

The baby.

A misbegotten baby in a long line of misbegotten babies.

Or perhaps, a baby fated to be made, fated to be born.

I shook my head frantically, pushing the thought away.

"The baby is fine," I whispered. "I'm the one who isn't doing all that well."

"I'm coming over," Carwyn said.

"No, you don't have to—"

But the line had clicked dead.

HE POUNDED ONCE, and then opened the door and let himself in, his face anxious.

I was pulling on my jacket.

"I need to go for a walk," I said, zipping myself in. I felt so cold. "Come for a walk with me."

"You're sure you're okay?" Carwyn did not look convinced.

"Just walk with me," I repeated. "Down to the river and back."

At the sidewalk, he took the outside, though there was no traffic in the cul de sac. He shortened his stride to stay beside me, though I walked as though driven. At the corner I turned to the left and headed downhill, toward town, and the park. The streetlights were beginning to come on. I felt his eyes on me, but could not bring myself to speak. Not just yet. In the trees overhead, some birds sang, and I did not recognize their song. I hunched my shoulders against their cheerful noise. Carwyn said nothing, asked no questions, and I was grateful for his quiet company. Calling him might not have been the wisest of ideas, but suddenly I was glad to have his number on speed dial.

The double lanes of Park Street were full of traffic even at this time on a Monday evening, and we got caught by the light on the island in the middle. A woman with a chocolate lab on a leash joined us there, and the dog sniffed at my shoes.

"He won't hurt," the woman said reassuringly, tugging gently at his leash, so he drew back and sat. "He's just a big baby."

Carwyn let the dog sniff his hand. The light changed, and we crossed the street. The lab and his person moved off toward downtown.

The park was dotted with groups of people: some hardy shirtless boys playing Frisbee, a man in a flowered vest busking on the corner. Two small girls were on the swing set, being pushed by their mothers. Overhead a plane buzzed. The globe lights along the walkways were strings of bright pearls in the darkening air.

"It's so—normal," I said.

"Just people," Carwyn agreed.

I laughed, and the sound was bitter.

At the river walk, I leaned on the rail and looked down at the boats docked at the marina. Close, but not touching, Carwyn did the same.

"What happened?" he asked.

Below, a man was swabbing the deck of a sailboat, skirting the furled mainsail, which was wrapped in a blue cover. I watched him, wondering what it would be like to know how to sail, how to guide a boat like that down the river to the ocean. What it would be like to keep sailing, far away, to another country, to another life.

"Howard came over," I said at last.

"Howard? Elaine's boyfriend?"

"Howard," I said. "My father."

I might have punched him. Carwyn reeled back, his mouth working.

"Your father is dead," he finally managed.

Having finished swabbing, the man below us leaned his mop against the rail and went belowdecks. On the pier next to the sailboat, a pair of seagulls stood guard.

"I *thought* my father was dead," I corrected. "I was *told* my father was dead. Until I was informed that he wasn't. Not really. Surprise, Emily! Just kidding!"

Apparently my voice carried. One of the seagulls swiveled its head to look up at us with his beady black eye. Its accusing gaze reminded me of my mother's—except not green.

"Stay here," Carwyn commanded. "Don't move."

He jogged away, along the promenade to the snack shack. I watched him dully, then returned my attention to the two seagulls. The man had returned above deck, and now he leaned against the rail, drinking a beer.

"Here. You need this." Carwyn was back, and he handed me an ice cream cone. "Chocolate chip cookie dough. I hope you like that kind."

"It's my favorite." He had, I saw when I peeled back the napkin, also ordered a sugar cone. I looked to his face as I licked the ice cream; he looked inordinately pleased.

We ate our cones in silence as the night drew on. The man on the sailboat finished his beer and stowed his mop and bucket away. The he went into the cabin and a light went on down there. When I turned, I saw that the children and their mothers had abandoned the swing set, where one of the swings swayed gently, as though with a ghostly occupant.

"So Howard is your father," Carwyn prompted after a while.

"So it says on my amended birth certificate."

"Wait, there's another?"

"A gift from Elaine. She didn't know how to tell me she'd lied all those years, so she gave me a new birth certificate. Classy, eh?"

Carwyn raised his eyebrows, nodding. "I suppose there's no easy way to admit that whopper of a lie." He turned the cone in his hand to attack the melting side. "And there's never a right time to bring it up, either."

I was further along than he at demolishing my ice cream cone. I took a bite out of the cone itself. "You make it sound so prosaic."

"Thanks. That's what I'm here for." He grimaced. "Better than let you twist yourself up into knots about this, which is, I suspect, what you've been doing."

"Wouldn't you?"

He held up his hands. "No comparison. My people were tired and busy and didn't give me as much attention as I would have liked, but somehow I'm beginning to think that that's better than the lot you were handed."

"That's what Howard said—that it was far too difficult being a member of this family. Far too much responsibility." Slowly I recounted the conversation, and Carwyn listened with his eyes narrowed. When he had finished his ice cream, he wiped his hands thoughtfully, then crumpled his napkin and shoved it into his pocket.

"So your family drove your father to drink," he said, once I'd run out of steam.

I shrugged. "I think that might be too simplistic an explanation—Howard's an alcoholic, after all. If it wasn't one thing that prompted the drinking which sent him into his spiral, it would have been another. The disease gets a person eventually." I sighed. "But he wants to make amends. He wants to work on his step nine with me, he says. I just don't know if I'm ready to have a father dropped into my life, after all this time of having none. Especially a father who might have been there, somewhere, had he and my mother not conspired against that happening."

"I can see why that might be a problem," Carwyn said. His mouth quirked in sympathy. "Remember our agreement? *Slowly?* That might just be the way to take things with him—with them both, if their intent is to reestablish their relationship as well."

He faced me, leaning his elbow on the railing. Beyond him, the streetlight came on, and his shadow fell away on the pavement. I finished my ice cream, looking around at my own misshapen shadow on the ground. No sign of a rounding belly yet. But soon. I thought ahead to Thursday morning and the appointment at the women's clinic.

"And I told her, Carwyn," I said.

"WHAT WAS ELAINE'S reaction?" Carwyn asked, taking my key and opening the apartment door.

Inside, I shuffled off my jacket and hung it on the peg next to the door. "She's not happy."

"And we're beginning to understand why?"

He'd taken a single step inside the apartment, rather as though he was unsure of his reception. I reached around him and shoved the door closed.

"There's so much I don't understand. I think I catch a glimpse of it, and then it fades away." I took my accustomed seat on the futon, curling my legs up under me. I waved him to a seat at the other end, the only other choice being the hard stool at the counter. I could still see the image of Howard Mitchell seated there. My father. After a moment, Carwyn sat at the very edge, looking uncomfortable. He was careful to keep his distance. In the confined space of the efficiency apartment, memories took up most of the room.

"But you understand why your mother is like she is, don't you?" He looked down into his folded hands. "You understand why she behaves the way she does toward you."

"She's a terrible mother because she had a terrible mother. I've got that line down intellectually. It's going to take a while to get there emotionally." I gulped suddenly. "If that's the way everything works, then I'm bound to be a terrible mother as well." I put a shaking hand to my abdomen. On my daughter. I looked up into Carwyn's wide face, noticing for the first time the spattering of freckles across his nose. He looked, tonight, surprisingly young. "I'm going to be a terrible mother, Carwyn."

He placed his hand over mine, over our child. "You won't. I won't let you be. Just as you won't let me be a terrible father. Because whatever happens, Emily, and why ever any of it happens, we will both be parents to this child."

"My family history—"

"To hell with your family history," he said fiercely. "We will not be dictated by your family history." He laced his fingers between mine. "I'm going to be here from day one for this child. I want you to know that."

"I want that," I whispered, looking at our clasped hands. "I don't want this girl to grow up without a father, like I did. I don't want her to grow up without a father like Elaine did."

"And Eleanor? Her father died when she was young."

"He did, but her mother didn't force him away. Her mother didn't lie to her."

Carwyn did not move. "We don't know that. We don't know what her life was like with her mother. We only know she got away from it as quickly as she could, joining the ballet company as soon as she was able."

"You're defending her."

"She was kind to me. I've told you that. I can't undo a lifetime of impressions that quickly. And I'm trying to understand her motivations, like I'm trying to understand your mother's, and—even yours." Carwyn paused, drew a breath, as though trying to summon his courage. "It's easier, I guess, for me to forgive her because she was kind to me when I needed kindness. It would make it even easier to forgive her if I could just understand what she was doing."

"But that's it. We still don't know exactly what she thought she was doing." The frustration was thick in my throat. "How can I possibly avoid making the mistakes she and my mother made, if I have no idea what is really going on?"

"We'll have to talk to your mother."

My mother. I tried to pull my hand away. Carwyn held tight.

"I don't want to talk to her," I hissed.

"Maybe not now."

"Maybe not ever."

He lifted my hand and ran a finger over my knuckles, which I clenched so hard they whitened.

"Maybe not," he agreed. "But remember—if nothing else, your mother has some of the puzzle pieces you need. You'll have to figure out which is stronger: your anger with her for her lies—"

"A lifetime of lies."

"Yes. Your anger at a lifetime of lies, or your curiosity about the reasons behind those lies."

He made it all seem so logical. Rational. Almost. "And you think you know which I'll choose."

He smiled, a full smile this time, no bitterness, no irony. Then he lifted my hand and bent his head to kiss my white knuckles. "I think I do. I've learned a lot about you since we've met again, and I think I know what makes you tick."

He kissed the back of my hand now, and the gesture was so sweet I thought I might cry.

"And that doesn't make you hate me?" I asked, and sniffled.

"No," Carwyn said. "It makes me love you, Emily."

63

"I'M FRIGHTENED," I said, peering across the parking lot at the front door of my mother's condominium. Elaine's Buick was backed into her slot, and next to it, the low-slung blue Malibu Howard drove.

"Don't be," Carwyn advised. He squeezed my hand. "You are in the right. You have questions it's about time someone answered for you. And Elaine is the only person who can answer them, now that Eleanor is dead." He withdrew the key from the ignition, then paused. "Do you even need me? I should have asked this before, since you're probably going to be talking about some rather intense family secrets."

"Provided she even talks to me," I interjected.

"Well, there's always that chance. But I think—somehow I think she will. Do you want me there? It's your family."

I took a deep breath. "For better or worse, Carwyn, it's your family now, too. You've been roped in." I thought of his words of the previous evening, but pushed them away. I couldn't think about them now. I had to get through this. We had to get through this.

"Now I'm frightened, too," he said. Then he winked and shoved open the car door.

"I'M GLAD YOU'RE both here," I said, trying to inject confidence into my voice and feeling as though I'd failed miserably.

Elaine looked pointedly at her gold watch. "We *are* going out," she said. My mother was, in fact, dressed in pale silk, with the strappy high heels she favored.

I bit my lip, but before I could say anything, Howard put his hand on my mother's arm. "We've got plenty of time," he said gently, as much to me as to Elaine. He peeled off his suit jacket and folded it over the back of a chair.

"Mitch—"

He raised his eyebrows. "Let's listen to what Emily has to say," he said slowly. "We owe her that much, Elaine."

Pressing her red lips together, Elaine seated herself on the sofa and crossed her ankles. Patience on the proverbial monument. I waited a beat, to see if there'd be any invitation for us to sit down as well. None was forthcoming. Elaine's posture made it clear that this was going to be my show, and the sooner it was over, the sooner she could resume her date.

"I have some questions." Despite the lack of invitation, I sank down into the deep cushions of the love seat opposite the sofa. Carwyn took a seat beside me. After looking from my mother to Howard and back again, I opened my purse to withdraw the muslin-wrapped tapestry. I set the roll of fabric on the coffee table between us.

Both Howard and Elaine looked down at it, unmoving. Neither seemed at all curious about the cloth packet or its contents: it might have been familiar to them both. However, if it was at all possible, Elaine's pale face grew paler beneath its powder.

"You had it," Elaine managed at last, her words strangled. "All the time, you had it."

"You know what it is, then," I said.

Without answering, my mother jerked herself up off the sofa and went upstairs, her footsteps muffled by the thick carpet. When she returned a few moments later, she had the small carved mahogany chest between her fingers. She set it down abruptly on the table before sitting again and reaching blindly for Howard. He took her hand in both of his.

"You might as well have this," Elaine said, looking away almost as though the casket would burn out her retinas.

I sat frozen, shocked. "You've had it all this time." My eyes flickered to Carwyn. *I'm sorry,* I thought confusedly. His expression altered the tiniest bit, then smoothed again.

"Yes," Elaine said.

"You took it. Out of Eleanor's bedroom at the Willows. You stole this from your mother."

The fury rushed up into Elaine's face, staining her pale cheeks red. She flipped a dismissive hand. "Just as, Emily, you stole the tapestry from her."

Stalemate. There was no answer to that.

"But—why?" I finally asked.

"Because—" Elaine seemed to have as much difficulty with the answer as I had had with the question. "Because I didn't want her to give it to you."

It suddenly seemed to me as though I was watching the scene transpire from somewhere outside myself. My own confusion and outrage, and at the same time, my own detachment. Across the table, the slow cracking of my mother's veneer, the hardness I had knocked against for all these years. Both Howard and Carwyn faded away toward the periphery, and there existed only the two of us.

"Why not?"

"Because I didn't want the damned thing to ruin your life, like it ruined my life, and your grandmother's, and probably every single woman's in this family since the dawn of time."

"Since *creavit ex Beatrice.*"

"Yes. Since Beatrice made this. By doing that, she cursed us all."

Over the years, I had grown used to the anger in my mother's voice, the impatience, and the bitterness; but this level of bile was shocking, and I rocked back on the love seat before the waves of it. I eyed the scrap of muslin, and longed to unroll it, to examine the cherub with its green eyes and its red-gold hair, even though I saw the figure clearly in my mind's eye without having to look. At the same time, my mother's violent reaction made me uneasy even to be in the presence of the cloth-wrapped package. I had thought the tapestry beautiful. But it was obvious that Elaine thought it to be evil.

"I didn't want Eleanor to give this to you," Elaine repeated. Her grip on Howard's hand was fierce, as though he was the only thing that kept her tethered—and maybe, I thought with a gasp, he was. "When she tried to give it to me, I refused it. I didn't want it. I didn't want the responsibility of it."

The responsibility. That was the word the dying Eleanor had used, the word which had made her own daughter turn away from her in fury.

"And I—" Howard started, then halted; his voice came from far away and was startling. "And I couldn't handle the responsibility of it. You see what it did to me." He looked at me steadily. "You asked me whether it was Eleanor who drove me to drink. That wasn't it at all. It was *this.*" With his free hand he pointed to the rolled tapestry and the small dark casket. "This is what damned near ruined my life. This is what drove our mother and me apart. This is what caused me to fail you so badly, for all of your life. *This.*"

I could no longer stop myself. I unrolled the muslin, and the tapestry lay between us, its colors rich and vibrant, the cherub glowing in the afternoon sunlight.

"But what is it?" I whispered, looking down into the face which looked so much like my own, and like my mother's, too, less the anxiety lines etched around Elaine's mouth and between her eyes.

Elaine didn't answer. The cherub didn't answer, either. It was, I thought, smiling in a secretive sort of way, and wondered why I had never noticed that before. Like Eleanor, who loved keeping secrets.

"You refused this when Eleanor tried to give it to you? And you stole the casket to prevent Eleanor giving it to me."

"I didn't realize she had already shown it to you. I knew she planned to, since I wanted no part of it." Elaine was close to tears, and the thick sound of her voice was unnerving. "I hoped to get it out of her apartment before she had a chance to pass the curse on to you. I thought, when I'd taken the wooden box, that I'd saved you. I didn't realize until I'd got home that the secret compartment was empty. And that you most likely already had the tapestry." The breath she drew was ragged and painful. "I wanted to save you from this."

My mother raised her eyes to my face, her expression haggard.

"And then the other night I found out I was too late." Elaine dropped her face into her hands. "Too late."

"Because of this baby."

Elaine flung herself to her feet, and paced from the sofa to the hall door to the window. Her hands were fisted at her sides, her shoulders stiff and straight. "Yes, damn it. Because of this baby. The baby that, if your grandmother, and my grandmother, and all the grandmothers before them, were to be believed, you were destined to have. Doomed to have."

I reeled back. "Am I the baby you were *doomed* to have?" I gasped out. "Is that why you've always been so hard with be? Because you think of me as your doom?"

It was as though glass shattered, and the pieces scattered their prisms all around us. I couldn't look at her. Everything I felt and thought was too sharp.

Elaine whirled. "No. I don't mean that."

"Then what *do* you mean?"

"Jesus, I need a drink for this," Elaine said, dragging a hand across her forehead.

Howard looked at her with concern. He turned toward the kitchen.

"Don't make him do that," I cried out.

But Howard waved her objection aside with a hand. "I'm fine, Emily."

Carwyn was on his feet. "No. Let me take care of that." He slipped around and down the hallway.

Howard turned away in frustration, hurling himself onto the sofa. His eyes were still on Elaine pacing like a caged animal. She wiped the back of her hand across her forehead once again, then ran her beringed hand up into her curling hair.

"I wanted you to stay with Rob," my mother said, her voice low, urgent. "It looked as though you were going to escape." She laughed dully. "Rob. Tall, dark, and handsome Rob. He was what I always wanted for you."

"*Rob?*"

She turned. "Yes. Rob. Your husband who had the wrong DNA. Did you ever wonder why your grandmother set herself so against him? Why she was so against your marriage? Because he would probably have had dominant genes, and you'd more than like have had tall dark children. Rob would have broken the curse for you. When you married him, I had such hopes."

"Yeah?" I laughed harshly. "Strangely, so did I. I thought I was marrying the man of my dreams, for better or for worse, 'til death do us part, and all that garbage. I had no idea whatsoever that after eleven years he'd find the woman of his dreams, and it wouldn't be me."

My mother stopped in her pacing. "I'm sorry about that, Emily. I truly am. I'm sure it must have been painful."

"Yeah. It was." The sarcasm, my last best defense, was lost on Elaine.

"The other part, or course, was that as long as you were living in Wilmington, you were out of Eleanor's reach." My mother sighed. "I didn't want you to move back. I missed you while you lived so far away, but at least I knew you were safe there."

Carwyn returned with a tumbler, which he handed to Elaine before resuming his seat. This time he sat close enough that our shoulders touched. I could feel his controlled breathing.

"Tell me now," I said, after Elaine had downed nearly half the gin and tonic on one gulp. "Tell me about this doom. This doom that you said I am not. Tell me what you mean."

Carwyn had found a little plastic stirrer somewhere in the kitchen and had stuck it in the glass. Eleanor circled it around, spiraling the ice, spiraling the drink. She stared down into the whirlpool she had created.

"I always wanted a child," she said finally, not looking up; she sounded infinitely sad. "Many children. Three or four or five. I was an only child. I dreamed of a big family, in a big house, with a handsome husband, and probably a dog."

"Romantic."

Carwyn hushed me with a touch. "Let your mother answer your questions."

"Well, you've seen what happens to dreams in this family. You get one child. One. A daughter. And the father of that daughter will always be a blonde, blue-eyed man. And you will love him with all your heart"—she threw an awkward glance at Howard—"but you will not keep him. And you will learn where all this baggage came from, and you will try your damnedest to break free of it all, and somehow, somehow, no matter how you try, you'll be sucked back into it. Alone, with a daughter you love and fear for and try to save and fail."

There were tears now, coursing down Elaine's face, streaking her mascara, and she made no attempt to stop them. She downed the rest of her drink, and then, shockingly, hurled her empty tumbler to the floor, where it shattered. The sparkling prisms were, now, all around us in reality.

"You hate what your mother has done to you and to your life, but you can't change it. You're like an animal in a cage, struggling against the captivity, and you can't get out. You want something else for your daughter—love and laughter and no more of this—*responsibility*—and you can't give that to her."

Elaine collapsed into full sobs, but when Howard stood to comfort her, she pushed him away.

I stared at my hands. I had heard it. I had heard what she said. The words she used. I had heard it.

"Mom," I breathed. "Mom." The word seemed pulled out of my chest by something outside me. I stood and stumbled over Carwyn's legs, trying to navigate around the coffee table. Glass crunched under my feet. I gripped Elaine's wrists and held on, as though to save her—to save us both—from drowning. "Mom. Say it again."

Elaine's flowing eyes raked my face. Her lips were quivering. "Say what?"

"I can't remember your ever saying you loved me before." My voice was still a whisper.

My mother tried to pull away, but I tightened my grip.

"Of course I love you, Emily," Elaine said, falling away into her old impatience. "I'm your mother."

"Say it to me," I pleaded. "Say it again."

For a long moment I gazed into my mother's face, noting every wrinkle beneath her eyes, every line in her forehead, the way the skin around her lips pinched in a kind of perpetual dissatisfaction.

Elaine swallowed, looking back to Howard for help. He took a step nearer, but stopped, hovering, right behind her shoulder.

"I do love you, Emily," she said, uncomfortably. "I just didn't realize I always had to say it."

"Not always. Just sometimes. Instead of telling me what you think I've done wrong, tell me you love me." I closed my eyes and leaned forward, slowly, until my forehead touched my mother's shoulder. Then I stood there, tentatively, feeling the rise and fall of her breathing, listening to the slight sniffle as she cried. After a moment, Elaine loosened one of her hands from my grip and patted my hair awkwardly.

"I do love you. Believe me." She shuddered with the strength of a sob. "And I wanted to protect you from all this, and I've failed."

64

"THE CURSE, THOUGH," I said as we sat down to the Chinese food Howard had run out to buy. My head was swirling: so many things said, so many things still to say. I was having trouble ordering my thoughts. I spooned a mound of pork fried rice onto my plate, then reached for the spare ribs.

"The curse," Elaine repeated uneasily.

"Yes." A couple of fried wantons appeared on my plate, courtesy of Carwyn, and I dunked one in the little cup of duck sauce. "And you told me, the day we were talking through Eleanor's funeral, that she had only ever loved one thing. I assumed it was the dancing, the choreography."

"It wasn't." Elaine had switched, perhaps out of deference to Howard and Emily, to iced tea. A sprig of mint stood at attention at the side of the glass. She took a drink now, looking as though she wished she'd stuck with the gin and tonic.

"Then what?"

"The mystery."

I stopped with a chicken wing halfway to my mouth. I set it back down and plucked the napkin from my lap to wipe the sauce from my fingers. "The mystery."

"All right, the legend. The one thing she held close to her heart. The one thing she worked for and protected all her life. The one thing she tried to pass on to me, and then to you, and if I'm not mistaken"—her eyes flickered to Carwyn, his blonde hair, his blue eyes—"to your daughter." She took a breath and rolled her heavy fork between her long fingers, as though she'd forgotten its purpose. "That mystery."

"The tapestry?" From my seat at the dining table, I could just see, looking through the door and down the hall, to the coffee table in the living room, on which sat both the casket and the roll of cloth. As I had all afternoon, I felt both drawn and repelled by the small piece of weaving.

"No. The tapestry, Emily, is your clue. To the mystery itself. And your proof, should the day arise—God hope us all if it does—when you need to give evidence of your bloodline."

"The family tree." Carwyn set his fork aside.

We all turned to him.

"Eleanor charged me with finishing her research—she told me she already knew what was there, but she wanted it down in writing, and she asked me to do it for her." He shifted uncomfortably on his chair, took a drink from his water. "I didn't know at the time she was using me."

Elaine tilted her head and looked at him, her expression wry. "You *are* the kind she'd have wanted for Emily. Blonde, blue-eyed: Mr. Recessive Genes himself. Because the red-haired, green-eyed look is key for the bloodline. It has to be retained. At just about any cost."

"The five-hundred year old curse?" My tone matched hers.

We stared at each other.

"I'll get the genealogy," Carwyn said. "It's in the car."

"It's always in the car," I murmured. He didn't hear me. I picked up another crab rangoon, broke it in half, and examined the cream cheese filling. I set it on my plate, wondering if I really wanted it.

He was gone for only a moment. I filled the time by piling his plate with rice, with beef and broccoli, with whatever came to hand. It hardly mattered, however, for once he was back, he pushed his plate to the side and laid out the now-familiar pages.

"We thought," he said, thumbing through them, "that we had come to the root of the puzzle of Beatrice." He set out a sheet before Howard and Elaine, pointing. "Here. We found Beatrice ver Vloet, and her parents, and her sister Elisabeth."

Howard's gray head and Elaine's red-gold one leaned together over the paper.

"It's from Elisabeth, then," Elaine said. "We're all descended from Elisabeth. I was certain we came from Beatrice."

"As was I," I agreed. "I thought for certain the child in the tapestry was the daughter of Beatrice, since she made the damned thing. And it was a play on words, you know? She made the tapestry. She made the child."

"Except according to this, she didn't make the child." Carwyn pointed again. "Her younger sister did."

"And you never got a chance to show this to my mother?" Elaine asked. She brushed her hair back behind her ear; when it fell forward again, Howard leaned over and tucked it back for her. Elaine glanced up at him, and for the smallest of moments, I thought—she looked happy. My breath caught in my throat. I couldn't remember ever seeing my mother *happy*. Not even for just a moment.

Carwyn had not noticed the silent exchange, nor the expression, or if he had, he did not remark upon it. "I didn't finish any of this until I was in Ludlow. I'd nearly forgotten all about it, but Emily asked me if I could trace the matrilineal line. Ironically, that's exactly what Eleanor had requested. Her mother, her grandmother, her great-grandmother. So I went as far back as I could, before the information petered out."

"And the pieces to the puzzle don't fit." Elaine reached for her iced tea. Only ice now. She grimaced.

"I don't even know what the puzzle is supposed to look like," I protested.

"Oh, I think you know more than you realize," Carwyn said. He glanced at Elaine. "You called this a curse, whatever it is. Wouldn't it be better to just—I don't know—drop it? And walk away from it? You and Howard go your way, the way you should have gone all those years ago. Emily and I go our way, once we figure out what that way is. We pile this mess somewhere and set fire to it or something. Exorcise it."

"My God," I whispered, amazed. "This from a historian."

Carwyn sat back, both his hands on the table before him. "I'm a human first."

But Elaine shook her head, tapping the edge of her plate. "No. We have to know it all. Emily has to know it all. This thing, this curse, is like some sort of spider's web. Sticky. We get all tangled in it, and we can't escape, so we keep reliving the same fate."

"And the men," Howard said. "We're like the prey of that spider. We get caught, and then we all end up wounded, or dead. Somehow we need to break this. And we can't do it without all the pieces. We have to know what we're dealing with, so we can eradicate it entirely."

"The black widows," Carwyn murmured, and Howard nodded.

"*Creavit ex Beatrice,*" I murmured, squeezing my face between my hands. "I know that's the key. I know it." I looked again through the hall doorway, along to the table where the rolled-up tapestry lay. The evening light fell from the window and shone on the piece like a spotlight.

"The things that don't fit: your grandmother decided to become Ludlow. Your grandfather even ended up living there. Ludlow is important," Elaine mused. Setting aside her tumbler, she too picked up a crab rangoon and pulled it apart, making no move to eat it.

I looked to Carwyn and cleared my throat. "Yes. Ludlow. Where, according to Eleanor's sly wording, all the answers are."

"Home of a castle," Carwyn added. "Where Arthur Tudor died. Home to a church where his heart is buried." He reached for my hand, and I let him take it, let him lend me that reassurance. "Place where your daughter, who is a sensitive, had a terrible reaction."

"Reaction?" Elaine's eyes shot to my face.

I tried to think of a way to explain it that wouldn't sound stupid. "It was so cold, and so heartbreakingly sad." The explanation seemed superficial, without weight. "*I* was so cold, so sad. I felt incredible grief."

"Like when Eleanor died?" Howard asked.

"Worse. Much worse." I swallowed, closing my eyes momentarily. The feeling echoed, as though far away. "It was *all* I felt. It was all I *was.*"

"Arthur Tudor?" Howard frowned.

"Henry VIII's elder brother," Carwyn said. "First husband of Katharine of Aragon—after whom, you should know, Nolan Harris named his other daughter. Arthur died when he was sixteen. Before he ascended to the throne. He and Katharine might or might not have consummated that marriage: she said no, her second husband Henry first said no, then said yes when it became politically expedient. In any case, Arthur had no children."

He reached across the table and took back the folder of papers. He then withdrew a final sheet and turned it on the tablecloth between them.

"This is Arthur Tudor," he said quietly.

No one spoke.

I recognized the print-out as of the painting at Hever Castle, the one hanging in the Queen's Chamber. I found myself studying the long-fingered, delicate hands, the flower held between them. The only contemporary portrait of the boy who would, tragically, never grow up to be king. I raised my eyes to the rest of the portrait.

At the red-gold hair.

At the green eyes.

At the narrow face.

I looked up at my mother.

I looked over into the mirror over the sideboard.

"Creavit ex Arthur," I said.

"BUT IT CAN'T be," Carwyn argued. "Arthur died in 1502. *1502.* That's the year Elisabeth was born. He could not possibly have been the father of her daughter. She was born after he died." He sorted through the pages of his family tree, until he came to the last entries, or the first. To the ver Vloets. He jabbed an accusing finger at Elisabeth. "Unless you want to argue that she's Arthur reincarnated—except that the reincarnation theory falls flat in the next generation, when nobody dies in time."

Howard reached for the page. "Can I see that? Do you mind?"

He squinted at the page, then reached into his shirt pocket for a pair of reading glasses. "Everyone here seems to have one child. Except the ver Vloets, with two, if I'm reading this correctly?"

Carwyn nodded.

Howard examined the paper again, still frowning. "But the ver Vloets waited an awfully long time to have a second child," he mused. "Beatrice in 1486, and then Elisabeth in 1502. Beatrice was sixteen. Well—" and he squinted again— "sixteen or fifteen, depending on when her birthday was."

"Children died." Carwyn shrugged. "The infant mortality rate was much higher in the middle ages and the Renaissance than it is now, remember."

"No," Elaine breathed. "No, Carwyn." She seemed to be trying to think through something she did not yet have the words for.

"What is it?"

"If there had been other children born," she said slowly, leaning to the side to look at the sheet of paper Howard held, "they would have had their births and their deaths recorded somewhere."

Carwyn straightened. "Yes. Perhaps—"

"And you would have come across them in your research, wouldn't you have?" I was feeling the edge of excitement. "I mean, you found Beatrice born in 1486, which, you said, was early for this kind of research. Then you found Elisabeth. It only makes sense that you would have found any brothers and sisters born between the two. Even had they died as babies, as children."

"And you found none. None." Elaine looked up.

Carwyn might have been holding his breath. "I found none." He licked his lips. "I think you need to say out loud what you're thinking. I think I need to hear you say it."

"It happens," Elaine said.

"Say it."

"Illegitimate children are born, and are absorbed into their mother's families. Disguised. Everyone pretends that that mother is actually a sister. It happens."

"So . . . we could be right." My breath was caught in my throat. "We could have been right all along, that Beatrice is the root, as you call it, of this family tree. She's contemporary with Arthur. They were born in the same year. Beatrice and Arthur could be Elisabeth's parents."

"Except we found her in Flanders," Carwyn reminded us. "Not in Ludlow." He made a face. "And in order for them to become parents to a child, they'd have to sleep together—a difficulty we have of several hundred miles." He sighed. "Again, you know how it goes in research: you have a hypothesis, and all the facts don't fit it—but you can't just jettison all the facts that don't make you happy."

I slumped again. I forked up some of the pork fried rice and found it was cold. I satisfied myself with a chicken finger dipped in duck sauce, even though that was cold, too. Somewhere in the back of my mind a thought was niggling, and I tried to ignore it, hoping it would ease out into the open. Chicken finger gone, I reached for a chicken wing.

"The tapestry at Hever," I said.

When no one answered, Howard took up the slack. "What tapestry is that?"

"The girl protecting the fawn. The one from the ver Vloet workshop." I pulled the wing bones apart. "It's small. But it has the ver Vloet signature on it—the two-arched bridge." Elaine and Howard looked at me curiously, so I explained: the two brothers, the two arches, the workshop. "The ver Vloets did some tapestry work for the Tudors. There was contact."

"We need slightly more than simple contact to make this work," Howard said drily.

"We need one hell of a contact, actually," Carwyn agreed.

"Well, Mr. Historian," Elaine said, standing to scrape her plate into the trash. "I guess this is where you come in. Can you find it?"

"Find it?"

"We need to get Beatrice ver Vloet into England."

"Into England?" I scoffed. "We need to get Beatrice ver Vloet into Arthur Tudor's bed."

"That's what I mean," Carwyn said. "One hell of a contact, that."

65

WHEN I FINALLY got back to the apartment, I found the mailbox stuffed. Flyers, the electric bill, the cell phone bill. And one heavy square envelope with a UK stamp and a gold-embossed sticker holding down the flap. I let myself in, dumped the junk mail into the trash, and stumbled to the futon.

You are cordially invited
to join in the celebration of the marriage of
Katharine Mary Harris
to
Helen Octavia Olmer

I scanned the rest of the invitation breathlessly, then groped on the side table for my laptop. I flipped it open and hit Facetime before checking the clock. Five in the morning at Viviane's house, I realized with a flush of guilt. Hurriedly I exited the application, hoping I'd hit the button before the computer had rung on the other side of the ocean. I set the computer aside again and picked up the invitation. The first Saturday in September. I'd be back to work at the library then, with any luck, for the coming academic year; but I'd have to take a couple of days off to be able to make the trip there and back. Madeline would not be pleased.

I would also, probably, be chubbily pregnant.

But, I decided, I would not miss this. Not for the world.

The ringing from the computer made me jump. I opened it up again, to find a call coming in from Helen.

"Sorry," I said quickly, when we'd connected. "I didn't realize the time. I didn't mean to wake you up." I waved the invitation in front of the screen. "But I got this in the mail. And I'm beyond excited."

Helen had her fine blonde hair pushed back with a wide band, though strands fell down around her cheeks, still flushed from sleep. She yawned, tugging at the neckline of her sweatshirt.

"Not half as excited as we are," Helen said. She wiped a hand across her eyes, which were at half-mast. "I'm having a bit of trouble sleeping. So you didn't really wake me up, don't worry about that." She yawned again. "So much to do."

"But you're getting married there. At Viviane's house."

"Still so much. Cake, dresses, someone to officiate—we've hired a company to come clean the house, and take care of the garden, because we don't want Viviane to worry about any of that."

"Makes sense." I chewed my bottom lip. "Listen. Helen? I feel kind of weird asking this—"

From across the ocean, Helen laughed and pulled the band from her hair, which then tumbled down around her shoulders. "It says *guest* on the invitation. You can bring him."

I felt my face flush. "No, no. It's not that. Not really." I pressed my hands to my hot cheeks. "And where would he sleep?" I coughed and pointed at Helen on the screen. "Don't you dare answer that question."

"Okay, I won't," Helen shot back. "What's your real question, then?"

I flexed my fingers nervously. "My mother. Elaine."

Helen raised her fine eyebrows. "What about her?" There was skepticism in her tone.

Now I raised a hand warningly. "And now, wait for it." I took a deep breath. "And my father. Howard."

"*Your father?*"

"That's what I said."

Helen raised her hands and then dropped them, looking around the room— the kitchen, and she had her laptop on the table; I could see the line of worry stones on the sill over her shoulder—as though for some elusive answer to a question she hadn't heard correctly. "Your father. What the hell. Am I hallucinating here? Am I hearing things?"

There was a creak, and then a sleep-mussed Katti appeared beyond Helen's shoulder. She smiled and waved.

Helen turned to her in shock. "Emily's talking about her mother and her *father,* Katti. Her mother and her *father.*" Helen spun back and glared. "What about your mother and your father? You never said."

"You never let me," I countered. "I'm kind of embarrassed to ask this, but do you think you might invite them to your wedding as well?" I took a deep breath. "I think they need to meet you all. I think it's about time."

"*Your father?*" Katti's tone echoed Helen's.

I shook my head. "Long story. Long, *long* story. But—he's not dead. He's very much alive. And I've met him."

"You thought he was dead." Katti drew up a chair and sat beside Helen, leaning her head on Helen's shoulder.

"I was told he was dead." I shrugged, uncomfortably. "But he's been resurrected, and I'm trying to get over being furious, and maybe get to know the guy. And I'm trying to understand why my freaking crazy mother would do these things to me—and to herself. It's hard. But I'm trying."

"Is Carwyn helping?" Katti asked, yawning.

"He was. He *is.*"

Helen smiled. "So he's forgiven you for being freaking crazy and doing these things to him—and to yourself?"

They were both smiling, as though I was a child who might just be on the verge of understanding. They radiated comfort with one another, and I felt some of that comfort reach out through the miles and the technology toward me. I felt my own lips curving slowly upward.

"It's hard," I said. "But he's trying."

Katti blew a kiss through the screen. "That's all you can ask, really."

Helen nodded. "I'll send your mother and father an invitation."

66

"I'D LIKE TO come with you," Carwyn said. He looked as though he wanted to say more, but couldn't quite bring up the words. He still wore his sunglasses, having stepped inside without so much as a greeting. His hands were in his pockets. He sounded as though he fully expected me to put up a fight.

"Well, this is awkward." I checked the stove, turned off the coffee maker, had a quick look around the tiny apartment to insure that nothing would combust while I was out.

He was as still as though carved from stone, one of the statues from the Italian garden at Hever. "Why?"

I gathered up my purse. "It goes against everything the family curse stands for. There's five hundred years of precedents. You're supposed to abandon me, one way or another."

Carwyn lifted his sunglasses and stuck them atop his head. He took a deep breath, and leaned in to kiss me. "I'm not going to abandon you," he said when he pulled back again. "We're going to break this damned curse once and for all."

I nodded, followed him outside into the brilliant morning sunlight, and turned back to check the lock on the door. "Have you ever been to an ob/gyn before?"

"No."

"Well," I said, and slipped my own sunglasses on, "this is awkward."

"YOU'RE DEFINITELY PREGNANT," the nurse practitioner said, turning the monitor to show us the results on the display.

"I've suspected. I took a home test a bit ago, which came up positive."

"So this is a planned pregnancy?"

I looked down into my lap, then threw a sideways glance toward Carwyn. "I wouldn't exactly say that."

"*We* didn't plan it," Carwyn added.

I spoke over his quickly. "I was on the pill, but then I was prescribed antibiotics for a sinus infection."

"Ah." The nurse practitioner nodded and adjusted her glasses, to look at me steadily. Her eyes were enormous behind the lenses. "Antibiotics will sometimes affect the pill's efficacy, it's true." She tapped her capped pen a couple of times on the desk top. "Well, as it's an unplanned pregnancy, we'll need to discuss your plans. Will you be continuing the pregnancy, or terminating it?" She looked from me to Carwyn. "I take it, Mr. Gray, that you are the father."

"I am."

"We are continuing the pregnancy," I said. "It is unplanned, but it is not unwanted."

After a moment I felt Carwyn's touch on my shoulder.

The nurse practitioner nodded. "Very well, then. We'll need to do a full exam. Then we can discuss what happens from here."

Interlude

HER GUARDIAN'S EYES were stern, steady, and Beatrice could not hold her gaze.

"You have shamed us," Lady Eleanor said.

"I could not have done otherwise," Beatrice answered, her voice small but determined.

"Who is the father? Some churl, no doubt—we can bring him to the altar. We can force this marriage, legitimize the child."

But Beatrice shook her head.

"You won't tell me?"

Again Beatrice shook her head.

The sound Lady Eleanor made was of impatience, perhaps of disgust. "You cannot hope to protect him, a man who would dishonor you and leave you. You cannot be that stupid, girl."

A third shake of the head. Beatrice felt herself growing dizzy, nauseated. "I cannot say, Madame."

"Stupid, stupid girl," her guardian repeated. She stepped to the window embrasure, looked out for a moment, then turned back. "I could slap his name from your mouth."

"Madame, I cannot speak his name." Beatrice felt weak, and the sweat prickled around her hairline. She gasped, and whirled toward the chamber pot. "He is not at liberty to marry."

Beatrice bowed over the stinking cesspool long after anything further came from her roiling stomach; the sweat now mingled with the tears on her cheeks. Slowly she became aware of the movement behind her, and then she felt the cool damp cloth against the back of her neck. Slowly she straightened.

Still the eyes of her guardian were fixed on her face, but there was something changed in them. A kindness. And a speculation.

"That's the way it is, then," Lady Eleanor said.

Beatrice dropped her eyes.

For a long moment neither spoke. Lady Eleanor withdrew for a moment to rinse the cloth in the basin, then knelt beside Beatrice once more and bathed her face with a surprising gentleness.

"We'll have to devise a plan," she said, tucking a bit of hair back into Beatrice's disarranged coif. "You know you are not safe. The child doubly so."

Beatrice's eyes shot to her guardian's face. Lady Eleanor did not look away.

"Come now," she said. "Surely you must have thought of that. Think Lady Margaret's brother, or of Perkin Warbeck, or any of the others. You are a threat now. And you know," she said slowly, each word a stone in a still pond, waves rippling outward, "what happens to threats."

IN THE MORNING her guardian wrapped her securely in a heavy cloak, bending to button it high up under her chin. She handed her a basket, a cloth tucked down over the contents. Then, uncharacteristically, she leaned forward and kissed her on the forehead.

"This is for the best," the older woman whispered.

She nodded, too tired, to confused, too frightened to cry.

"Master Arnaud will be kind."

Another nod.

They slipped through the still-dark passages, down staircases Beatrice had not known existed, until they reached a small gate. The sun had not yet risen, and smoke from the surface of the river swirled around their skirts. A figure detached itself from the fog and approached, footsteps making no sound. He bowed slightly, but did not lower his hood from his face.

"You have horses?"

"Beyond the market."

A small purse was passed from hand to hand.

"Godspeed, then," Lady Eleanor whispered. "To both of you. Remember the price of discovery."

"I do not forget, Madame."

Then her guardian was gone, the hush of the gate closing behind her the only sound.

"Come, then, my daughter. For so you are, from now on. Your mama awaits at the end of our journey." He turned and led the way along the stone wall. "Follow close, now. Until we are away, there is danger."

Part Four

Creavit ex Beatrice

67

WE REACHED THE train station in the early afternoon, and as the cars eased alongside the platform, I caught sight of Helen and Katti, arm in arm, scanning the windows as they passed. The expressions on both their faces, so expectant, gripped me so I couldn't breathe. *They are looking for me,* I thought, surprised. *There are people on the train platform looking for me.* I felt the wideness of my own smile. As we ground to a stop, I met their eyes, and their faces looked like mine felt. I gripped the handle of my small blue suitcase and shoved it off the train as soon as the doors opened, leaving Carwyn to follow as he might. On the platform, I was enveloped in their arms.

"Can I play, too?" Carwyn demanded, approaching. Helen loosed an arm and pulled him into the embrace. I suddenly felt like crying.

"Come on, then," Katti said at last, her voice muffled from the crush of the group hug. "Mum's waiting at the house. She was desperate to come meet the train, but we wouldn't have all been able to fit on the way home unless she rode in the boot."

"And she's a little too old for that, bless her," Helen added.

"We need to load your cases in there, anyway."

We rolled the suitcases out to the car park, the wheels bumping over the ruts in the tarmac.

"Mom and Howard will be along tomorrow. They've taken a room in Ludlow." Having deposited my case in the boot of the car, I climbed into the rear seat. When everyone else was in and clicking seat belts into place, I added, "Mom's a bit nervous about this."

Katti met my eyes in the rearview mirror. "I can imagine. I'm feeling a bit anxious about it myself."

Helen snorted.

Katti slapped at her shoulder. "Hush, now, and keep your eyes on the road," she ordered sternly.

"But you're different." I made a wry face. "You haven't spent your entire life living with a baseless anger at your step-mother and half-sister. This is complete rearrangement of her world-view. I don't think it's easy for her. I *know* it's not."

"Nor for you?" Katti asked.

I shrugged. "I've almost given up worrying about it. My brain exploded long ago."

"Well, as Mum would say, at least you're beginning to see things from Elaine's point of view now. You're developing sympathy. Empathy, even." Katti smiled at me in the mirror. "She'll be so proud of you, Mum will be."

68

"DINNER," VIVIANE ANNOUNCED, carrying the platter to the dining table, "is served."

The scent wafting from the rack of lamb was divine. Spread about the meat on the platter was a mix of roast potatoes, fennel, and radishes.

"You *cook* radishes?" Carwyn exclaimed.

Viviane looked taken aback as she sat in her chair at the head of the table. "Why not? It's a root vegetable like all the others."

Helen filled their goblets with ice water, then set the pitcher, shaped like a large blue fish, and which gurgled when tipped, at the center of the table.

"Are we all set?" she asked, before lifting her own goblet, which winked gently in the fading sun from the big window. "Because I'd like to propose a toast." She looked around the table, her eyes resting on each of our faces in turn. Then she focused on Katti, to her left. "To the woman who is going to make me the happiest person in the world, tomorrow, by marrying me." She grinned, delighted, as Katti's round cheeks grew red.

We all touched glasses and drank.

"Really," Howard protested, not for the first time. "If you'd all like a glass of wine to do this up properly—"

He was quickly shouted down. Again.

"I'd like to say something," Viviane broke in. She too looked in turn at all of us, the small placid smile playing about her mouth.

"Don't be all mushy, Mum," Katti interrupted. "I'm embarrassed enough already."

"Katharine," her mother said sternly, "the world does not revolve around you." Then she winked at me. "No, I wanted to say how pleased I am that you are all here. *All.* Finally." She turned her steady brown gaze on Elaine. "Especially you, Elaine. You don't know how long I've longed to be able to see you seated at my table. Your father always wanted it, too: to have his two girls together." For a moment she looked close to tears, and I imagined her straight back and her quiet grief at the graveside of her husband. "I'm sorry he's not here with us to celebrate his one wish. And I'm sorry he's not here to celebrate the wedding of Katti to her absolute soulmate. But—as they say—better late than never. I'm glad to have you here, finally, Elaine. I've wanted you for so long."

Elaine was very still, and had gone very pale beneath the careful perfection of her hair, splashed gold from the sinking sun. She was looking down into her plate.

"We have, you know," Katti said softly. "I'm so glad to have my sister, at last." She reached back to the window sill for one of the worry stones, and handed it to Elaine. "This is for you. From Dad."

Elaine wrapped her hand around the stone. Without looking up, she nodded. I thought she might be crying. After more than thirty years of never having seen my mother cry, I'd witnessed it several times in recent weeks. It was like meeting an entirely new mother. Or perhaps a new and improved one. I looked around the table, at everyone: strange or changed within the past few months of my life. Perhaps I was strange and changed as well.

"I've a toast as well," I heard myself saying in a voice that seemed not my own. I waited until they had all raised their glasses. "To our strange and difficult and—patchwork—family. We're all a mess"—I took a deep breath—"but we can make it better. We *are* making it better. Because there's love here. To us all. Together."

We all touched goblets again, and the sun sparked off them like fire.

I leaned over and kissed Carwyn on the cheek.

69

IT WAS TO be a small ceremony, and the mid-morning sun shone onto the back deck. In the corner nearest the kitchen door, a young man with a bouzouki—Viviane had introduced him, but I had immediately forgotten his name—played a background music that segued from classical to folk to soft rock and back again. The birds seemed to think of that as some sort of competition, for they sang more loudly than I could remember having heard them. The garden filled slowly, with friends of both Katti and Helen, and out of the corner of my eye, I could see Viviane welcoming them all, a gracious hostess in a lavender high-waisted dress. Until, from the depths of the house, the clock struck eleven, and the bouzouki player launched into a delicate version of the Handel.

We all stood, and from the rear of the garden came the brides, one on each of Viviane's arms. I felt the tears prickle at the back of my eyes, and leaned slightly backward, until I was up against Carwyn's warm presence. He placed his hands on my shoulders and rested his cheek against my hair. As the three women reached the front, they broke apart and moved along the row, each to kiss me, Carwyn, Elaine, and Howard. Katti and Helen approached the officiant, and Viviane took her place next to me, twining our fingers together. Carwyn's hand slid down to my free one, and I could see, on his other side, my mother's hesitant acceptance of his left hand.

"Together," Carwyn whispered.

Then Katti and Helen spoke their vows.

70

WHEN THE LAST guest had departed—Katti and Helen had long since gone, to begin their honeymoon journey to Venice—Viviane took Elaine and Howard to the cemetery.

"Let's walk up to the common," I suggested. I still wore my flowered sundress, but had changed my heeled shoes for Tevas.

"Bring your jacket," Carwyn advised. "It's beginning to cool off."

I grabbed one of the windbreakers from the hook beside the back door, and slipped my arms into the sleeves. The jacket was too big, and a vague scent of pipe tobacco hung about it. Nolan's? After all this time? It made no sense, but I was beginning to understand that not many things in this family did. I pushed up the sleeves, and they promptly slid down again over my hands.

"This way," I said, and we turned up the lane to the right, ascending the slight hill. Carwyn had been right about the cooling air as the afternoon moved into early evening; no sun reached down to us as we entered the tunnel of intertwining branches.

"Can I hold your hand?" Carwyn asked.

I held mine out, palm up, and after a moment, he took it. We walked on.

"Are we going to be okay, Emily?"

I felt his eyes on me.

"Slowly," I said.

He half-laughed. "No. I mean really. Is there any hope for us at all?"

We came out from beneath the trees, and the shadowed common, with its tufts of bushes scattered about amongst the tall grass, spread before us. I lifted our clasped hands and studied them, turning them over and back again.

"I'd like to try, Carwyn. I'm willing to work at it." I looked up into his face, at his furrowed brow. "If you're willing to risk it."

His smile was wry, self-deprecating. "I'm willing to risk my life on us."

"Don't joke about that." My voice was sharp.

"Why not?" He stepped closer. "Why not?"

I tightened my grip on his hand. My palms were damp.

"Because my mother might be right. Because I might ruin your life. Because I might be living under a curse."

"But you might not be," Carwyn countered. With his free hand he drew forth a folded piece of paper from his pocket. He held it out.

"What is it?" Too many shocks in too many pieces of paper. I did not take it.

"A fair copy of a letter from Eleanor Croft to her husband."

"Who is Eleanor Croft?"

"A woman whose husband, Sir Richard, was comptroller of Arthur Tudor's household, in Bewdley and Ludlow. In the letter, she writes that"—he flipped the folded sheet open and read—"*our Beatrice continues well under Master Arnaud's tutelage on the hand loom.*"

I snatched the paper from his hand. I scanned the letter quickly: questions about Sir Richard's journey to London, information about the winter weather and the rising of the river, and the line Carwyn had read to her.

Our Beatrice.

Master Arnaud.

I lifted my eyes to his, my mouth dropping open.

"The two we want, in the place we want, in the time period we want."

"Where did you find this?"

"The copy came in an email this morning from a colleague from my grad program. Your mother called me Mr. Historian, remember? I couldn't find any information anywhere about Arnaud ver Vloet bringing his daughter to England on his visits. So I threw the question out there to people I could trust, who might have had other connections. And I got this."

"But what does it even mean?"

Carwyn took the page, refolded it, and slipped it into his pocket.

"It means she was here. It might also mean she's not the daughter of the ver Vloets, that she knew and perhaps was working with Arnaud, and that she was sent to them for some other reason."

"What other reason? I don't understand."

"For some transgression," Carwyn suggested delicately. "Or for her own safety."

It was too much information. I released his hand and walked away, up the hill between the scraggly bushes. At the top, I could look down over the other side, and see more of the common. Somewhere in the western distance, I knew, was Wales. I whirled back to look along the track to Carwyn, standing, waiting.

"A transgression?"

"Sleeping with a boy already betrothed to a powerful princess—that might work."

"Being impregnated by a man already betrothed to another woman."

Carwyn dipped his head in acknowledgement.

"But—for her own safety?"

Carwyn made his way up the incline to join me. The sky overhead, a beautiful deep blue all morning and afternoon, had begun to gray over. The sun, soon to set, slipped behind a cloud. I shivered.

"The baby—if Elisabeth is Beatrice's daughter—would have a claim to the throne."

"She's a girl. She's illegitimate. That's a tenuous claim."

Carwyn shrugged. "Perhaps. But consider the time. Arthur's father's claim was through an illegitimate line; that's part of the reason why he married Elizabeth Lancaster, whose claim was more legitimate than his own. And our Elisabeth, remember, was born the same year Arthur Tudor died, and Henry became heir presumptive."

I held up my hands, clenching my eyes shut. "It's too much. Too much."

"To some parties, a child of Arthur could have been someone to rally around. Even a girl. Even an illegitimate child. And you know what happened to pretenders during the Tudor reigns. That family was ruthless."

As is my family, I thought.

"And if what we've got here is true, you're a Tudor," he added, as though reading my thoughts. "Directly descended from a king, on the matrilineal side."

"A prince. From a prince." Even *that* was bizarre, and the thought made my head spin. "It's all *ifs.* It's all supposition."

Carwyn nodded in agreement. "And we're lacking proof of many things. You're right. But the hypothesis takes into account the pieces of the puzzle we have. Even"—he stepped forward again and put his hands on my shoulders— "even the grief. You felt it where Arthur had fallen ill, where he had died, where he was buried. If what we think is actually true, you're feeling Beatrice's grief. The grief at the death of the father of her child."

"The grief the women in my family have been channeling in every generation since. The grief that made my grandmother determined to ensure the continuation of the line." I took a deep ragged breath. "I don't want to feel that, Carwyn. I don't want to feel that *for you.* "

He wrapped his arms around me and crushed me to his chest. I felt the slightest flutter, the baby kicking. I didn't think Carwyn noticed.

"I told you, Emily," he said. "I told you. I'm willing to take that risk."

THE WIND WAS picking up when we turned back down the lane toward the house. The branches overhead moved uneasily. The early evening smelled of rain.

"It is all *ifs,*" Carwyn said, fitting his stride to mine. "And because of that, it could be that none of it is true. In which case, we have nothing to worry about."

Up ahead, the familiar rustle, and I put a hand to his arm to stop him. I pointed, and out of the underbrush came the fox. This time, she was followed immediately, not just by the kit—a bit bigger than the last time I had seen them—but by a third fox, this one larger than both the others.

"I've seen the vixen and the kit, but never him. If it is *him.*" I leaned close to Carwyn, hoping the sound of the air in the trees would cover my whisper. But the wind was blowing the wrong way, and the two adult foxes lifted their noses, sensing the humans on the air. The vixen turned her head slightly and looked up at us. After a moment, at some silent signal, the three dashed together into the underbrush at the other side of the lane.

"I guess we'll never know for certain," Carwyn said. He looked down at me, brushed a strand of hair back from my cheek. "Can you live with that? Never knowing for certain?"

I looked again down the lane, where there was now no trace of the foxes. After a moment, however, the headlights of Viviane's car turned in from the main road, then came to a halt on the verge beside the house.

"I can live with that," I answered.

Postlude

"HUSH, NOW," MATHILDE whispered gently, kissing her damp forehead before laying the swaddled baby to breast. "Feed the babe, and love the babe, but remember: to keep her safe, she is to be your sister. Always remember that." The kind round face floated above her in the candlelight, the softest of touches brushing the hair from her brow.

Beatrice had never spoken of this matter to Mathilde, nor, as far as she knew, had Master Arnaud, and in her stolid kindness, and her unmitigated happiness at having someone to care for, Mathilde had never questioned.

"Do you know—?"

"Hush," Mathilde said again, pressing a finger to her lips. "I do not know, and I do not care to. Some things, child, are best left unspoken." She smiled tenderly, touching the damp gold curls of the baby, awkwardly rooting. "You are my daughter. This babe is my daughter. That is all anyone needs to know."

"Master Arnaud—"

"Papa," Mathilde corrected.

"What does he—?"

"Papa only wishes to make me happy," Mathilde said softly. "And having daughters makes me happy. You are blessings from God, brought to me by a good man." Again she bestowed a gentle kiss, then withdrew to the chair near the embers of the fire. "I am grateful, Beatrice. Now rest, if you can."

In only a matter of minutes, Mathilde's breathing deepened into sleep.

In her arms, the baby whimpered gently, then fell to suckling. Beatrice touched the red-gold hair with a finger, then kissed the nursing child.

"I will never let you forget," she murmured against the warm skin. "I will never let you forget who you are, and from whence you come. Never."

Much research went into the construction of this story, and many many thanks are owed.

To Amtrak, whose Writer's Residency made it possible to have time to write. The residency also allowed me the opportunity to visit Chicago and the Art Institute of Chicago, as well as New York City and the Cloisters of the Metropolitan Museum. In each case I was able to examine Medieval and Renaissance tapestries, including the wondrous series of the Cloisters' Unicorn Tapestries.

To Alison Palmer, Conservation & Engagement Assistant at Hever Castle, for information about the castle's Tudor-era tapestries, and about the painting of Arthur Tudor. The Beauty tapestry and the ver Vloets are fiction, but the rest are real.

To Frances Gies and Joseph Gies, and their book *Life in a Medieval Castle,* for information about daily life.

To The Getty Museum, and their video *The Art of Making a Tapestry,* for information about tapestry weaving, and the Gobelins.

To Alexandra S. D. Hinrichs and her book *Thérèse Makes a Tapestry,* for information and inspiration and synchronicity.

To Ian Blake, for information about paths of desire.

To every librarian I've ever known, from Ann Westerveldt to Heidi Conroy, for everything. There's a reason why my main character is a librarian.

To the British folk-punk band Merry Hell, for their CD *Bloodlines*—especially the title track; shamelessly, I stole their title for Part III. Cheers!

And, of course, to Julia Hawkes-Moore and Roger O'Neill, for the castles, the pubs, the laughs, Arthur Tudor, and especially, cake!

So many more people, so many more places. For a story that had part of its genesis at the Stonecoast Summer Writing Conference in 1991, this has been a long time simmering. Thanks to everyone who added to the pot.

Anne Britting Oleson lives with her family and cats in the mountains of Central Maine. She has published three novels, *The Book of the Mandolin Player, Dovecote,*and *Tapiser,* and three poetry chapbooks, *The Church of St. Materiana, The Beauty of It,* and *Alley of Dreams.*